Ann Arbor's Typhoid Epidemic

Print Edition
ISBN-13: 978-1497589957
ISBN-10: 1497589959

Copyright 2014 by Rohn Federbush
Book Cover Design and Book Formatting by Rebel Ink Designs

All rights reserved. No part of this book may be reproduced in any form or by any electronic or mechanical means, including information storage and retrieval systems—except in the case of brief quotations embodied in critical articles or reviews—without permission in writing from the author at RohnFederbush@RohnFederbush.com.

This book is a work of fiction. The characters, events, and places portrayed in this book are products of the author's imagination and are either fictitious or are used fictitiously. Any similarity to real persons, living or dead, is purely coincidental and not intended by the author.

For more information on the author and her works, please visit Rohn's Website at www.RohnFederbush.com.

Table of Content

Acknowledgements:
Chapter One
Chapter Two
Chapter Three
Chapter Four
Chapter Five
Chapter Six
Chapter Seven
Chapter Eight
Chapter Nine
Chapter Ten
Chapter Eleven
Chapter Twelve
Chapter Thirteen
Chapter Fourteen
Chapter Fifteen
Chapter Sixteen
Chapter Seventeen
Chapter Eighteen
Other Books by Rohn Federbush
About Rohn Federbush

Acknowledgements:

My appreciation goes first to Paul Federbush for his loving, undaunted support. I value the time stolen to write when I neglected my family and friends to create fictitious worlds. Also, as a voracious reader, I value my fellow writers in MMRWA, RWA, ACFW Great Lakes Chapter, RWAPro, Ann Arbor City Club, as well as Elizabeth George, and Northrup Frye for their continued inspiration and encouragement in this long, humbling voyage.

Chapter One

Ann Arbor, Michigan, June 1879

Humidity from a threatening storm wilted the starched-lace on the pleated front of Abigail's engagement gown. At the head of the table, Grandpa drained his water glass and then dabbed at his substantial white moustache with his napkin. Hoping for twilight's first shift of air, Abigail directed the butler, "Isaac, the windows."

Isaac followed the Breckenridge house rules and pulled the dark green shades below the table top's level, in order not to let breezes snuff out the candles. Behind the blinds and white filigree curtains, fly-paper curls ambushed insects drawn to the savory aroma of roast duck. Cooler air reached Abigail's ankles, but harsh barking from the neighbor's collie only added to the jangled state of Abigail's nerves as did Grandpa's continuing challenges to her darkly, handsome fiancé, George Lott.

Grandpa's subject was George's finances. "You think you can keep this girl in fancy dresses?"

George stiffened in the straight-backed, dining-room chair. "All she will ever ask of me."

On her left, Charles Van Aker, her blond, curly-headed friend since grade school, smiled and then attempted to lighten the mood. "You could terrorize our Abigail, so she'll never open her mouth." No one cracked a smile, but Charles plowed forward. "Or, keep her in the house so no one will notice she's out of fashion, no longer in harmony with society."

George didn't raise his eyes from his plate. Abigail scowled a warning at her grandfather, but he refused to look her way. Finally, Grandpa realized the ill-advised line of questioning. He frowned and then smiled at Abigail, his faded blue eyes twinkling with mischief. "Did I tell you, Abigail, they found Confederate gold out at the Husted's?"

Abigail relaxed with the change of subject. Under cover of the tablecloth, she raised her skirt above her knees to take full advantage of the cooling breeze. She planned to share this secret of staying serene with Dolly Colt at the next opportunity. Where was her beautiful, redheaded friend? Dolly's empty chair across from Charles reminded Abigail of their Jewish neighbor's Seder celebration, where an extra place was set for an absent, invited guest. The prophet, Elijah, was welcome to occupy the Breckenridge chair any time, but she expected Dolly Colt.

Lightning struck nearby, shaking the house and making the candles flicker. The collie outside hushed.

Then Abigail screamed jumping up to escape whatever had grabbed her knees.

Isaac couldn't rescue her chair fast enough and it crashed to the floor.

George and Charles leapt to their feet. George raised his steak knife, prepared to attack from across the table. Charles moved Abigail behind him for protection. She peeked around his shoulder as Isaac dragged Taffy, the maid's black baby, out from under the table. Taffy, just starting to stand, would pull herself up to anything available, in this instance, Abigail's knees. Taffy's large eyes threatened to spill tears and her mouth puckered.

Abigail offered a sugar-cube bribe, hoping to avoid any howling. "Oh, sweet, don't cry."

Grandpa motioned for everyone to sit down. "Dinner is resumed." Raising his voice, he called, "Cotton, come get your scamp."

Cotton hurried in stammering, "She…she gets away from me, Sir."

"Don't fret," Grandpa spoke softly. "No one has been unduly injured."

Cotton continued to prattle, "Look at her eyes, big pools of sorryness, sweet pumpkin." Isaac herded Cotton and the child toward the swinging door to the serving room. They could hear Cotton croon an explanation to the rest of the staff. "Dis here heat's too smothery for my baby."

Abigail tried to fan away the warmth on her cheeks. She did hike her skirt up an inch or two, but refrained from exposing her knees to further infractions.

Grandpa asked, "Now, what was I talking about before all hell broke loose?"

'Don't swear' was on the tip of Abigail's tongue, but Grandpa's habits were impossible to cure.

"Confederate gold," George reminded him. "How much gold did they find?" George re-attacked his large portion of duck.

Abigail smiled. Grandpa's gruff, low voice with its hint of hillbilly twang from his Illinois home calmed the worst case of nerves she had ever experienced. Maybe she wasn't the only fiancée to feel shaken by the prospect of marriage. She stopped fanning herself to listen.

"The runaway's name was Tess," Grandpa said. "I reckon, her master's son, Jamie, must have had those fifteen English sovereigns on him when he brought Tess up here, probably just days before the firing on Fort Sumter. Tess's letter shows they were in love." Grandpa directed his final comment with undue emphasis directly to George.

George shifted in his chair.

Abigail considered asking if the gentlemen wanted to remove their coats, but thought better of it because George was too formal for shirtsleeves. Admittedly shortsighted, Abigail compared the dark, tanned complexion of George to Charlie's sunburned redness. George's dark, curled moustache enhanced his good looks, while Charlie's full lips detracted from his square jaw. Grandpa was impolitely rumpling his thinning white hair, still waiting for a comment from George.

"Forbidden love," George managed, wiping his brow. His voice was perfectly modulated with a melancholy cadence. "Who found the gold?"

"Yep," Grandpa continued his story. He intentionally avoided answering George's question about the money. She stared at her future husband, tried to envision living with him. Grandpa had, no doubt, wanted to emphasize George's monetary interest in the love story.

"They used Tess's mother's trip to a cancer surgeon as cover for their escape. Jamie's mother must have been particularly keen on keeping her cooking slave, to send her north for surgery. Their plan was meant to delay any search for Tess, who they hoped would reach Canada with the money. Jamie promised to rejoin Tess as soon as he delivered her mother back down south. The large amount of English money was probably meant for rebel troop provisions."

George wiped saliva from the corners of his mouth.

Grandpa nodded to Abigail at the added proof of greed before finishing the story. "After Tess heard the war had started, she stashed the gold in the Husted's dirt basement with a long letter."

"Unusual for a slave to be able to write." George laid his napkin next to his empty plate.

"Guess Jamie taught her." Entranced with the romantic story, Charles leaned forward forgetting to keep his elbows off the table.

"Tess's note said the Husted boys took too much interest in her," Grandpa said.

"Some refuge," Charles interrupted again.

Grandpa disregarded the comment. "Tess propped a chair against her bedroom's doorknob each night. She wrote she was returning down south to find Jamie."

"What happened to Tess and Jamie?" Abigail asked.

"That's the whole story," Grandpa said. "We don't know."

"They probably crossed paths," Charles said dreamily, "maybe several times."

"Sister Grace dreamt the gold was under canned carrots in the Husted cellar, and sure enough the widow found those English sovereigns." Grandpa added for Abigail, "Come in handy now."

Abigail explained for George. "Grandpa is referring to Mrs. Husted's need for funds. Her late husband didn't leave a will and her sons want to sell the farm." Abigail's words raised an octave with her heightened outrage.

Grandpa said, "Mrs. Husted refused. Now the estate distribution will be decided in court. I understand why Abigail is incensed by the sons' behavior."

An uncomprehending look on George's face showed he didn't realize how outrageous the demands of the children were. Not everything was easy to explain thoroughly, but Abigail appreciated Grandpa and Charles's continued efforts to acquaint George with Ann Arbor lore.

Motivated by the Husted probate case, Grandpa had finished drawing up all the particulars of his own will with Mary Foster, the only female attorney in Ann Arbor. Mary was a widow too, but well provided for. The lawyer inspired Abigail to apply for entrance to the law school for the coming fall, but then George began courting her in May.

George had refused to consider a career for his wife. "Pushing yourself into unseemly situations? Highly objectionable for the Christian mother of my children," he had said.

The mention of children filling her life had stilled Abigail's initial rebellious reply. Grandpa told her not to worry. Her trust money for law school would be waiting should George change his mind.

"Who is Sister Grace?" George asked Charles.

Charles finished the home-made beer in his crystal mug before answering. "St. Andrew's." He must have thought better of his cryptic reply, adding, "Sister Grace has the gift of second sight."

Abigail touched Charles's shoulder as she explained further for George's benefit, "And, she isn't shy about offering her insights to parishioners."

George shook his head. "Your minister encourages this chicanery?"

Grandpa sighed. "You missed the point entirely."

Charles and Isaac found other places to look besides George's face. Abigail did find the ignorance of George, a stranger to Ann Arbor, perplexing at times.

Charles led the talk to safer ground. "Another St. Andrew's name you'll come into contact with is the Loomis family. They provided a station on the Underground Railroad. That's where Grandpa found Cotton."

"Good people, William and Caroline," Grandpa said. "They went to Fortress Monroe in Virginia to see their only son after he was wounded, but they brought back his body." The room held a respectful silence. "He was the Civil War's first casualty to be buried in Ann Arbor. Then his parents had the fortitude to raise one thousand dollars in twenty-four hours to bring the wounded home from Gettysburg."

George's head snapped to attention at the mere mention of money.

"Those were hard times." Abigail hoped to shift the conversation away from that sad war. "Brother killing brother."

Grandpa acknowledged the ill-timed subject, as he stood and ushered the group into the parlor. Instead of logs, lilacs and bridal-wreath branches decorated the fireplace grate. Grandpa had suggested a quiet dinner at home before the engagement dance at the Hill Opera House. As it was, Abigail worried about feeding these few guests in the suffocating heat. Mrs. McConnell had worked hours on the cherry sauce and trimmings for the duck feast to impress George. Abigail touched her throat with her fingertips, as she recalled the cook's opinion on the matter.

"Someday, God forbid, if Mr. Breckenridge should cease his good walk on this earth," after a brief pause for prayer, Mrs. McConnell's musical, Irish brogue continued, "Mr. Lott might be paying my wages. I mean to please his fancy palate, early like."

Removed from the dining room, whose warmed floor was directly over the hot basement kitchen, they now enjoyed a flower-scented breeze in the crowded parlor. The gilded-edged furniture from New York was part of Grandmother Salome's dowry. The small room was stuffed with two triple-back sofas, two armchairs and eight side chairs. Chairs sat in front of the Allmendinger grand piano and each window, with enough chairs left over to surround the elaborately carved center table. In the corners, ferns flourished at varying levels, supported by mahogany pillars.

Abigail hadn't seen the color of the walls for years. Every available space was decorated with dried-flower wreath arrangements framed under glass, or nature prints of damsels with flowing hair. Terribly old-fashioned, but there was no sense in disturbing Grandpa's memories of his dark-headed, beautiful late wife, Salome, who everyone said Abigail resembled.

Not that Abigail hadn't dreamt of redecorating. As the room was arranged now, there was hardly space for Abigail to walk past the crowded breakfront display cabinet to get to the front windows without snagging her lace hem on one of the claw-footed chairs.

Grandpa mentioned the Hill Opera House again to George. "That family of Hills from Massachusetts has funded many a building for Ann Arbor."

George reached in his pocket for notebook and pen.

"What do you have there, son?" Grandpa peeked at the small pad of paper. "Husted, Loomis, Hill?"

George's tone was unctuous. "You are a font of information about Ann Arbor families. I want to take full advantage of any contacts I can make to provide for Abigail's future."

Abigail had to give George credit. He was seriously pursuing knowledge of Ann Arbor's wealthiest citizens.

Grandpa tapped George's pen. "Don't do that at the engagement dance." Precipitously, they all heard their horse, hitched to the double-seated shay out front, neigh with impatience. "Old Prescott's getting up there in years," Grandpa said. "Hope he makes it to the dance."

George's austere demeanor was broken by a nodding smile and he didn't write down the horse's name.

Grandpa slapped her fiancé on the shoulder. "My friend, Gardner, says Prescott may not live to wear out his new shoes. Course Gates tells me my carriage won't last much longer."

"Your cronies know their business," Abigail said.

George found a place for his elbow on the slate mantle already crowded with a clock, vases, candlesticks, and bric-a-brac. He swept the top of the Plymouth clock with his fingertip. Abigail hoped he hadn't found any dust. Cotton was more of a lick-and-a-promise housekeeper, but George seemed inclined to appraise the piece rather than worry about lint.

He has good taste, Abigail thought, and then smiled at his reflection in the mirror over the fireplace, as she remembered his words.

"You're the gal I picked to marry," George had said last week in front of the ambrotype photographer of their engagement picture. His uncharacteristic remark, calling her 'gal' had made her smile even as she tried to move away from the metal clamp holding her head absolutely still.

Without a female relative to rely on, Abigail hadn't been sure of her engagement dress until she saw the finished print. Quite romantic, the eerie yellow light gave the impression time had passed and she and George were old people. It was comforting to look mature and content. Maybe her plague of nervous blushing would diminish with time.

"With the railroad spur going through Trist," George said, diverting his attention from the clock. "I plan to take Mrs. Hanson's suggestion and buy up all the land available out there."

"The old Mrs. Hanson or the younger?" Charles asked, but George ignored him.

"Mighty romantic theory." Grandpa pulled at his nose as if to stop a sneeze. "Not sure I'd be willing to vote for another spur. Haven't seen any profit on the north-south bond yet, and it's been ten years."

"But the line has only been running a year, sir," Charles said. "Nothing like a small town in a rural landscape that cherishes an arcadian image."

"You're planning to buy land out there, too?" George asked.

"No," Charles said. "The description referred to Ann Arbor."

Grandpa followed the conversation's direction. "Last year the newspaper quoted a professor saying Ann Arbor has 'an air of beauty seldom seen in places of sudden growth.'"

"Didn't that professor get a lot of help from an older woman?" Abigail asked.

"Don't know about that," Charles said, "but St. Andrew's is mighty grateful."

"Why is that?" George asked.

"The lady funded one tenth of the money needed to remodel St. Andrew's," Charles answered.

"She was in love with the professor even though she had twenty years on him." Abigail laughed.

"Stranger things have happened," Grandpa said. "One can have platonic and deeply felt affection for young people."

The men continued to chew on the subject of the city's sylvan beauty, but Abigail escaped into her own world. After George kissed her in the garden in May, she had accepted his proposal of marriage, rushing straight away into the house to tell Grandpa.

George took every opportunity to steal a kiss or hold her close when no one was around. George held an unsettling, animal attraction. He gripped not her soul but her entire body which reacted on its own volition to every glance from him the way it jolted at the neighbor collie's first siege of barking, or the strikes of lightning. Thank God, George proposed after his first disturbing kiss.

George was the oldest man to have kissed Abigail. Charles hadn't kissed her since they were eight. Charles's tepid flirtation didn't provide the physical stimulation that George did. However, she did look forward to Charles's visits. They were like fresh breezes invading the room, not at all like the smothering presence of George, who managed to send everyone off on errands in order to be alone with her. It was disconcerting to be interrupted in a perfectly good anecdote by a sweeping embrace and intrusive kiss.

Often when dressing for the next encounter, Abigail wished she could make some excuse, illness or any reason to avoid George's visit. Abigail's dressmaker on Main Street complained about the need for so many dresses to be buttoned in the back. Abigail couldn't reveal George's hands were less tempted by the style. Besides front buttons, Abigail avoided her favorite lilies-of-the-valley scent. George had mentioned perfume caused his passions to escalate. But marriage would sanction all the rampant rushing about of blood and nerves. A messy business, matrimony promised order for the chaos her mind and body experienced around George.

The married women Abigail knew complained about their husbands, too. The young Mrs. Hanson had said her husband,

"…snuffed out reasons to breathe." Another bride mentioned stumbling over her man at every corner in the house. The surprise element in grabbing and rumpling surely caused the wifely displeasure.

George was ready to move in, anytime. Grandpa said the sooner the better, after walking in on them when George had stopped her piano practice with a long, exploratory kiss.

Her friends, Charles and Dolly, were not awfully fond of George. Abigail's close affinity with Dolly had developed when Dolly gave her piano lessons. Dolly played piano like an angel and she agreed Abigail could study music without the fear of enduring a recital. Dolly said curiosity had nothing to do with the urge to perform. Abigail admired Dolly's independent life as a University professor…Mary Foster's, the lawyer too. Both women managed to be happy without the constant travail of courtship.

What could be keeping Dolly? Abigail hoped she would be on time for the dance.

Charles leaned in Abigail's direction and gave her a comforting smile. "All will be well," he said, as if he sensed her worry.

Abigail turned back to the windows searching for Dolly.

Charles, an amateur poet, never referred to himself with the singular first person pronoun, which often created confusion when he quoted other poets. The habit gave Charles a cultured air. For instance, when Abigail first mentioned marrying George, Charles quoted Henry James, "If a man is free not only in respect to outward compulsion, but free also in respect to inward constraint, he is essentially devoid of obligation to his fellow man or to himself, in a word, his own sole law."

Abigail wasn't sure how the quote applied to poor George, but somehow it sounded criminal if applied to anyone else. She'd mentioned Charles's comments to Grandpa and George at dinner the previous night.

George had said, "The Civil War made rules of conduct as arbitrary as the domestic rites of Pharaohs."

One thing would need to change about George after they were married. He'd have to stop bringing up the war with Grandpa. Each time the harsh memories whitened one more hair on Grandpa's head, and George appeared to enjoy diminishing his future grandfather-in-law. When Grandpa brought up the subject, it fit into the conversation easier, a gentle addition to the fabric of words, not a subtraction.

Grandpa had only asked, "Who are you quoting, George?"

Perhaps the chill toward George was jealousy on both her friends' part, as George intimated. Dolly was older, 26 and not married, and Charles had been especially fond of Abigail since they were in school together. It did worry Abigail that after marriage they all might not remain friends, so she insisted Charles be George's best man and Dolly her maid of honor.

George had wrinkled his perfect brow but agreed. He was sweet really, pliable. Surely he would eventually see the social niceties of having a wife with a professional life of her own as a lawyer. It did occur to Abigail that she hadn't remembered what George did for a living. Maybe he was a land developer. Who knew? Surely Grandpa had inquired.

George's family hailed from Maryland, she thought he had said. Abigail liked the idea of being the only one in George's life. Charles had an entire village for a family. He was one of eight children. As an orphan, Abigail envied Charles's closeness to his mother and father. Of course Grandpa and the rest of the Breckenridge household made up for it. Seven to ten, Abigail compared the number of people in each house. No, now it would be eight to ten, with the addition of George. She liked *not* learning about George's family during the last month. It was as if George and she were two orphans meeting in a tempest of storm-tossed nerves.

Abigail tried to resist pacing in front of the windows. The three men chatted congenially around the flowered fireplace. Dolly did possess a poor sense of time.

Finally, Abigail spotted her friend tugging at the sleeve of a thin man, coaxing him to follow her up the front walk. Had Dolly misunderstood? She didn't need an escort for the dance. Charles was available for her partner.

Once inside Dolly introduced the man. "John is the desk clerk from the Cook Hotel, where George is staying." Then, she moved behind Abigail whispering, "I must speak with you, privately!"

Across the room from them George fumbled with his glass of sherry, dropped cigarette ashes on his suit, and became increasingly flustered.

"What's wrong?" Abigail asked him.

George responded by purposefully walking past her and roughly grabbing Dolly's forearm.

"Stop that!" Abigail shouted, surprised at her vehemence in defending her friend. "Grandpa!"

"No reason for roughness," Grandpa said, prying George's hand from Dolly's arm.

The hotel clerk cowered in a corner of the sofa, whimpering. "I shouldn't have come. My uncle will have my hide."

Abigail was at a loss.

Dolly shakily explained, "I brought John here to refute any of George's denials." Grandpa escorted Dolly to the sofa and stood protectively behind her. Dolly took a deep breath. "George Lott already has a wife and a child."

Abigail made a surprised outcry.

After the disclosure, they all stared at George as he adjusted his shriveling neck to fit his shirt collar. "…a flagrant spy," his only comment.

Grandpa and Charles pushed George out the front door, into a freshly arrived downpour. Abigail heard them harangue the man on the steps of the porch until Cotton entered the parlor to light the gas lamps.

* * *

Abigail's summer of 1879 began with the uncovering of betrayal, perfidy at its worst. Devastated, Abigail wished she could disappear or just drop through the floor of the crowded parlor. Unable to listen to more of Dolly's condolences, Abigail escaped to the dining room.

The ambiance of the glittering, candle-lit table mocked Abigail's stricken state. Would she ever know happiness? She picked up George's emptied crystal mug and walked to the window.

Isaac retrieved the glass before she could toss it out into the rain. "Events seem frightfully great when ruined," he said, not meeting Abigail's unladylike, angry eyes. "These are squally times."

Dolly stood in the doorway to the parlor, so Abigail hurried through the servants' waiting room, where dishes remained stacked from the dinner courses. She covered her ears not wanting to hear Dolly calling. Then, gathering her skirts, Abigail ran up the servant stairs.

A cold fear gripped her throat as she entered her sitting room on the second floor. Maybe she would live alone forever. Someone knocked softly on her door. Abigail coldly locked it. "I need some…time, Dolly."

"He's not worth prostrating yourself with grief," Dolly said from the other side of the door. "I'll call tomorrow after lunch."

Abigail wanted to unlock the door and rush into her friend's arms, but it was all too humiliating. She pulled her spoiled, damp dress over her head and threw it into the corner of the bedroom instead of carefully hanging it in the wardrobe. She kicked her slippers after the defiled promise of her engagement dress.

The rooms were cool. Isaac had been thorough in his charge to open the windows. The shutters rattled from the rising wind. Abigail wanted to howl with the storm's fury. Her wet stockings let her know the rain had blown in. She shut the south window and wiped up the wood floor with her chemise. Without lighting the bedside lamp, Abigail unclasped her hair pins, letting her dark hair fall past her shoulders.

Numb with shock she climbed on top the covers. The shadows of tree limbs and leaves rush across the ceiling. Had that ever happened before, black shadows frightening her? How close had she come to being taken advantage of physically? If they'd been left alone long enough, would George have forced himself on her?

The stranger in their midst certainly held no scruples. Could she have stopped a prolonged attack? If not, she might have had a baby like Cotton did, without benefit of a father in the child's life.

Abigail had never had a father in her memory. She could almost remember her mother, Bernice. Or, perhaps she internalized the memory Grandpa offered of her mother's braided crown of blonde hair. Still, she associated a warm sensation of protection with her mother's spirit, or memory. Not so her father.

Abigail refused to remain fearful. If something could hurt her more than she already was, let it happen.

"Please, Lord," she prayed. "Give me the strength I need."

A wave of relief overcame her embarrassment. Call all the demons and fiends of the world, she could face them down, with God's help, before she'd perish.

Chapter Two

Charles preferred to follow his poetic temperament. He didn't often take advantage of his muscular frame, one of the benefits of building furniture in his father's factory. But once on the plank walk in front of the Breckenridge home, with Grandpa's sanction, Charles marched George down to the end of Wright Street. Neither of them had retrieved his hat. The rain left George's black locks a stringy, sodden mess. Formidable at six-foot-five, Charles shook his head of blond curls. More water splashed onto George's face.

To make it perfectly clear, without rhyme, Charles said, "No further contact with any of the Breckenridges can be healthy for you."

George sneered up at Charles. "If you want to stay single for a year or two, you should avoid the Breckenridge house, too."

"What is your insinuation, Sirrah?" Charles found George's collar in his fist. The smaller man's face was running with rain and getting paler. No doubt about it, George wore paint like an actor and smelled like a woman. Charles let go, and George wiped at his forehead with a darkening handkerchief. Charles used his finger to wipe at a streak coming from George's hair. He shoved his blackened finger in George's face. "How old are you?"

"Old enough. That imp of a child stared at me just as you are. I kissed her to back her off. She almost fainted and asked if I loved her."

Charles wanted to run, but he felt hypnotized by the talkative snake.

"I told her everyone surely loved her. Then with her arms wrapped around my neck, she asked me if I wanted to marry her." George spread his arms as if beyond blame. "Of course I said I did, and off she ran to crow to Grandpa." George tried to adjust his tie, but only smeared dirt on his shirt. "Abigail is a trap ready to spring!"

Charles hit George so hard he rose in the air before falling a foot away from where he originally stood. Charles helped him up and lent his handkerchief for George's bloody, no doubt broken nose. As Abigail's immediate champion, Charles warned, "The sheriff might provide permanent lodgings if you don't relocate on your own volition."

"Sheriff Leonard's lodgings on Main and Williams are my favorite stomping grounds." George's taunt was muffled by his bloodying handkerchief. "Why don't you send that hellion detective, Dolly Colt, over there?"

Dirtied by even listening to the scoundrel, Charles's supper churned in his stomach with a threatening taste of bile at the back of his throat.

* * *

Back inside the Breckenridge home, after Cotton had given Charles a towel to wipe off some of the rain, he entered the parlor in shirt sleeves. Even with all the gas lamps lit, the room was as mournful as a Sunday morning. A profound silence had ensued. The desk clerk had scurried off into the rain. Abigail escaped into the upper recesses of the house. Charles wanted to ask about her, but Dolly caught his arm to stop the query.

Grandpa tore at the remaining bits of his hair. "Should we put a notice on the Opera House door?"

"It's too late to reach all the guests to cancel." Charles stood at the fireplace, afraid to leave any dampness from the rain on the upholstery.

"We might as well have the dance," Dolly said. "Everyone is already dressed and looking forward to the event."

"That will add fuel to the gossip," Charles argued. "All those people in one room, talking about Abigail's broken engagement."

Grandpa sat down hard on the sofa. "I should have been more careful. Asked for references."

Dolly spread her skirts next to him. "His manners fooled us all," she said, trying to reassure him.

"Post a notice at the Hall," Charles said. "Fielding questions shouldn't be a problem."

"I'd be happy to oblige," Isaac offered.

A long discussion followed about the wording of the note. 'A family emergency' won the contest as the most innocuous.

The rain stopped, and after Grandpa retired, Dolly and Charles waited on the front porch for the butler's return. Cotton made sure the rocking chairs were dry and served a decanter of peach liquor. "Help you sleep after all dat commotion."

After Cotton left them, Dolly whispered her opinion of George Lott, "That wretch."

Charles wanted to say he would step in as groom, but he couldn't ask Abigail now. "What possessed the man to disgrace such a fine young woman?" The smell of rain mixed with the fragrance of flowers in the front yard. The overwhelming beauty of the air debilitated Charles. Funny how thinking of Abigail left his chest tight.

"That was probably it, possession of innocence and beauty," Dolly said.

Charles raised his voice, hoping Abigail might hear. Her bedroom looked out onto the roof of the front porch. "Poor George. He couldn't have known the finer qualities of Abigail, her gentleness, her luminous intelligence, her good heart."

They heard someone scurry past the front parlor windows. Charles got up hoping Abigail might be listening.

"It was only Cotton," Dolly said. "Do you plan to ask for Abigail's hand?"

"As soon as she's over this tragedy." Charles hung his head. "Maybe a few years from now. What did Abigail see in the man?" Charles poured another glass of brandy.

"He was good looking and spoke well," Dolly offered. "But, of course, he had no concept of integrity. I'm sure Abigail didn't consider very long. Does Abigail know your feelings for her?"

"Eighteen is too young." A strange weakness overcame Charles.

His own father told him exactly that before they knew George Lott had begun to court Abigail. "Give it ten years," his father had said. "You'll have less of a brood to feed, and you'll be able to provide properly for Miss Breckenridge the way she's used to."

So Charles started paying closer attention to his father's business. "There is an incredible amount to learn in a furniture factory," Charles said. "The banking and accounting jargon make figuring out how to increase profits almost unsolvable. Instead of fresh lines of poetry, new efficiencies and cost-saving ideas bubble up now."

"As the oldest of eight, Charles," Dolly said, "I understand why you think money is important to establish a home."

"Every nickel Father pays is saved for the higher purpose of providing for Abigail's future; or was, before George got into the picture." Charles remembered how easily he could have spent all he made on the wants and desires of his two brothers and five sisters. "Father says the old farm out on Plymouth Road is intended for the eldest."

"How soon will you speak to Abigail's grandfather?" Dolly asked again.

"A few years will pass in no time," Charles said. "Abigail knows my plans." Or, Charles thought, George was too good of a catch to pass up. The sweet brandy was not cheering his mood. "If Abigail's grandpa hadn't cautioned me, George would be laying out behind the carriage house."

Dolly shook her head.

Back from his errand, Isaac informed them, "There were no questions."

"You'd best walk me home now," Dolly said.

Charles rubbed his forearm. The muscle twitched as if eager to beat on George's head. "How did you find out about George?"

"I told you, they were painting my rooms at the University," Dolly said as she allowed Charles to help with her shawl.

"Tell it again," Charles said. Five sisters had taught him to be patient with women. Unlike his habits of speech, they often forgot antecedents. Actually Charles concentrated on listening to their communication in reverse order to surmise the logic. As a man, he took time to construct the necessary transitions before barging into conversation.

"I'm living, temporarily, at the hotel," Dolly explained. "John loves to gossip about the other guests. I can't even invite the string quartet to rehearse there. I'm afraid he would impugn the reputation of the young men."

Charles nodded to encourage the story.

"He was chewing on George Lott's personal life, so I mentioned that he was quite attractive."

Charles raised his left eyebrow. It was a habit of his mother's. He had determined to break it after Abigail first mentioned the similarity to his mother's grimace. Charles placed his hand over his eye, forcefully pushing the eyebrow down to imbed the reverse pattern into his mind. After eight years, the remedial action had not found a home in the revised-behavior part of his mind. At least he'd stopped repeating her favorite phrase, 'Really!'

"That's when I got an earful tonight," Dolly continued. "John showed me a secret drawer in the hotel hall's writing desk. It had a note in it addressed to George." Dolly sighed. "I can understand why John thought his uncle might beat him for carrying bad news. I should be caned for bringing so much pain to Abigail and her grandfather."

"You only saved her from ruining her life!" Charles walked to where Dolly was standing and embraced her in gratitude, thinking, *you saved Abigail for me.* As he let Dolly loose, he said, "By the way, George mentioned you should devise a way to look into Sheriff Leonard's place on Main and Williams."

"That whore house?"

Charles felt his eyebrow twitch.

"Everyone knows the sheriff runs it."

"Is that why Father voted for the other guy?"

"Well, there you go." Dolly straightened her hat. "Do you know the quickest way to the Cook Hotel? My slippers aren't the best for hiking. Most of the trek is downhill, but it's too late for the trolley from the train station."

"Imagine you're dancing," Charles said. "When Abigail shared the same 5th Ward School, we lived around the corner on Moore Street."

"You're the same age?"

Sticking out his chest, Charles said, "Six months older. When the household got too big, Father moved us down to Madison."

"It's growing awfully dark," Dolly said, as they walked toward the river.

Charles offered his arm. "One more bridge on Broadway, then downtown by Division."

"I've only lived here since I received my appointment in the Music Department."

"Is it true, if you marry, you'll lose your position? So unfair."

"But true. Did you know Abigail wanted to start law school in September, before George said, no?"

"Why did she ask him?"

"You don't believe a husband has a right to say no?" Dolly stopped to loosen the straps on her shoes.

"Curiosity should be encouraged."

"For a young man, you're very mature."

"Maturity isn't the only quality needed to share Abigail's life." Charles rumpled his hair, another bad habit he wanted to conquer. "Tariffs must be learned, the price of stoves, and roofing."

"It would help Abigail's reputation if she married quickly now."

"Here's St. Andrews," Charles said, uncomfortable with Dolly's probings. "You can see the engine house and the fire tower on Huron."

"John wasn't the first to hint George was bad news. When Abigail and I attended the Ladies Library meeting at the Presbyterian church last week, several matrons stiffened at George's name. The young Mrs. Hanson actually blushed."

Charles stopped abruptly, turning Dolly toward him. "Why did you not ask them for particulars?" He let go of Dolly, embarrassed by his actions. "Excuse me, Dolly." He bowed to her. "Are you hurt?"

"Your concern for Abigail does you credit, but you're right to apologize." Dolly rubbed her arms. "I'm not accustomed to men laying hands on me."

They turned at the firehouse to walk west, continuing slowly down Huron.

Dolly said, "The women told more by their reactions than words could. Besides none of us wanted to ruin Abigail's happiness." Dolly hung her head. "Don't listen to me trying to push you into immediately proposing to Abigail. I'm interested in making everything all right for her."

"We all are." Charles beat a tattoo on his forehead with his index finger. "But there is so much that has to be accomplished."

"Abigail and her grandfather would love to have you move in with them. You don't need to bankrupt your family to provide for her."

"A man has to be able to support a wife to gain her respect. Can't you see Abigail running to Grandpa, when she's told, 'No. We can't afford it.'"

Dolly shook her head. "Better strike while the iron is hot."

Charles laughed. "It's best to wait until things cool off."

"Could you see me to the desk?" Dolly asked, as they stood on the new court house side of Huron.

"Do you think George, or that kid, John will give you trouble tonight?"

"I'm…I'm not sure." Dolly held back.

As they crossed Huron in the middle of the block, Charles offered his arm. "The Breckenridges are asleep by now."

"I wish I'd had this trepidation while I was there."

"Mr. Breckenridge would have taken you in." Charles rubbed his knuckles which still ached from punching George. "If either of them is in the hotel, you'll come home to our house. Mother isn't normally friendly, but a college professor may improve her memory of good manners."

"Funny how that works. Being a professor I can count on invitations, even return visits, but Abigail's the only true friend I have."

"Maybe you threaten their way of life with your independence. Your feelings of isolation are not unusual." Charles's invitations to dine were predicated on his ability to recite poetry. Memorizing his lines took attention away from the factory's complicated production schedules, but society's acceptance was worth the resulting mistakes and accounting errors.

"Even Abigail has enemies," Dolly said. "Truly. They hint Grandpa buys her way into every club."

Charles shook his head. "The Lord knows, Grandpa just wants her to be happy."

"And the rest of them are such skinflints. Unlike the Breckenridges, they're afraid to see a dime of theirs end up in the pocket of some poor tramp in town."

Charles rang the desk bell for news of John or George. The hotel's marble floors and staircase let the echo reverberate. The polished mahogany of the registration-desk cage and the plush lobby straightened Charles's spine. Grandpa's house was the only elegant home he felt comfortable in. His renown as a local, albeit unpublished poet, allowed him access to the homes of the elite of Ann Arbor where he experienced the same stiffness in response to the disparity of finances, his thin wallet's charming response to opulence.

The manager appeared. "John came by to quit. You would have thought blood hounds were after Lott. Someone had socked him pretty good."

Charles flinched at the comment.

The manager winked, "Good job, kid."

Dolly shook Charles's hand goodnight. "Don't delay in asking for Abigail," she said right in front of the hotel manager.

As Charles continued south to Madison Street, where the Van Aker home stood in the same block as their furniture factory on the old tannery site, he mulled over his prospects of claiming Abigail someday as his wife. They were not bright.

The two of them, Grandpa and Abigail, were worth ten times the Van Aker family, if you counted dollars per head. Charles's mother, Elizabeth, might be higher in society in her own mind than Abigail, but being born into a Vermont first family didn't count for much in

Michigan, unless money followed the blood line. Even though Grandpa's wife, Salome, had family money, Grandpa Breckenridge lived frugally after she, and his son, and daughter-in-law, Bernice, perished. Grandpa lit up more when Bernice was mentioned than when his wife's name, Salome, came up.

The beauty of youth, Charles explained to himself had to be the reason. The tintype of Salome on the mantle showed she was not an unhandsome lady. Grandpa told Charles his wife blew with every breeze in her head. Abigail's tall mother, Bernice had come from solid Swedish stock.

Apparently, Abigail's dark eyes and hair favored her grandmother more than her blonde mother. He believed Abigail and he were kindred spirits. She was affectionate and emotionally driven. Not that Charles wanted to go around admitting an unreasonable weakness, but he was comfortable calling himself a poet.

The power and pleasure of language overcame barriers and opened epic territories of narrative, when they organized themselves into stanzas under his pen. Charles knew writing was all about controlling his own universe. He'd heard some preacher or was it the orator talking about prohibition say, "Words are little shards of amber, crystalline housings for the magnetic art of meaning." God have mercy, that was beautiful. He lost the name of whoever wrote the words, but they kept their beauty intact.

In school, ten inches above the heads of his classmates, Charles tired of being called 'Oaf.' Somehow his ears never outgrew the name, even when he hadn't heard it for eight or nine years now. He remembered sounding stupid, stammering, "I…I…I…." Now words calmed him. He constructed every reply before its utterance and carefully avoided the first person, singular pronoun. His habit allowed time for polite responses. Poetry bridged the gap between laborer and intellectual, he hoped. He wanted to understand compassionate people not become falsely demonstrative.

Charles grew up knowing Abigail was never a fake, like some of those dewy-eyed, dramatic girls who acted as if his presence caused ecstasies of emotion. Abigail had minds, too. Her expressive face showed heartfelt interest in new ideas. Her engagement to George made her more nervous, even high-strung.

Charles opened the gate to his family's yard on Madison. He decided to knock on his parents' bedroom door to wake up his dad.

They sat on the back porch to smoke their pipes over the evening's fiasco. "Was she heartbroken?" Mr. Van Aker asked.

"She was upstairs by the time George's nose got broken." Charles wished he could light the pesky pipe as easily as his father.

"You didn't talk to her? Shame. She could have used a kind word."

"Dolly was there, but Abigail wouldn't talk to her. Probably too humiliated."

"Abigail has nothing to be ashamed of, has she?"

Charles began busily puffing away on the off-center coals in his pipe. "Bad judgment, like everyone else. His manners, you know."

"Your mother got me that way. Now I can't please the woman."

"You won't give in about dressing for church?"

"If there is a God, he brought me into this world without clothes, and I'll not give a month's earnings, take the food out of my youngsters' mouths, to throw away on a new cut of clothes!" Conversation stalled as they dispensed great clouds of fragrant tobacco smoke into the heavens. "Abigail's not like your mother, boy. She doesn't mind being fancy, but I've seen her comfortable as a milkmaid in the yard." His father pointed to the chicken coop. "Picking up chicks and holding them to her face. She's earthy and has God's own good sense."

"George was a slippery one to fool Grandpa Breckenridge."

"You've got that straight." His father knocked out the spent pipe and clapped his son's shoulder. "Get some sleep. Morning will come fast enough."

Charles stayed on the back porch, losing track of time. When the ominous George Lott appeared in the Breckenridge parlor in May, Charles tried hard not to think of Abigail's charms, her slim waist, her graceful neck. After Abigail asked him to be the best man, Pastor Tatlock told him not to worry about his continued interest in Abigail. "The friendship of childhood sweethearts doesn't count as lustful coveting of another man's wife."

Childhood sweethearts didn't quite cover the Charles's emotions. If Abigail had asked him to lie down in the street in front of the entire St. Andrews' assemblage so she could walk on his back, Charles would have done it in a heartbeat. Now, with George Lott out of the picture, Charles released the reins on his heart. His affection could gallop into any territory, free of constraint. But, Charles reminded himself, he would have to market mountains of furniture around the world to provide for her.

He drifted into the quiet house drawn to the incongruous silhouette of his mother's writing desk. Even in the darkness, he knew the color of the richly polished cherry. The lid was always locked, but Charles lingered near, as if all the secrets of the universe were contained therein. Here was a box of plenty in a room of near want. He wet his finger and smudged it purposefully against the cabinet's mirror, hoping to upset the pristine, private world of his mother.

As if thus summoned, the door across the hall opened and his mother emerged. "Charles, stop stomping around the house. If you can't sleep, take a walk. For heaven's sake your father's exhausted beyond sleep. He's rolling around in there like a whirling dervish."

Thank God it was dark. Charles knew an infantile blush spread over his face, as if caught at a naughty, childish deed. "Sorry, Mother."

He walked around the block, stymied by his financial prospects. Even if he figured out how to double his father's furniture business through exports, his immediate army of brothers and sisters would need the proceeds. He couldn't put the future of his siblings in jeopardy. How could he break free to provide for Abigail?

Perhaps he could teach poetry on the side, if he ever got published. Charles thanked the Lord he believed his Creator would not instill interest in Abigail, if he wasn't meant to love her. And love her he did. The future was thrilling with Abigail in it. He would be careful, calculate every event. He felt like a criminal planning some robbery of his family's finances to marry Abigail.

Maybe he should seek out Reverend Tatlock again, sort out his needs. Then a Bible verse flitted through his mind. "Forsake…forsaking all others."

As he approached his gate, the first light of dawn arrested his attention. He tiptoed up the stairs to the room he shared with his younger brothers, John Eric and Little Ben. Finding the concordance and Bible on his bedside table, he crept back down the stairs. The porch would take advantage of the morning light, enough to read by.

He looked up 'forsaking' but found nothing of relevance. The listings under 'mother' were endless, but the first promised something, Genesis 2:24. He found the passage in his worn Bible, "Therefore shall a man leave his father and his mother; and shall cleave unto his wife: and they shall be one flesh."

His body responded to the promise in irreligious ways, but his mind, or his heart, couldn't dismiss the Van Akers' needs easily. Still he needed Abigail. Maybe his father could talk more sense to him. No, better not add to his father's mountains of worry.

Abigail, could she help? "I want to marry you, Abigail," he whispered, "…someday." Then he asked the author of the Bible for help, too. "Lord, lead me in paths of righteousness for your name's sake."

Chapter Three

Barking intruded on Abigail's sleep. Her dream had held warmth and palpable expectations of Dolly's arrival in the empty Breckenridge foyer. The expansive, two-story hallway widened in the dreamscape; but Dolly remained missing. As the collie's woofing continued, the dream faded. So, Abigail awoke thinking first of Dolly.

Why hadn't she asked Dolly to stay the night? George and John might have waited at the Cook Hotel with less than welcome arms. At least Grandpa should have offered the carriage. Charles. He would have walked Dolly home and seen to her protection.

On her feet from the anxiety over Dolly, Abigail wondered what the new day held now that George was no longer in her future. As she poured wash water into her basin, she thought of poor John Guiteau. His uncle, Professor Maynard, was unhappy enough after John failed his freshman year. If he lost the job at the hotel, he'd probably be thrown out on the street.

Why had George delighted in his spiteful hoax? Abigail sobbed bitterly into her face towel. Why had she known no harbinger of evil in George's caresses? She faulted her monstrous conceit and outrageous ignorance not to have asked about his past. A gnawing, guilty pain for her participation in the scandal consumed her.

She faced her mirrored image and pushed back her waves of dark hair. She frowned at her stupid eyes, which revealed their lack of judgment. Even Charles found her too unattractive to touch. She knew she would not miss George's intrusions on her person. All she experienced in his direction was relief, as if Dolly had blocked her leap over a terrible cliff.

Delaying as long as possible, Abigail crept through her sitting room. The door to the hall was still locked. Cotton had surely tried the doorknob this morning. Abigail blushed as the dregs of her temper tantrum presented themselves.

In the hallway, the door to her grandmother's suite on her left was closed. The room was filled with stored items: trunks, used clothing, and other paraphernalia from the household. Grandpa's door on the other side of the open stairwell was open. Abigail stood near the door of her mother's old room at the back of the house. One peek through her mother's windows with its view of the garden would suffice.

Her mother's room was stuffy from yesterday's heat. Opening the window, Abigail hung her head outside for a minute to take in the cool morning air. The garden below was a shambles of flowers, weeds, and trash from the recent storm. Abigail hadn't attended to its needs after George's first kiss in May. He demanded all her free time. Perhaps Cornelius, the cook's helper, wouldn't mind hauling the garden's rubbish for her. At least the garden was something she could set herself to accomplishing.

Sitting down in the rocking chair at the window, Abigail wondered what her mother, Bernice, would have said about George. According to Grandpa, she hadn't been wise about Abigail's father, Orlando. But where would Abigail be without her mother's error in judgment? "Please, Lord," Abigail prayed, "Give me guidance in this time of trial."

Abigail went back to Grandmother Salome's rooms to open the windows, sweeping out the old air and bringing in the new. The furnishings were fussy, the room cluttered, whereas her mother's had room to spare. Abigail remembered the story of a neighbor widow keeping ducks in her attic in the winter. Other neighbors complained all the way to city hall, but Grandpa refused to join the outcry. "A widow's mite must be respected," was all he would comment.

Grandpa wouldn't allow storage in Bernice's rooms, calling them the guest suite. Mrs. McConnell added Grandpa considered them a shrine to his clear affection for his daughter-in-law.

Drawn by the smells of bacon, coffee and fresh cinnamon rolls, Abigail finally went below to face the world.

Isaac served breakfast. "Mr. Breckenridge planned to make an early call at the newspaper."

Abigail held her coffee cup with both hands, like a scared child. "What will he tell them?"

"That absolutely nothing need be printed about last night," Isaac's voice steadied Abigail, " in any of the journals."

"Thank you, Isaac." His loyalty was sweet. "Would you ask Cornelius to help me in the garden before dinner, when my afternoon callers have left?"

"I'll instruct him," Isaac said. "I've already asked him to pick up the dead twigs and branches from the storm after he finishes in the kitchen."

Unable to swallow much of anything, Abigail wandered back upstairs into her grandfather's empty rooms, as she had as a child. She opened both doors of the large medicine chest over his wash basin. His collection of shaving mugs and fancy razors rested on a snowy towel on the first shelf.

What was she looking for, some remedy?

The second deep shelf held tall cobalt blue jars of Rogers Worm Syrup, Baker's Pain Panacea; and shorter, stock vials of Mott's Liver Pills which Grandpa swore relieved his back pain. Abigail's back wasn't aching and she didn't want to even think of worm medicine. Nevertheless, Abigail anticipated a slight dizziness might be caused by any gathering of people, even though they would never allude to the fact that she *had* to reject George Lott.

Maybe, Grandpa had something in his chest of remedies she could keep in her reticule for emergencies. The golden label of Fellows Syrup of Hypo-Phos-Phites promised to reform and vitalize her blood. Smelling the white liquid reminded her of George's breath. Alcohol, she reasoned, would be a temporary cure for what ailed her. Abigail recapped the bottle and moved it to the side.

A small, octagonal white jar with its advertisement folded under it claimed Abigail's attention. Hagan's Magnolia Balm promised to do away with redness, shallowness, and to overcome the flushed appearance of heat, fatigue, or excitement. Without wondering why Grandpa might need such a thing, Abigail pocketed the newspaper clipping with the jar.

"Physician, heal thyself," rang in Abigail's head; besides trusting others was not a crime. "Help me trust you more, Lord," Abigail earnestly prayed.

Then she decided a book might take her mind off her troubles. Grandpa wouldn't return until lunch. The shelves of the downstairs library offered: Playfair's "Euclid," Brocklesby's "Meteorology," and Mrs. Willard's "Universal History and Republic of America." Abigail did open Olmstead's "Natural Philosophy," re-shelved the book and picked out Watts's "On the Mind." Nothing intrigued her to do more than flip through a few pages. Even Abercrombie's "Intellectual Powers and Moral Feelings" failed to inspire any comforting thoughts.

Finally, Abigail opened the King James Bible, as Robinson Crusoe did while he was stranded on his lonely island. She found

Esther 4:13 "Think not with thyself that thou shall escape in the king's house…"

What? How could her grandfather's house not be safe? The outside world held danger. She tried the New Testament, ignoring chapter and verse. "do thy diligence to come before winter."

Two warnings. Abigail didn't have a clue what either of them meant; except perhaps she should prepare. She closed the Bible and decided to tour the house to see what needed doing. Perhaps she should straighten out Grandma's rooms. St. Andrews might not arrange yearly rummage sales, but the Fuller Street church certainly could stand another fund-raiser. Cotton could fill the carriage and Isaac could drive down to their church to store or give away the junk. Grandpa would have to approve use of the carriage, since their poor horse, Prescott, was not getting any younger. Wasn't it a sin to keep things when others could put them to good use? Maybe hoarding was one of those errors mentioned in the Book of Common Prayer, "…sins known and unknown, things done and left undone."

She never should have let George kiss her. At least then she wouldn't have seen the need to bless the deed with marriage. She couldn't remember if she'd had much choice. Now she'd lost all semblance of face with society. She hoped Charles and Dolly would help see her through this time of trial.

Abigail asked Cotton to help with the sorting of Grandmother Salome's room.

Cotton tugged at her head scarf. "I can't be doing dis now, Miss Abigail."

Isaac stood in the hall surveying the growing mountain of clothing, old draperies and linens the women were tossing out of the room. "Cotton is in the middle of laundry, Miss Abigail."

'Of course," Abigail said, "I'm sorry, Cotton. Go ahead now. I can finish this."

"And den I got to lay out your afternoon clothes."

"Really, Cotton, I'll manage." Abigail began throwing everything they'd stored on the bed out into the hall. "Is Cornelius busy, Isaac?"

"I'll fetch him from the garden." Isaac's frown indicated he thought there was enough to do without making more work.

Abigail ignored him and continued sorting the mountain of clothing.

Cornelius showed up in time to see a pile of dusty drapes thrown over the front banister to the downstairs hall. "Let me take dem down the back steps, Miss Abigail. Cotton ain't gonna like all dat duck fluff landing on dat parlor furniture."

"You're right," Abigail said. "I'll stuff the clothing into pillow cases."

"We could put some on a bedsheet," Cornelius said, "den tie the corners together."

"An even better idea," Abigail said. She worked for two hours on the room, filling the hall with bundles of clothing. The mindless work let her mind play with ideas of the unending boredom of housework. No wonder Grandmother Salome was called flighty. A caged bird, Salome, must have flung herself against the endless walls of duties and imbecilic chores.

It was only June after all. She could still apply for law school with Mary Foster's help. In September, she could start on her career plan. Grandpa had encouraged her to ignore George's opposition.

Abigail dragged the last bundle to the back stairs. She looked up the staircase to the third floor. She hadn't been up to the servants' quarters in years. "Cornelius," she called down the steps to him. "Are all the windows open upstairs to let in the cooler air?"

"Oh yes, Ma'am. They been open since Master Lott left."

Soon enough, Abigail thought. When had she last taken refuge in Mrs. McConnell's bed on the third floor, as she often did when school chums had tormented her to the point of tears? More than once the teasing was about being sweet on the giant, Charles Van Aker. She cried not for herself, but because they made fun of how fast he had grown: past their ears, past their shoulders, past their minds. They used him as the butt of their infantile jokes. Her feelings never wavered for Charles, except when George's physical attentions had overwhelmed her good sense.

She left her last clothing bundle in the L-shaped keeping room behind the dining room.

Isaac appeared, still frowning. "Are you finished, Miss?"

"Yes," Abigail had almost responded with a 'Sir.' "I'll just slip down to the basement. Mrs. McConnell might need something from the market."

Isaac shook his head. No doubt Mrs. McConnell had already taken care of business but Abigail suffered a certain restlessness waiting for Grandpa's return. Grandpa's daily routine included meeting with caretakers at the Kellogg nursery on his way to the University, where a retired regent's secretary kept him abreast of the latest developments on campus. Grandpa's physician had cautioned Abigail not to discourage Grandpa's tramps all through the town even in bad weather. "It keeps him fit," Dr. Wells had said.

In the basement kitchen, Mrs. McConnell was slicing vegetables for the luncheon soup. She smiled and put a hefty arm around Abigail. "There's my girl. Up and about without being any the worse for wear."

"There's that." Abigail appreciated the cook's good nature and ready affection.

The basement usually stayed cool even while Mrs. McConnell cooked. Last night had been an exceptional day with ovens going from early morning to make all the necessary pies and breads.

Now the door to the garden was wide open. Abigail watched Cornelius clean the gardening tools before storing them in the lean-to next to the basement entrance.

"I thought you liked George," Abigail asked Mrs. McConnell, while she kept gazing outside in order to let Mrs. McConnell arrange her face without scrutiny.

"There's leftover raisin pie and a cup of coffee to help wash it down. While George was good to you, sure." Mrs. McConnell went back to slicing carrots. "But you remember when he thought you ought not attend law school?"

"Yes?" The raisin pie hit the spot. Abigail could hear thumping in the laundry room, where Cotton sang ditties to her baby, Taffy.

"I wasn't a bit fond of him, then." Mrs. McConnell wiped her hands on her apron after dropping the slices of carrots into the kettle. "In fact, I was that put out with old George. Grandpa said to wait until the deed was done and he'd bring up the subject of schooling again."

"Did he now?"

"Shore and why not; doesn't your grandpa love you more than his own teeth?"

Abigail hugged the cook. "I love you, too. The dastardly man lost a good cook, he did."

Mrs. McConnell went off into a cloud of laughter, as Abigail slipped back upstairs to the main floor. Abigail wondered how Grandpa would explain George's previous family to people he met in his morning rounds. At lunch she found out.

Grandpa was convinced he had predicted the disaster. "George? That southern cracker rode too high a horse to be sincere. He's a cussed, vilified man!"

"He abused no one," Abigail said. "He spoke only of himself and himself he praised without stint. It was trying at times, talking to a man looking at himself in the mirror."

"Benjamin Franklin said, 'If I have to choose between pudding and praise, while I yet live, I'll chose pudding.'" Grandpa circled the table to hug his ramrod-straight granddaughter. "I love you my Abigail. You're not one of those hysterical souls…like Salome"

"But I suffer from a great imbecility," Abigail said.

"Nonsense," Grandpa retrieved his spoon. "You've seen the elephant."

Abigail finished her soup. "A Civil-War reference, no doubt."

"Death and dying," Grandpa said. "Soldiers came to terms with their own mortality during their first battle."

"You think I've suffered death in polite society?" Abigail asked, "Am I cast out? Is that what they say at the greenhouse and on campus?"

"A mere indisposition, a cold, a slight blight, as these things go. I didn't stop at the nursery or make my trip to the campus. I doubt any serious war clouds are lowering." Grandpa broke his bread for soup dipping. "Maynard's nephew fared worse than you."

"Was he thrown out?"

"Maynard says he joined a group of prohibitionists, praying for a liquor-free America. Said John was going to Washington to baptize Congress in the Lord's truth."

"Mercy," Abigail said.

"Exactly." Grandpa laughed. "Maynard needs to walk all the way to Washington with his nephew. Must weight all of three hundred pounds. Looks bloody awful. Sorry."

"Grandpa?" Abigail asked. "Why do you think I look like my grandmother?"

"The hair, I guess. But you've always been a serious child, more like Bernice." He scooted his chair away from the table. "Let me find those tintypes of Salome and your mother. You'll see, when you compare your expression with Bernice's."

Abigail didn't want him to leave the table. She wanted to discuss George, college, Charles, Dolly, everything.

Isaac refilled her coffee cup, then he placed a large piece of strawberry-rhubarb pie in front of her grandfather's place at the table.

She smiled at Isaac, the mind reader, and waited for Grandpa to return.

Grandpa handed her the photo from the parlor and then spied the desert on his side of the table. "You are of inestimable value to me," Grandpa said. "You manage the house with infinite ease. Don't determine to become inconsolable. Get up from your iron couch of introspection. Go out with your friends."

"Dolly promised to call after lunch," Abigail said as she studied the dim image of her grandmother. "Do I get my minds from you or Mother?"

"It's true your father was as scatter-minded as your grandmother, running off to make his own money. I thought Bernice was the perfect match for him. She was our housekeeper back then, about four years older than Orlando. Maybe six. He was good-looking, good bones like you and Salome. Your mother did love my boy. She was as strong as an ox. He tried to sock her once, so she threw him over the fence into the neighbor's yard. Strong minded woman, too. Wouldn't leave Salome and me when he abandoned her. Said that wasn't the deal. I think I loved that woman. Never touched her you know, even after Salome and Orlando died. Miss her every day, all of them really. Your mother would have seen right through George Lott." The pie was gone. "Thinking of college again?"

"I am. Mrs. McConnell said you were set on bringing up the subject of my education once I married George."

"Thought about doing just that. So that's one hurdle we've jumped." Grandpa got up to leave. His nap was long overdue.

Turning at the door to his study, he said, "And Abigail, your own neat, incisive manner will serve you well in law school."

Abigail forgot to ask about the carriage trip to the Fuller Church, but Isaac would take care of it when he settled Grandpa down for his nap.

Checking to see if Cotton had placed the laundry in compliance with Grandpa's military standards, Abigail paused at the upstairs hall mirror. Did she look like Salome? At lunch, Grandpa had said she did when he showed her the shadowy tintype of the laughing girl. But it was difficult to see the resemblance. Women dressed so oddly back then with yards of material over wide hoops. Her grandmother's hair flowed over her shoulders, plaited with white flowers.

Mimicking the gay face, Abigail could see her own hair was styled too high to soften her cheek bones. The nose was the same. Grandpa had agreed, but said her eyes were different. Abigail peered at her serious expression, which Grandpa said leaned closer to her Swedish mother's temperament. Both had died before she was two. Abigail missed being mothered.

Just once to hear from a woman that she was lovely might have helped her smile more. George's flattery found a willing ear. Charles rarely rhapsodized about physical attributes in his endless poetry. He was more apt to name her faults and his own. Charles was charming, but his self-deprecating fixation didn't leave him with any inclination to praise her. George's false compliments surgically removed any budding confidence in Abigail.

Changes needed to be made. She hung over the banister to calling Isaac. Abigail resisted the impulse because Grandpa would be disturbed from his nap, besides being upset by her unladylike caterwauling. Meanwhile, she had to attend to a social routine suddenly reversed back to the one she had kept before George appeared.

George. How had she allowed him into her life in the first place? Reverend Tatlock had brought George over after services for dinner the first Sunday in May. Grandpa's hospitality and Mrs. McConnell's cooking probably convinced George to return. But Abigail remembered almost the first words out of his mouth. He congratulated Grandpa's good fortune, "…on this beautiful young woman for a granddaughter."

But George was entertaining, too. He could talk on any subject as if he'd written the original book in Eden. "Knowledge by hearsay," Grandpa called it.

"Doesn't check his facts," Charles had agreed.

Abigail expected men to have all the answers. They ran the world didn't they? Voted idiots and scoundrels into office. So she listened to George's rubbish about the continents being one land mass and the moon falling out of the Pacific Ocean to cause the Bible's flood.

George also teased that Jesus must have had a pet whale under his feet on the Sea of Galilee. He liked to explain away miracles: how unconscious people were often buried as Lazarus had been and the feeding of the loaves and fishes resulted when selfish people hid their lunches until Jesus told his apostles to hand out their scant supplies.

George said to ask any woman who survived childbirth about the possibility of virgin birth. The concept had worried Abigail. She accepted belief as the greatest miracle she could witness. The Episcopal Creed used the plural pronoun 'we' instead of the singular 'I,' so Abigail had no qualms when repeating the grand myth of perfect birth, perfect womanhood. She did share her own story of Mary's pregnancy scenario with George.

In Abigail's version of the annunciation, the glorious light of the Angel of the Lord was the morning sun radiating off the golden armor of a Roman centurion. The soldier's beauty and Mary's swoon of desire produced the man who was taller than his countrymen, Christ. An intelligent woman, Mary was secretly educated by her Aunt Elizabeth. Mary decided not to be stoned for adultery; but turned the indiscretion into a means of saving her Jewish nation from the tyranny of Rome.

Using chapter and verse from the Torah, Mary taught Jesus he was the Messiah, able to arm his people with spiritual weapons strong enough to defeat any force on earth. After being baptized by his cousin John the Baptist, for 40 days and 40 nights Jesus sought to find the answer his mother claimed he knew. Jesus did successfully teach a proud people to survive by turning the other cheek...for eons.

The Sunday school teacher heard the whole thing and sent her to Reverend Tatlock, who complimented Abigail on her imagination. "We don't know what happened and that you can be sure of." Abigail settled for the importance of the incarnation mystery.

The context of George's words never mattered to Abigail. His voice affected her, all those dulcet tones directed toward her. He required few comments, but she imagined a kinship between them. George's conversations were so unlike Charles's. True, Charles was modest and his poetry beautiful, but George asked about personal things: her rings, her teeth, even laughingly how often she cut her toenails. He wanted to know all about her grandmother, living cousins, the family finances. Would they need many servants? Abigail hadn't realized the implied financial assessments. She'd been too entranced by his attention. Even Charles never sat with her as long as George did -- just to talk.

And then the kiss happened and the disaster. Thank God, she hadn't thought much about a wedding dress. The engagement party took enough arranging. What a waste. Could he have actually married her with a wife already in tow? Men were strange creatures.

In her sitting room, Abigail looked around for more things to alter outside herself. The pictures were babyish: Ivanhoe, Robin Crusoe, deer and rabbits. She took all the pictures off the walls and stacked them next to the door in the hall. Maybe Taffy or Charles's sisters would want them. Abigail did like the new photographic arts; too bad the only one she possessed contained George's likeness.

She could relish a shopping errand for new pictures. The photographer, who took their engagement picture, had his walls covered with scenic views, serious Indians, and prancing horses. Were horses too childish? They certainly looked powerful. Abigail Breckenridge was finished with childish coyness, which hadn't produced good results in real life.

Cotton came into her bedroom and busily laid out Abigail's afternoon-calling outfit. "Will you be needing the circlet hat or the white plumed one?"

"I doubt I'll do more than receive Dolly." Abigail removed her morning dress. "The heat convinces me a corset should be avoided."

Cotton shook her head in disapproval. "Mrs. Miley says bustles add no heat."

No sense arguing over the corset-shop owner's advice. "I'd like to wear the yellow skirt." Cheerful, it was, spread out on the eyelet bedspread.

"There's no jacket or hat to go with it," Cotton said.

"Perhaps, I'll stay in." Abigail reached for the spritely colored skirt.

"No, ma'am. Isaac said your Grandpa wants you out da house, often as possible." Cotton was going to wear her neck out wagging her head 'no.'

All right, all right," Abigail acquiesced. "You're so fastidious, Cotton."

"Best bees careful." Cotton's head still shook from side to side. "Didn't serve me well though, being careful like."

"Cotton, don't worry so much about Taffy. You're a good mother, and Isaac can discipline her when she needs it."

"Isaac? I've set my cap for Cornelius."

"Why, Cotton, that boy's ten years younger than you."

"Don't matter. It's not like I needs takin care of. Besides I likes someone I can rest my elbow on."

"He'll grow past that soon enough."

"I'll have him trained by den." Cotton held up a depressing black jumper and a lighter striped fabric. "Taffy taught me 'bout men."

"The brown and white striped skirt." Abigail hoped to avoid any further head wagging. "You never told me about Taffy's father."

"Taffy didn't get no father." Cotton lifted her chin. "Mama seen to dat."

"Did she disapprove?"

"I should say!" Cotton laughed. "Caint talk bout dat, Miss Abigail. I promised. But don't worry yourself 'bout Mama. She did me a favor."

Something shivered up Abigail's spine. Promised? Had Cotton implied some violence took place? Abigail bent to Cotton's ministrations. She still planned to stay in with Dolly. "I hate this jacket. The tassels blow up in a strong wind and look ridiculous."

"Caint have that." Cotton rushed out and returned before Abigail finished buttoning her many-pleated, white blouse. It was relief to button herself up. When George was about, she wore dresses fastened in the back to keep George's fingers from straying.

Cotton returned in a flurry. "I just borrowed Cornelius's fishing weights to tie in back of dem pesky tassels. Take a hurricane to get 'em flying up off your bustle now."

"Better sew my hat to my head, too."

"We'll just jam it down close to your ears." Cotton practiced the act. "Dat head of hair of yours will keep her down." Cotton stepped back to admire her handiwork. "You's looking audacious, Miss Abigail."

"Audacious? Did Isaac teach you that word?"

"No, ma'am. Twas Cornelius."

Abigail removed the hat and jacket. "If I need them," Abigail said, not planning to. She did allow herself to add a touch of her favorite lily-of-the-valley perfume.

* * *

Ensconced in the darkened parlor, Abigail practiced Bach's 'Invention in A Minor' until Dolly arrived.

"A little faster, when the weather is cooler," Dolly suggested.

Abigail frowned at Dolly's assessment of the difficult, short piece.

"Abigail, yours is the saddest face I ever saw."

"George shook me to my very depths. I hope Charles saw you back to the hotel last night."

"He did. John and George were both checked out by the time we walked back."

"Dolly, let me apologize. Grandpa and I forgot our manners. We should have lent our carriage and Isaac."

"We managed." Dolly sat on the piano bench next to Abigail. She removed Abigail's hands, then played the lovely piece with ease relinquishing none of the melody's overt joy. When she stopped, she took Abigail's hand. "Abigail, did you think it mean of me to make sure you found out about George?"

"All I wanted to do was close my ears and scream."

"George's refinements were spread thin."

* * *

"Until it was skin-deep only," Charles arrived, unannounced by Cotton. "Thought Abigail's playing had improved."

"That was me," Abigail lied for some unknown reason. Had George's habits rubbed off on her? She rose and motioned for Charles to sit on one of the sofas. "Dolly thinks my eyes have sunk into cavernous depths." Mercy, Abigail had asked him for a compliment. Charles wondered when she would pull herself together?

"You have glorious eyes." Charles didn't take the offered seat. "Snagged this poster off your hitching post. P. T. Barnum's circus is at the railroad station on their way to Detroit, but a parade is scheduled near campus."

Pushed out of the house, with hat and jacket, Abigail faced her first steps back into society with a good friend at each shoulder. At the railroad station three blocks south of Moore Street, they caught the horse-drawn street car. A large enclave of students had already left campus for the summer, so the State Street crowd was not a crush. Awnings over the shops provided enough shade to make the day pleasant.

Charles showed Abigail the circus poster. "This is from a new steam printer at the Courier."

"Are you thinking about your poetry book?" Dolly asked, before Charles could explain his interest to Abigail.

"Self-publishing," Charles lowered his head, "is not the way to go."

"I agree," Abigail said, "but you could run off copies for your friends to read."

"Too costly." Charles carefully pocketed the folded poster.

Abigail persisted, "Seventy-five cents a book isn't very expensive."

Charles took her arm and smiled down at her. "It is, when you have bigger plans."

"Little steps toward bigger designs are very effective." Dolly winked at Abigail.

Before Abigail responded to Dolly and Charles's hints, the parade arrived, headed by six elephants. A crazy man, an acrobat, in red silk tights performed wonderful leaps and triple somersaults on the elephants' backs. Then a giant, over nine feet tall walked by the hushed onlookers. There were no stilts.

"I thought you were tall," Abigail said to Charles, as he overlooked the rest of the crowd.

Two sparkling-dressed, bareback riders hurtled among twelve prancing champion stallions. The stunt people cavorted back and forth from one horse to another.

"It's enough to make you feel stodgy at twenty-six," Dolly said. "I'd like to go to the arena in Detroit."

"We could see a museum and a menagerie, according to the poster," Charles said excitedly. "One of the elephants is supposed to be twenty-five feet tall."

"Children," Abigail laughed. "You are both children."

Dolly hugged her. "Your laugh is worth ten three-ring performances."

Two women older than Dolly elbowed past them. "...not in the newspaper," one said. "A hurried affair," the other answered.

Dolly's face blanched and Charles could feel his shoulders square up in a defensive stance.

"So this is the blight Grandpa mentioned," Abigail whispered to Charles, "Should I act like a widow or a hussy?"

"Neither," Charles said too loudly. "You be your sweet self, Abigail Breckenridge, untouched by any scandal."

Chapter Four

Sunday, two days after the George disaster, Abigail attended church. To avoid curious stares she fixated on the chancel's stained-glass windows. The center panels of the three long narrow windows contained a different symbol. The Lamb of God on the left, St. Andrew's saltier or diagonal cross in the middle and the dying swan feeding her young with blood plucked from her own breast graced the right window. The pitiful swan held Abigail's attention throughout most of Reverend Tatlock's sermon. Whose death was symbolized by this tortured neck, bloodied and bedraggled feathers?

She prayed for Charles, Dolly, Grandpa and the rest of her family: Isaac, Mrs. McConnell, Cotton, Taffy, and Cornelius, paid servants but family nonetheless. Were children worth the pain of sucking the life blood out of a mother to feed them? Maybe, eventually. Charles could continue to work for his family's sustenance and live with them. But men had such gigantic egos. Even the roof over their wife's head had to be provided by their efforts.

Look at old Mr. Van Aker. Eight children. Who needed eight children? True, one child seemed prettier than the next but, my heavens. Charles's father looked drained by overwork the last time she saw him at the Van Aker home.

None of Charles's social beliefs in equality would allow him to accept help from the Breckenridges. Actually, Abigail's goal for law school originally recognized the fact that Charles might never court her while she was of child-bearing age. Sad really, because she was sure of his affection, but no passions would hurry his decision. He didn't even object when George swept her off her feet. After communion, she prayed for forgiveness for George and Charles and for the Lord to relieve her resentments.

On the way out, Abigail planned to ask the pastor who the swan represented. Was it the Lord, or his mother?

Mrs. Earl, the previous preacher's widow, wasn't aware Abigail and her grandfather followed closely on her heels. Walking in front of Mrs. Earl were the young Hansons, long-time parishioners. Slightly deaf, the old woman had a voice louder than she intended. She turned to Miriam Pettibone, and said, "…disreputable associates," clearly in reference to Mr. and Mrs. Hanson, who had also been friends with George Lott.

At Abigail's side, Grandpa was terribly chopfallen at the insult. "That daunted me," he whispered. No noisy bluster, just fretting and fuming on his part. After shaking hands with Reverend Tatlock, Grandpa took a deep breath and approached Mrs. Earl, who stood next to the pastor. "Madam, would you honor us with your presence for dinner?" Grandpa Breckenridge retained the woman's hand until she finally agreed.

* * *

Abigail chided him on their carriage ride home. "Why did you invite that fierce woman?"

"When you can't avoid talkers as you should alongside fire, famine and pestilence invite them to dinner and take the wind out of their sails." He smiled. "I knew she wouldn't pass up a chance to eat Mrs. McConnell's cooking."

Better an ally than a gossipy enemy, Abigail surmised.

Cornelius turned around in the driver's seat. "Isaac will have a fit. Table's already laid for three more now."

Grandpa frowned at him and Cornelius righted his position to attend to their progress up Broadway.

"Charles and his father plan to join us with Dolly," Abigail explained.

"That's why you pay servants." Grandpa did not lower his voice. "They can't complain to your face. You should know I've taken care of them in my will…to stay on in the house."

"Of course, Grandpa." Paid indeed. They were family once under the roof of Israel Breckenridge. "Mrs. Earl will no doubt bring an escort; hopefully the roast will stretch."

"We can always put more water in the soup," Grandpa said, helping her down in front of their porch. "I'll bet it will be the vestryman, Chinks."

"Chinks? Mr. Koelz, that frail fellow?" Abigail tried to knock the dust off her short train with her parasol, so Cotton wouldn't scold her. "I'll bet fall's tuition to law school Mrs. Earl will bring Miriam Pettibone."

At the door, Grandpa stopped her entrance with his arm. "No bet, but I'm happy to hear you are attending law school this fall." He let her pass and then stood in the still open door, pondering some decision.

Cotton clucked her tongue; before Grandpa remembered to step in and pull the door shut. "I'll throw in a trip to Europe this summer."

"To get away from the talk?" Abigail bluntly asked.

"You could say that." Grandpa shed his coat and hat. "Or we could say you were expanding your world. You'll need a chaperone."

"Charles?" Abigail asked.

Cotton coughed loudly and Grandpa heeded her censure. "I suspect he'll be too busy with his father's business. Dolly could go along. She won't be teaching in the summer. Maybe she can arrange a concert in Europe. It might improve her stature at the University."

"Will it be terribly expensive?"

"That's what money is for, Abigail. Time is money, and money should be enjoyed." Grandpa found his pipe on the mantle in the parlor. "Mrs. Earl will be here any second. Abigail play 'Amazing Grace' for us."

Abigail was singing along nicely when Cotton stopped her by announcing Mrs. Earl.

Miriam Pettibone arrived with Mrs. Earl and Robert Koelz, the vestryman everyone called Chinks. Miriam commented on the parlor suite while they waited for Dolly and Charles to arrive for dinner. "Rocco rosewood from Meeks, I believe, in New York?"

"I haven't a clue," Grandpa said.

Miss Pettibone insisted they up-end a chair to clear up the matter. "Marvelous," she said, as Robert showed her the undercarriage of a side chair. "Abigail, this is money in the bank."

Mrs. Earl touched her lips with her handkerchief. "Great resale value."

Abigail could tell Miriam's mouth was watering, too, as George's had over the Husted widow's find of Confederate gold. "My grandmother, Salome, brought the furniture with her from New York."

"Yes, yes," Grandpa said. "How many books have you stocked at the Bibliopole now, Robert?"

"Two thousand more volumes. Must have six thousand by now. I believe I may have twenty duplicates," Robert said. "I purchased the Justin estate. A lawyer you know."

"Abigail might like to buy those law books from you. I plan to build her a gazebo to study in."

"Really," Miriam and Mrs. Earl said in unison.

"A new interest," Abigail explained, still thinking it must be difficult for Grandpa to have his belongings assessed while still sitting on them. "Shall I play a piece before Dolly arrives, Grandpa?"

He smiled his gratitude at the diversion from the inventory Miriam Pettibone continued to make of the mantle.

"Sit here with me, Miriam." Mrs. Earl poked her with her fan.

Robert added, "Now your ears will have the same feast your eyes have had."

Thank God, Dolly arrived in the nick of time. "Dolly," Abigail begged. "Come play us a short piece while we wait for Charles and Mr. Van Aker."

"Happy to oblige," Dolly said. "Scarlatti's cat inspired this sonata."

Abigail envisioned a cat running across the keys as Dolly played.

"Once more should do it," Grandpa said.

* * *

Sure enough, Charles arrived with his father after one repetition of the piece. "Now that was Dolly." Charles kissed Abigail's idle hand. "Mrs. Earl, Miss Pettibone, Mr. Koelz. Missed you at church." Charles looked up smiling after he kissed Abigail's hand. He was surprised and pleased when she had blushed. He wished they were alone, in order to kiss her sweet lips, too.

"We attended the earlier service," Mrs. Earl said. "Mr. Van Aker, I haven't seen you lately."

"Refuse to attire myself to my wife's liking." Mr. Van Aker bowed to the ladies.

"Dinner is served," Isaac announced, as he slid the dining room doors open. The delicious aromas emanated from the room wetting everyone's appetite.

"Benjamin," Grandpa directed Mr. Van Aker. "Sit down here next to me so I can kick your shin whenever you mention improper subjects pure minded ladies never touch upon, even in their thoughts."

"Are there such subjects, Grandpa?" Abigail had always been a terrible tease.

Mrs. Earl nearly mewed at Miss Pettibone's frown.

"I'm starting law school, Mrs. Earl," Abigail said as if to divert the conversation.

"Good show," Isaac interrupted, then excused himself to bring more food.

Mrs. Earl's eyebrows nearly reached her hair piece. "Are there enough legal difficulties in Ann Arbor for two women lawyers?"

"The new sheriff, Oliver Martin, thinks so," Charles's father said. "Especially after that student killed himself for one of the prostitutes. Ouch. Israel Breckenridge, that hurt!"

"Improper subject," Grandpa said handing him a plate of roast beef.

"More proper to keep the house of ill repute open?"

"Benjamin!" Grandpa shouted, spreading his hands in supplication to the offended ladies.

Robert Koelz said, "Abigail's good mind would be a great advantage to the profession."

Abigail bowed her thanks at the compliment. "Mary Foster has agreed to sponsor my application. And Grandpa has given me a European tour as a pre-reward."

Charles's breath left his body. He laid down his suspended fork.

"Goodness," Miss Pettibone sighed in envy.

Robert asked, "Have you talked to Mr. Shyler, the general freight agent for the Michigan Central Railroad? He lives just down the street from you. I bet he can make arrangements for the entire trip."

"Charges a fee, does he?" Grandpa asked.

"I believe so, Israel, but you can afford it."

"Dolly and Charles, I'd like you to accompany my granddaughter," Grandpa said. "Dolly, perhaps a recital abroad would add weight to your appointment at the university."

"I'm sure," Dolly said. "Charles, are you able to get away."

"No," Charles said to his father who was motioning for him to include himself. "There is too much to learn about the business right now. Abigail, understands."

"I'm sure I don't, Charles," Abigail said. "I want you to come, too."

"Some other time, Abigail." Charles's noticed his voice was almost condescending.

Grandpa intervened, "Abigail," in the tone he used for crowning misdemeanors. Abigail said no more, and the conversation turned to town gossip. Charles wished he wasn't driven to learn everything about his father's business right now, wouldn't a month from now do as well? He wanted to explain his compulsion to Abigail. She glared at him. Maybe this afternoon was not a good time to try to get her alone for an affectionate kiss.

Robert was holding forth about the city's lack of clean water. "Well water can be easily contaminated with fevers."

"Since the war, I never drink anything but boiled water," Grandpa said. "I thought the counsel assigned a contractor as drain commissioner."

"They did," Charles said. "but Schlenker's mostly interested in manufacturing pipe. They need to tear up the streets, install indoor plumbing and purify the supply."

Miss Pettibone said, "Prince Albert died from tainted water."

"He was worn out by that royal brood mare. Ouch." Charles's father had obviously been kicked again by Grandpa.

"Sorry, again, ladies." Grandpa said, as Isaac offered Charles's father more dinner rolls to stuff in his mouth.

Charles shook his head. "Father, your conduct is embarrassing."

"I said I was sorry," he mumbled in his crumbs.

"My husband, Reverend Earl," Mrs. Earl said, "Could curl your hair with comments which went straight to one's heart."

"He never misfired," Robert Koelz said.

"Ministers are allowed," Charles said into the bottom of his empty wine glass, which he held almost over his head. "'…though Christianity is best shorn of its miracles,' Butler."

Isaac approached in a huff, grabbed the glass and filled it.

"No thank you." Charles looked at Abigail questioningly.

"We don't often request help without using Isaac's name," she explained to the silent table.

"Butler lived in England…" Charles tried to clarify his use of the author's name. "Abigail tells me people don't know who is being quoted."

Isaac frowned, and Grandpa stood. His face was flushed with anger. Charles, stood, too.

Isaac turned, stepping deftly around Mr. Breckenridge, staying eye to eye with Charles, "Before I was freed, my master. Professor Isaac Demmon, traveled to England. Then, Mr. Breckenridge hired me at Professor Demmon's demise."

Charles tried to touch Isaac's shoulder, but Isaac flinched away. In a quiet repentant voice, Charles said, "Apologies. The statement about Christianity is a quote from Samuel Butler."

Isaac glared at Charles for a moment, then grasped his hand. "My apologies. I am afraid I am quick to anger."

"And as quick to forgive," Grandpa said. "Dinner is resumed."

Mrs. Earl chimed in, "The essence of Christianity is forgiveness."

"Here, here," Charles's father said.

The party offered relieved laughter.

* * *

Abigail could see Charles had a lot to learn about people and servants. She recalled the old Mrs. Hanson's advice at a recent Ladies Library meeting, when one of the wives complained about her husband refusing to shave. Mrs. Hanson said, "After you raise your children, you'll notice your husband needs a certain amount of mending. Sometimes you have to start from scratch. It's not just forgetting where their socks are, they forget the proper use of table utensils and how to open doors."

Abigail grinned at her thoughts, and sweet Charles misunderstood her smile for a flirtation. He smiled warmly back at her. Maybe one kiss could be ventured.

During the dessert course, Mrs. Earl continued to preach in her usual, rare form. Abigail bit her lip more than once not to comment. Grandpa's dinner rule was if you could not agree or add to a guest's opinion, it was best to let it lay like an unseasoned egg where it would finally rot from lack of attention.

"Women die in childbirth all the time," Mrs. Earl said smiling directly into Charles's face. "Remarkable men accomplish things, build edifices, start businesses rolling the economy into good times."

Not under the Breckenridge house rules, Charles countered, "Women are caretakers."

"Givers more than takers?" Dolly, always somewhat of a scamp, asked.

Mrs. Earl harrumphed her disapproval. "Read the obituaries. Women are forgotten for good reason. Who wants to hear how many loads of laundry they saw to in their lifetime?"

"Or how many children they birthed," Abigail added while avoiding her grandfather's scowl and enjoying seeing Charles's left eyebrow raise.

Charles quoted Proverbs, looking directly at Abigail, "Who can find a virtuous woman? For her price is far above rubies. The heart of her husband safely trusts, so that he shall have no need of spoil. She will do him good and not evil all the days of her life. Strength and honor are her clothing; and she shall rejoice in time to come. She opens her mouth with wisdom; and in her tongue is the law of kindness. Favor is deceitful, beauty vain; but a woman that feareth the Lord, shall be praised."

Mrs. Earl remained undaunted. "You left out all the hard work in those Proverbs, Charles Van Aker, and you act like you're courting our Abigail."

"Not yet. Not able to afford the girl, yet."

'Dear Jesus,' Abigail prayed, when would Charles understand he was needlessly wasting time. Time they could be spending together. Each off-putting word from Charles cancelled out his intended compliments.

After the church luminaries left, Dolly thanked Grandpa and Abigail. "I'm so pleased. My year has been difficult at the university. I appreciate your generosity. I have had offers to perform in Madrid and Portsmouth this summer, which I will accept now."

"Don't you think Charles should come?" Abigail asked.

"Charles has a time-table in mind he's afraid to change," Dolly said.

"Well, I wish he'd talk to me about his plans more," Abigail said.

"All in good time, my girl," Mr. Van Aker said, as if that should be the end of it.

Charles ignored their comments as if he had suddenly gone deaf. "Those august, severe Mrs. Grundy's revel in the power to make their claws felt."

"That's why it is best to keep them well stroked and well fed," Grandpa said.

"They've been planted in pews too long," Dolly said. "Love for others flies before everlasting posing and preaching."

Abigail's stomach hurt. All this sham because she agreed to marry the wrong man. "Charles," she said. "I need to clear something up with you."

Chapter Five

Charles couldn't think of much to say to his father on their walk back home from the Breckenridges' When Abigail had asked to speak to him alone, his father intervened, claiming the children needed their attention for the rest of Sunday afternoon. More than the lost opportunity to be grilled by Abigail, her pink silk dress occupied Charles's attention. Rows of pearl buttons had curved down her back, past her waist. Starched pink lace encircled the bustle with a final layer flirting with the pleated mini-train. The lace hadn't bothered him, but the lithe body of Abigail Breckenridge beckoned.

"...could have asked Abigail to dinner," his father was saying.

"It's a short walk back to the Breckenridges."

"Talk the invitation over with your mother first. Tell me again about the export company."

"You could export your own furniture." They passed Bach and Abel's furniture store on south Main. "Plenty of retail outlets in Canada, Europe, and Australia."

"Should we fight those tariffs Congress has been filling the paper with?"

"You ought to because they can retaliate. Eat into profits when you export."

"How soon could you get an order from one of those countries?"

"Two are on your desk now; but, the shipping costs need to be known before quoting prices to the companies. You'll very likely double your profits."

"I wanted to expand the place; maybe build your mother a bigger house."

As Charles approached their house, he tried to see it through Abigail's eyes. The Van Akers had no servants, so a third story wasn't needed. Would the size of the home he planned for the acreage on Plymouth Road be grand enough. "Will Abigail need many servants?"

His father said nothing for a few seconds and Charles remembered servants were a sore subject between his mother and father. "Son, you might try talking more and quoting other folks less. Butler and Keats can't really say all of what you feel." Benjamin raised his hand to stop his son's repetition of avowed affection. "Women like to hear about themselves. We all do. I realize you have trouble speaking because of all the torture you went through growing up too fast. If you tell Abigail what she means to you, in your own words, she'll wait until you amass whatever fortune you seem to think you need." His father pulled on his suspenders. "I don't know if you recognize, Son, but your mother is fonder of me than you think. I started out telling her about our future and she believed me. We make such beautiful children together and neither of us has the sense to quit. Get sidetracked we do, just loving each other. Life's been pleasant, though we do get along by the sweat of our brows. Rich folks don't have it any easier. Do they seem happier?"

"It's not the money. Abigail is accustomed to a certain way of living. Should she be denied what she doesn't even realize are not necessities?"

"Didn't kill your mother."

"Of course not, but Abigail..."

"Is a fine girl. Don't overestimate her needs or underestimate the value she puts on you."

"Quoting the words of others lets feelings speak."

"Your own words would sound truer. When you use the words of others you don't sound sociable, personal enough."

Charles laughed. "Who got kicked for speaking of unholy things in front of the church ladies?"

"Me? Twice, but you don't have to be saying anything about that to your mother."

* * *

Mrs. Benjamin Van Aker sat at her rosewood secretary writing one of her daily letters back to friends in Vermont. Charles noticed she glimpsed his entrance in the desk's mirrored cabinet doors. "What is it? I'm busy as you can see."

"Mother." Charles wanted to take off his suit coat because of the heat, but instead merely wiped his brow. "Would you consider asking Abigail Breckenridge to dinner...sometime?"

"When?" Came the crisp query from her still bent head.

"Next week, whenever it might be convenient." Charles hoped she wouldn't ask why. "She loves the children so."

Elizabeth stopped writing, turned, and even smiled at Charles. "She does, doesn't she?" She raised her left eyebrow contemplating the possibilities.

Charles wished he hadn't seen it. Now he could feel both of his eyebrows twitch, ready to arch in harmony with hers. "There is the fat hen that refuses to get off her nest. Well, see if Sunday suits Abigail."

"Thank you," Charles said, sincerely.

"And, Charles," she called him back in. "I like Abigail, if you're wondering. The debacle with George should be forgotten. Ask her father, Israel, too."

"Yes, Mother." Charles smiled warmly, almost ready to approach her.

"Now, leave me alone," she said, as if anticipating a warm unsettling hug before it happened.

* * *

Sunday shone bright and warm. A constant breeze across an empty lot of wild roses kept the chicken yard smells at bay. The Van Aker dining room table had been moved outside between two shady elms. Mrs. Van Aker allowed her best china, saying it had an even chance of surviving outdoors as well as indoors.

Charles's oldest sister and his father's favorite, Matilda, had made four pitchers of lemonade. His brother, John Eric, promised his mother there would be enough strawberry ice cream stored in the ice house to keep every child happy. Fresh rhubarb pies, asparagus, and new peas graced the table along with the roast chicken, mashed potatoes, coleslaw, and the last of the pickled beets filled.

Once Abigail arrived, Charles couldn't remember much of the conversation, except he thought his family hogged most of the time. He had it in mind to pass a few well-rehearsed compliments to Abigail.

During the luncheon, Abigail talked to Matilda about her high-school teacher, Madelon Stockwell. "She's been teaching so long, she puts everyone into different personality slots. I'm in the stubborn, dark-headed group."

"So was I," Abigail patted her dark coiffure. "And Grandpa says I'm the most pliable granddaughter he has."

John Eric nudged his sister's chair. "Isn't she his only granddaughter?"

The girls laughed until Mrs. Van Aker called Abigail to her side. "Are you ignoring me, child?"

"I'm sorry," Charles heard her apologize. "I should have sat with you, but the girls started me gossiping about Mrs. Stockwell."

Charles strained to hear everything said, but his mother spoke too softly. Only snippets drifted on the breeze to him. "Bernice and your grandfather…, ….when you make your own family," and more clearly, "Charles used to…," and "Charles doesn't like…."

Charles was about to walk over to them to put a stop to his torture, when Grandpa Breckenridge walked up and offered a fine cigar from his breast pocket for Charles and his father. "Let's get in the lee of the wind."

When the three of them were smoking on the far side of the house, Grandpa asked Charles, "Why don't you take my granddaughter for a walk around the block? The neighbors will be pleased, and you two can at least say hello to each other."

Charles immediately put out the just-lit cigar and asked Abigail to accompany him.

She took his arm. "Where to, Charles?"

"Around the block will do, Grandpa said." Charles smiled. "Will it?"

"It will," she said, squeezing his arm, "and nicely, too."

"Can you imagine living without servants?" He didn't want to miss the opportunity to ask this crucial question, since an entire floor might have to be added to his dream home.

"Do you cook, then?"

"It might be fun to learn."

"I can think of better ways to enjoy ourselves," Abigail said, no doubt trying to shock him.

He stopped walking. No words came to his mind. What a delight she would be as a wife. They'd probably never even find the kitchen.

Then, right in front of Mrs. Burns's house, he encircled her waist with his arm, bringing her close enough to kiss. She tipped her chin up and he placed his full lips on her dainty, warm mouth. A shock traveled to his heels. He kept looking into her open dark brown eyes wondering if he could ever stop kissing Abigail Breckenridge. Recovering some manner of decorum, he let go of her waist and took her arm again. She acted dazed. Would she ask him if he loved her, as George said she asked him? Maybe she was thinking of the same scene. That wouldn't do.

"Dad says all one needs is good loving and cool spring water."

"That will do fine for me, Charles." Abigail faltered a step on the plank walk.

She wanted him; that was all he needed to know. "Could you come down to the factory? To see the furniture samples and then come along to Amish country before you leave for the continent?"

"I'm sure I can arrange that." Abigail moved closer to his side. "I love being friends with you. You are so good not to let George's shenanigans come between us."

"You are held in my highest regard." Charles stopped again. They had reached the gate on Madison Street. "Thank your Grandpa for the great idea."

"What idea, Charles Van Aker?" Abigail said mimicking Mrs. McConnell's brogue.

"To walk a bit with you." Charles opened the gate. Surely she didn't think her grandfather told him to kiss her. "The kiss was opportune."

"It certainly was that." Abigail smiled up at him.

* * *

The next morning, Abigail visited the Van Aker furniture factory. Charles took her down each row of craftsmen stations as they added their touches to different pieces. He hoped she noticed the clean smell of wood chips flying in every direction, carpeting the wood floor of the factory. One man added scroll work to the sides of a beveled mirror, while another applied carvings to the panel between the mirrors of an oak wardrobe.

"The wood is beautiful without all the flourishes," Abigail said.

Charles wanted to sweep her off her feet right there. He'd hoped she hated the old-fashioned furniture in her Grandpa's parlor. It might be so. He guided her to the upholstered furniture side of the factory.

Abigail stopped at a remake of a Hennessey cottage bedroom suite. "The nice thing about this set, Charles," she had to add because he was continuing without her, "is that there is little woodwork to dust."

Charles walked back to her. Her saucy yellow skirt skimmed the floor. "It's only for cottage use," he explained, "for the summer."

"Why not use it year round?" Abigail touched the smooth wood. "It would eat up less space in a room."

"Our bedrooms will be big enough." Why had he said that? Now she could tell he was planning a house without her input. Was he struck dumb because he couldn't explain he wasn't prepared to fund the project yet. She'd already had a mortifying letdown from the broken promises of George Lott.

"I'm glad," was all she said. But her eyes spoke to Charles, the way the lids lowered then lifted with her sweet smile. She understood how important she was to him without speaking. Surely she did. "Eventually, I'll need a caned rocker," Abigail said, "in the nursery."

"Of course," he said. Now she'd gone too far. He couldn't talk about the nursery in public. People would think she was with child. Charles angrily pulled her along to the couches.

"What's wrong, Charles?" she asked, still not out of earshot of all the workers. "Don't you want children?"

"Abigail!" Charles motioned for her to follow him outside through a door nearby. "Do you realize you are creating material for a further scandal?"

Abigail rubbed her arm. "You hurt me."

"Hurt you?" His heart sank. "Oh no! Are you bruised?"

"You mean because I talked about a nursery," she said, still rubbing her arm.

"Yes." He couldn't go on, but he took a step closer.

"People think I was intimate with George?"

"No, Abigail." Charles kissed the hand of the arm he'd injured. "But people love to talk. Just be more careful."

She skipped up to kiss his cheek. "I'm sorry if I embarrassed you. Weren't we going to look at modern couches?"

"Yes," he said, relieved she hadn't gotten angry with him. "Come along."

Abigail wouldn't move past a blue stuffed sofa. The soft upholstery continued over the rounded arms. "Robin's-egg blue. The color is robin's-egg blue."

"It is rather ornate."

"I don't care. There's not much carving, at least no pierced carvings. Cotton says those are impossible to keep dust free." Abigail pouted as she plumped down on the couch. "I love the color. Who is it being made for?"

"The younger Mrs. Hanson ordered it, but her husband canceled last week."

"Could you set it aside?" Abigail's eyes welled up with tears.

Charles stood mute. He could think of nothing to alleviate her stress. No doubt she was thinking of the money George must have swindled from the Hanson's.

Finally she wiped her eyes, blew her nose and said to the floor, "…until I can have it?"

"Yes!" He was happy for an acceptable solution. At least Abigail gave up squatters rights. He picked up a bill of lading for the couch and marked it, "Hold." He showed it to her and she smiled at him with her whole heart. Her sweet warmth invaded him as she took his arm as they walked back toward the entrance. Charles hated to let her leave. It occurred to him when they were finally in the privacy of their own home, he might become accustomed to using the dreaded pronoun, '*I.*' Anything was possible. At the door he asked, "Is next weekend too early for the trip to Ohio? Mother said Matilda and Samantha should come, too."

Abigail was all smiles. "Thank you, Charles."

She meant the words, and he loved the way his name sounded on her tongue.

* * *

Charles had made the long trip down to Ohio several times. First he went out of curiosity, knowing the Amish made most of their own furniture. Then he went because he loved stepping back into time. The one-horse towns had post offices where people picked up their mail in person. Ann Arbor was moving ahead too fast for Charles; except for the no-account drain commissioner with the pipe he kept selling the city instead of providing clean water for the residents.

Abigail arrived at six in the morning, quoting her grandfather, "'You are not going to some strange town without a proper conveyance.' I told him you could manage the reins; but Grandpa would have none of it, so Isaac is driving the carriage."

The girls, Matilda and Samantha climbed in with their picnic baskets.

"Oh, I didn't bring anything," Abigail said, clearly mortified.

They laughed at her.

"What could you bring?" Matilda teased. "Mother says you have a cook."

"Mrs. McConnell would not be that happy with my stealing her hard work," Abigail admitted. "If I'd brought my piano, I could play for you."

"We'll sing on the way," Samantha said. "And you did bring the carriage."

Charles was stunned by Abigail's beauty. Her red-and-white striped frock was edged with red rick-rack. White eyelet lace graced her throat, wrists, and petticoat. Charles wasn't sure the petticoat should be seen, until his mother commented. "Oh, the latest style." She took Abigail's hands. "You look lovely, dear. Watch out for my chicks now. Isaac, keep them all within sight."

"Yes, ma'am, Mrs. Van Aker. Mr. Breckenridge already instructed me about how precious these young ladies are to you both."

The three grown-up young women laughed. Charles didn't think keeping the women safe was a laughing matter and was glad Isaac was accompanying the fragile women.

At noon they found a shady road-side tree and picnicked. The girls, Matilda and Samantha went down the road picking blue cornflowers and Queen Ann's lace. Isaac trailed after them.

Abigail moved her hip next to Charles's and sighed as she looked into his eyes. Charles grasped her shoulder with one hand and her chin in the other. Their second kiss was less hurried than the first. Charles finally noticed Abigail was pushing against his face.

"They've turned around and will see us."

"I don't care," he said, without thinking.

"Charles," Abigail flung both arms around his neck, pressing her lovely self to him. "You said, '*I*!'"

"Must have slipped out," Charles said with his nose happy in the bend of her neck.

"Miss Abigail," Isaac called. "The girls need your help."

Abigail let go, and Charles prepared to meet Isaac's, frown.

Instead, Isaac winked at him. "Nobody's business," he said.

Chapter Six

On the way home in the flower bedecked carriage, Charles asked Isaac to stop in a small town where one building combined a post office, feed store, and grocery store. Abigail bought a pipe for her grandfather with her pin money, and helped Isaac pick out a doll for Taffy. Matilda and Samantha discussed which colors in the stacks of material bolts went best with redheads.

"I think orange matches Bea's hair." Matilda held up a gaudy flowered print.

Samantha disagreed. "Maybe Lily could wear it, but Bea would clash with the colors."

Abigail negotiated the choice. "Green will set off their beautiful hair. You don't want to take away from their crowning glory."

"Is it too severe for Cassandra?" Samantha asked.

"Will the striped green work better for her?" Abigail clapped her hands. "This is so much fun. I always wanted sisters."

Matilda and then Samantha hugged her. The buying frenzy continued until they'd found material for tablecloths and pillow cases along with rolls of lace for trim.

Charles decided on a wooden boat model for John Eric and a miniature Amish wagon for Little Ben. "Is this too babyish for Ben," he asked Matilda.

"He'll love it, Charles," she said. "Dad will say it's a waste but he'll play with it too."

"All and all a good day," Charles told Isaac after the carriage was re-filled with the girls and their packages.

Several farmers along the road back home invited the party of pretty women into their yards for water, which usually turned miraculously into lemonade or apple cider. Charles introduced himself as a furniture maker and asked a dozen questions about each household's furniture. "Most of it is handmade," he explained to Abigail after another house tour.

"I do like the idea of hanging chairs on the walls," Abigail said.

"Easier to mop the floor," Samantha said.

His sisters were beautiful, Charles noticed, as if for the first time. As they laughed and talked non-stop with Abigail, the farmers and field hands took note, too. The day was magical as if nothing could ever be difficult or worrisome again. Birds chirped. The strong smell of winter wheat freshly cut and laying ready for binding in the fields added freshness to the slight breeze. The shadows were still cool, the grass sun warmed, and Abigail's kiss lingered on Charles's lips.

He overheard Samantha ask Abigail,.. "What's it like to kiss a boy?"

Before Abigail could answer, Matilda rushed in with another question. "Mother says rich woman know how *not* to have so many babies."

Luckily Abigail was interrupted again. A farmer in shirt sleeves approached. "The mother wants to see your shawl close up."

Abigail handed over the lovely piece of her Swedish mother's work. Then a shy girl asked Abigail to sit down on a handy bench so she could get a better look at her hat. The plain people made a fuss over Abigail's outfit.

Isaac whispered to Charles, "Time we left for Ann Arbor." He pointed to a queer old man coming from the barn yelling something at them, pitchfork in hand.

Apparently, the patriarch wasn't happy with his family's close encounter with outsiders.

Charles hastily ushered the group back into the carriage.

* * *

A week later, Abigail and Dolly invited Mr. Shyler, the train agent, for afternoon tea to arrange their European trip. Aptly named, the nervous man had difficulty answering direct questions from the ladies. Grandpa had to backhand each volley. Abigail leaned forward to present Mr. Shyler his cake. "Wouldn't the Erie Canal be more interesting than the railroad?"

Shyler accepted the cake, then looked from it to the tea cup in his other hand. Dolly suppressed a giggle. "Use thet table!" Grandpa barked, indicating the horrid, footed marble table slightly behind Mr. Shyler's chair.

Mr. Shyler bumped his elbow on the armchair as he sat the tea down nearly spilling it onto his trousers. The Oriental rug absorbed the gift without complaint. "I believe I've quite forgotten the young lady's question." Mr. Shyler appealed to Grandpa.

"Never mind," Grandpa said. "These delicate gatherings are beyond me, too. I usually end up swearing every time I attend one." Mr. Shyler smiled but said not a word. Grandpa rose politely to his aid again, "I believe, the Erie Canal boat ride would take too long to catch the steamship."

"Correct, too many stops for passengers." Mr. Shyler smiled again, as if recently delivered from the gallows.

Dolly tried her hand at the conversation. "I'm sure you know how long the steamship will take to get to Portsmouth."

Mr. Shyler accepted her smile, nodding. "Well, man, how long is it?" Grandpa's volume increased with his frustration, which only succeeded in spilling Mr. Shyler's cake to the floor.

"A month, or more." Mr. Shyler scrambled to pick up the cake nearly upending his chair in the process.

Dolly and Abigail foreswore further questioning, and Grandpa took pity on the man. He stood and showed Mr. Shyler the door.

"Bloody waste of time," Grandpa said, as he re-entered the parlor. "I'll go down and speak to him at the station." Then he grinned at them. "You girls are too charming for poor Mr. Shyler. I hope Europe is ready for you."

Abigail agreed with the final decision to put off a Grand Tour of the continent until she graduated from law school. The two settled for a short stay in England. Dolly arranged for two months off from her summer appointment at the Music School on Maynard Street. The train trip to New York would take three days. They planned to pack light suitcases for the sleeper cars. The steamship from New York to Portsmouth would use up most of July, so they readied larger trunks for use on board ship.

Grandpa had advised them to pack light. "You'll want room to bring home those new fashions."

Abigail was still bothered by Charles's refusal to accompany them. Everyone agreed the trip was advisable after Abigail's broken engagement, in order for the talk to die down. Abigail wanted to go, but she knew she would miss her greatest ally and champion, Charles Van Aker. Their first kiss at the Van Akers was completely different from George's. Charles was so gentle. Charles dominated her thoughts like the giant being he was. Her emotions kept her feeling as if she were floating.

The trip to Amish country more than increased what she had previously thought was a natural attachment to an old friend. When Matilda and Samantha conspired to divert Isaac's attention, and Charles repeatedly kissed her, he had relaxed enough to pronounce the one word he had dreaded since grade school, '*I.*' He couldn't have delivered a better gift, except of course, an engagement ring. England developed into a more daring trip without Charles's powerful, protective presence along. Poets needed to see the world, didn't they?

Dolly planned to stay in Bernice's old room the night before they left. The last afternoon at home, Abigail had tea sent up to her mother's sitting room for them to enjoy a last view of the flowering backyard. With Cornelius's help, Abigail had transformed the garden.

Grandmother's hollyhocks lined the picket fence. Rows of pink peonies hung their heavy heads in a row below them, interspersed with hybrid white roses and bright yellow daisies. A lower layer of lilies-of-the-valley, violets, and primroses ended at a curved line of whitewashed stones. A birdbath brought yellow finches, cardinals, blue jays, chickadees and an occasional woodpecker to the garden.

Abigail pointed to the blue jay, which was harassing the collie next door. The blue jay perched on the collie's feeding dish, causing the poor animal to howl and bark in frustration. The neighbor's cook came out and ordered the dog to hush. He obeyed until the bird returned to tease him into sounding off once more.

"How long does the bird keep it up?"

"Until the food is gone." Abigail laughed. "I'll be glad to come back home."

"We haven't left, and you're already homesick?"

"I guess I am. If only Charles…."

Cotton came dashing up the servants' steps, "Miss Abigail, come quick!" They heard her calling before she entered. "It's Mrs. Van Aker."

Abigail rushed down the front staircase. Dressed in mourning, Mrs. Van Aker stood in the entrance hall. "Isaac, why haven't you shown Mrs. Van Aker into the parlor?" Abigail admonished, trying to guide the older woman into the room.

"I can't stay, Abigail. I made that perfectly clear to Isaac."

"What can I do?"

"I've bought a ticket to accompany you to New York. My mother is near death in Vermont and I need to attend to her affairs."

Grandpa appeared, coatless but his vest was buttoned. "Of course, Elizabeth. Dolly and Abigail can share a bed if the sleepers are all taken."

"No, no. I have my own. I wanted to prepare the girls. Their journey is such a gay adventure; I didn't want to frighten them at the station dressed in black like an old crow."

"All my sympathies," Abigail said. "We'll be glad to have your company on the long journey."

Mrs. Van Aker petted Abigail's cheek. "You did a fine job, Israel, mothering this girl without the help of women around you."

"Thank you, ma'am," Grandpa said. "May I accompany you home?"

"Isaac will do. Thank you." Mrs. Van Aker delicately dabbed at her damp forehead with a black-edged handkerchief. "The trek uphill from the end of the tram was more than I bargained for in this heat."

* * *

At the depot when Charles arranged for their trunks to be shipped directly to the steamship, he appeared to recognize a further explanation was needed for his failure to accompany Abigail to England.

"Dolly will make a better traveling companion." Charles bowed to Dolly and took Abigail's hand. "Plans for the future don't allow such expenditures right now. Someday we'll see all of Europe."

Heartily sorry she hadn't made it clear, Abigail held tightly to his hand, lest he vanish. "You misunderstood. Your trip was a gift from Grandpa. He wanted you to come with me."

"He won't mind if Dolly accompanies you." Charles stepped closer. "Father's business requires all available time and energy. He's not well, you know."

The steam-engine train to Detroit made a tremendous racket, belching and spewing coal dust as it pulled into the station from Jackson. Porters began loading the tagged trunks and suitcases, shouting at the top of their lungs. A few harried passengers climbed off.

Abigail only had a minute with Charles when he helped them get settled in the sleeping car. "Charles, what's the matter with your father? He seemed healthy when I last saw him."

"He works too hard trying to support the family." Then he whispered close to her ear, "in the custom Mother demands."

"It's time," Dolly interrupted.

"All aboard," the conductor shouted.

"Now, if you'll excuse me," Charles kissed his mother good-bye.

"Kiss me." Half of Abigail's spirit was staying in Ann Arbor. "I'll miss you."

Charles bent down and pressed his warm lips to her cheek. "That will have to do. Come back as soon as you can." Then he whispered again into her ear, "Please understand, my Abigail."

"I do." Abigail rehearsed for their future, wanting to hear Charles repeat the two words.

Charles waved after he got off the train.

Abigail opened the window and hung half-way out of the train car to wave back as the train left without him. On the opposite seat next to Dolly, Mrs. Van Aker smiled at her shenanigans. Abigail wondered if she would ever be number one in anyone's heart; certainly not in the heart of Charles Van Aker…too many of his family members laid claim to that. Abigail closed the train window and sat down. She hid her tears not wanting to ruin Dolly's trip.

Dolly kept up a constant chatter with Mrs. Van Aker all the way past the village of Wayne, with monosyllabic replies from Abigail. Abigail's mind went over and over her time alone with Charles: the Madison Street kiss, the factory misunderstanding, the trip to Amish country. But now, they were getting farther and farther away from each other because of her trip. He'd only kissed her good-bye on her cheek, probably because they were in front of his mother. The miles between them didn't worry her as much as the measure of no kiss, no pronoun 'I.'

When Mrs. Van Aker left to check out her compartment, Abigail said, almost to herself, "Charles never grabs at me, like George did."

Dolly took off her hat. "I hope not. You're not officially engaged."

"That's true. George kissed me on the mouth before we were engaged. Why didn't Charles kiss me in front of his mother?"

"Charles is a thoughtful man." Dolly fidgeted in her seat. "Why should he try to excite you when he's not prepared to marry you, yet."

"Not prepared?"

"Financially."

'That's so silly. Grandpa has money."

"Abigail," Dolly leaned forward and touched her knee, "Charles wants to provide for you on his own, without your Grandpa's help. How else will you respect him?"

"I don't respect money."

"You would if you didn't have it so readily available."

Abigail knew her grandfather's will down to the crossing of the *t*'s and dotting of the *i*'s. Grandpa made the will when he thought George would provide for her immediate needs. God forbid, if she lost Grandpa, she'd have enough to keep the house running, maybe. Each of the servants was to be retained with salary. Grandpa wouldn't hear of them being turned out. There was an allocation for repairs, she remembered, groceries, gas for the lights, horse feed, carriage repairs, doctor and vet fees. No clothing allowance, except for the servants. She remembered that hadn't bothered her, then. There was the educational trust, even though they both knew George had refused to allow her to attend law school. "Things happen," Grandpa had said at the time.

"Things change," Abigail said.

"That's the only thing you can count on." Dolly said.

"Dolly, I know we're friends, but I've never presumed to ask you financial questions." Abigail sensed her face reddening with embarrassment.

"We learn from our friends, if we're lucky. Ask away."

"How much would I make in salary as a lawyer?"

Just at that moment, Mrs. Van Aker slid the door to their berth open. "Really," she said, with her eyebrows at their high point, "I don't know the figures. Most lawyers are as poor as church mice unless they have another source of income. Mr. Beal runs the newspaper and Mr. Fleming built the mill."

Dolly moved over for Mrs. Van Aker to sit next to her. "Of course, I'm told John Allen went out to California to search for gold."

"Can a lawyer make as much money as you, Dolly?"

"Mary Foster certainly makes more." Mrs. Van Aker answered.

"She told me real-estate, and title searches were lucrative," Abigail said. "She offered to let me apprentice in her office while I'm in school, because Grandpa's educational trust for me won't provide for my personal needs." Abigail unpinned her hat and placed it in the hat box sitting next to her. "He thought George Lott would take care of me."

Dolly said. "I'm sure your grandfather will change his will now."

"Certainly," Mrs. Van Aker said as if to confirm the obvious. "I'll arrange for a table in the dining car." Excusing herself, she asked, "Join me?"

"Of course," Dolly and Abigail said in unison.

"But, Dolly," Abigail detained her from putting on her hat. "Don't you think I should try to know what I spend…to let Charles off the hook. When I'm a lawyer, I could provide for myself. How much would I need to make?"

"More than I do." Dolly handed her the pert traveling bonnet. "Your taste in clothes would pauper me in a month."

Continuing the conversation as they maneuvered their way down the aisles to the dining car, Abigail said, "I need to ask my seamstress, Mrs. Stone, for a list of my expenses."

"You could economize," Dolly said. "I thought I noted two new dresses a week when George was around."

"Oh, that." Abigail laughed. "I had to get new dresses that buttoned in the back because George was so fast with hands."

"Good heavens!" Dolly's beautiful green eyes rounded in shock.

The dining car sported white tablecloths and roses at each setting.

"I should tithe, ten percent," Abigail said, as she slid into the booth next to Mrs. Van Aker.

"What is ten percent of zero?" Mrs. Van Aker asked.

They laughed together, but part of Abigail's mind started to count the cost of being Abigail Breckenridge. "I should keep a ledger of expenses," she said without adding the reasons for her task. She and Charles would have to know the cost of a tour of the continent, someday in the future, but if there were babies....

Charles said his father worked too hard to keep Mrs. Van Aker in the manner she was accustomed to. But, Mrs. Van Aker dressed very simply and the house was modestly furnished. Abigail considered them quite poor. Of course, all those children. Life must be awfully expensive for one person to bear as burden. Charles and she needed to be partners in providing for their family.

"What about children when you're a lawyer?" Mrs. Van Aker seemed to be reading Abigail's thoughts.

Dolly came to the rescue. "Other women drag their infants around. Taffy and Mrs. Miller at the general store."

Abigail tried to imagine. "A baby carriage in a court room?"

"That won't do," Dolly admitted.

Mrs. Van Aker delicately buttered a corner piece of bread. "Your grandfather's hired help could tend the babies."

"True," Abigail said. "How easy it is to talk to women."

Mrs. Van Aker swallowed quickly. "Not like managing the gigantic egos of men."

"Which often need such delicate handling," Dolly said.

Abigail giggled, "Like rotten eggs."

"We're missing the view." Mrs. Van Aker directed them to the sunset.

Abigail turned dutifully toward the window. Corn, orchards, cows…all costly. Poor Charles. He knew all about this and had already shouldered the responsibility, along with hers but without her asking. "I can change that," Abigail said.

Mrs. Van Aker asked to be let out of the booth. "Thank you for sharing dinner with me. I'm so accustomed to crowds at home when it's time to eat."

When Mrs. Van Aker left the dining car, Dolly asked, "What can you change?"

"Charles's share of the load."

* * *

In New York they helped Mrs. Van Aker find the correct train connection to Vermont before heading for their hotel near the shipping docks.

Once on the steamship to Portsmouth, Abigail had time to reflect further. The word travel did come from the root word for travail and journeys did require a lot of packing, hauling, remembering where things were, finding what was available to eat, demanding all the water be boiled and cooled before drinking, which she had promised Grandpa she would do. When following his instructions about the water became impossible, Dolly told Abigail to order wine, beer, coffee, or tea.

Learning how to manage money was more difficult. She portioned the money out, budgeting daily expenses and Dolly's pocket money. Grandpa told her to buy clothes in London with a letter of credit he had sent to their hotel, the Red Lion. However, Abigail wasn't sure there would be enough for the return trip. She hoped England's food wouldn't be too expensive.

"Let's see Stonehenge and Bath," she told Dolly. "I read in the New York Tribune that they've just uncovered more Roman ruins in Bath."

"After my performance at St. Mary's College, we'll be free to roam."

"Would you mind not staying in London every night?"

Dolly cocked her head. "I bet we can find good lodging in the country. Are you worried about how far Grandpa's money will stretch? I did bring my own money to share expenses, Abigail. Your grandfather understood that I would pay my own way."

"I apologize, Dolly. I thought Grandpa was making a gift to you."

"The idea to improve my standing with the university by performing overseas was the reason for my thankfulness." Dolly smiled. "Does that alleviate any budgeting problems?"

"Yes, if you're sure."

Dolly continued unpacking in their small stateroom on the ship. Abigail watched Dolly's efficiency, but her thoughts strayed to the time she'd spent with Charles. "Dolly, I can't stop thinking about Charles. When he kisses me and when he pulled me outside at the factory to scold me, I didn't feel the way I did when George…."

"Took advantage of your innocence," Dolly finished the sentence for her.

"My stupidity, you mean. Anyway, Charles's roughness…."

Dolly interrupted, "He hurt you?"

"My arm." Abigail waved her hand to indicate nothing untoward had happened. "He's so big."

Dolly banged the lid of her trunk shut. "I think you should tell me what happened."

"Didn't I? Don't get upset."

Dolly squeezed between the two trunks and pushed Abigail down onto her bunk. "You have not discussed this with me and I suspect Grandpa hasn't heard the story, either. He should have been stricter when old George was in the picture. We have 20 minutes before dinner."

"Well, he invited me out to the factory and we toured the aisles. I commented on the furniture I liked, not that dark carved stuff at home."

"He hurt you," Dolly was tapping her fan on one of the trunks, "Start there."

"I merely mentioned I'd need a rocking chair in the nursery."

"Abigail! Did anyone hear you?"

"That's what Charles was afraid of. So he pulled me outside. He scolded me and I told him that he hurt my arm, when he manhandled me. He was awfully sorry."

"The night George left, I thought Charles was going to shake my teeth out," Dolly said.

"What?" Abigail couldn't believe it.

"I told Charles I knew you should not be engaged to George, before John showed me his wife's note."

"When did you know?" Abigail was more shocked about Dolly's withholding information than in Charles's response.

"At the Ladies Library meeting. They gave knowing glances to each other behind your back. And young Mrs. Hanson blushed for half an hour." Dolly sat down on the other bunk and brushed imaginary lint from her lap. "Charles apologized."

Abigail was glad she hadn't witnessed the library women's reactions. She would probably have ended up defending that villain, George; but Charles was another matter. Abigail realized a further dimension to loving someone, especially when he was shown in an unflattering light. She wanted Dolly to like him as much as she did. "Charles doesn't know his own strength."

"You sound like a woman in love," Dolly said. "We better hurry and dress. I think we're scheduled to sit at the captain's table."

* * *

London was loud and hot. Thick smoke and ancient smells of mold and rat droppings hung in the air.

Dolly opened the windows in their narrow rooms, then wet half the hotel bath towels before stuffing them between the raised ledges of the windows. "This will cool and clean any breath of air that might agree to creep in here."

"I know a trick, too." Abigail sprinkled the sheets with talcum powder.

The weather cooperated for Dolly's concert-hall performance. Cool breezes swept through the open doors. Dolly appeared on stage, radiant with her red hair in a cascade draped with chains of seed pearls. Abigail realized she had never fully appreciated her friend's elegance.

The audience was entranced by the beauty of Mozart's 'Andante,' Handel's "Air in G Major," and Chopin's "Mazurka in A Minor. Other artists were included on the bill, but only Dolly Colt was applauded into an encore of Mozart's "Variations on Twinkle, Twinkle Little Star."

The next day when they were shopping for shoes and hats, Dolly seemed as carefree as a Samantha.

"Dolly, will you ever marry?" Abigail was suddenly mortified by her question. "Forgive me, but you are so beautiful."

"I'd lose my job." Dolly smiled, relieving Abigail embarrassment. "I've thought of babies, who become more adorable every day. If you knew my parents, you would understand why I chose a profession to delay making a family."

"How did they influence you against an earlier marriage?"

"I think they were a little insane." Dolly placed another tipped-brim hat on her head and admired herself in the shop's mirror. "If you met them alone, you'd think I was the crazy one to say that. But when they were together, something weird happened. A battle ensued, not physical, but a subtle test of wills, I guess you would call it."

"Not doing what the other requested?" Abigail choice of hats included one with two white birds with wings spread wide on the same hat. "Too many feathers," she said, putting it back on its stand.

"No, nothing that obvious. If Mother went for a walk with my father, he would instruct her about her need for more exercise, every day, maybe twice a day. By the time they returned home, Mother would take to her bed, ill from the amount of exercise he'd proposed. If she misplaced her house keys, he'd remind her of all the years she never knew where her keys were."

"Years?"

"Yes, he'd repeat each instance, leaving her feeling like a dithering idiot. I assure you she had some semblance of intelligence, although severely undercut."

"But all marriages…."

Dolly didn't hear. "It wasn't anything she could describe to ask him to change. And she told me whenever he wanted his marital rights, he would try to make her jealous by remarking on the intelligence, dress, or children of one of her friends. Mother told me she avoided intimacy out of pique."

"Not very truthful communications," Abigail said, finding the search for a decent hat wasn't as much fun as she had anticipated.

"I can't even blame my father. His upbringing was a war zone compared to the battles he unknowingly fought with my mother. His own mother and uncles used to chase each other around the house with knives, threatening murder."

"Why did your mother insist on staying with your father?" Abigail wished they had never started talking about marriage, because Dolly's happy mood had vanished, but Abigail didn't know how to begin another subject without hurting her friend's feelings.

Dolly walked to the shop's door. "I don't think she realized how negative her environment had become. She tried to act in the local theatre in Boston. I thought she did a fine job, but he commented on every wrong motion, every false inflection of her voice, every error she made from the scripted dialogue. When he died her career blossomed."

Abigail tried to cheer her friend's prospects. "You will avoid such a man in your life. You'll be able to recognize the traits."

"Actually, I think my mother almost asked for contrary input, as if she thought of herself as not being good enough." Dolly finally laughed. "Abigail I haven't closed any doors."

"Good, because someone will be awfully lucky to capture you."

"Capture?" Dolly laughed again. "I'll be the one deciding that. Look, there's a shoe store."

The next week in Salisbury, their carriage cleared the low entrance gate of another Red Lion Hotel. The flowering courtyard convinced them of their wisdom in leaving London. Their rooms were smaller than Cornelius and Isaac's room on the third floor. An ancient Black Forest clock in the hotel's reception hall towered over eight feet. Abigail imagined it might have come from King Arthur's castle.

A sturdy breakfast prepared them for the tramp through the monoliths at Stonehenge. They took an hour pacing around the outside of the circle of the collection of three-man-high gray rocks. Their placement on the gentle rise of the flat countryside demanded explanation.

"They look like they fell out of the sky," Dolly said.

Abigail had read a little about them. "The outer bank of stone holes were markers for blocks as large as dinner plates. The stones were moved daily in some ritual of combinatorial analysis."

"I thought they incorporated a Druid sacrificial church."

"Oh, no; before the Druids, other sun worshipers counted the days until the next eclipse of the sun. Then some powerful priest could unseat any unfit ruler with the claim of heavenly powers."

"They most likely were used to count off the days to the winter and summer equinoxes."

"You mean, solstices. I don't think I remember the reference. But did you feel the pull of gravity at the entrance? As if the dead were beckoning, tugging at your ankles with their lonesome spirits."

"Goodness," Dolly said. "Are you sure Charles is the only poet back home?"

"I don't know about that, but legends say the stones walk at night and scare roaming lovers and farmers coming home late from the fields."

"It's always good," Dolly pinched Abigail's arm with affection, "to have legends to scare roving lovers into staying within range of chaperons."

After another day of packing up and organizing transportation, Abigail found the steeply rolling hills surrounding the town of Bath conjured up visions of Roman soldiers traipsing to the river. The good, cool weather continued to hold, but Abigail thought the town smelled too much of sulfur to enjoy for long. The Pump Room entrance was a gaping hole in the process of unearthing treasures. The lead floor of the Kings Bath had been removed and the hustle and bustle of construction created so much noise and dust that the weary travelers returned to their hotel.

The desk clerk growled, "If Major Davis had not insisted on tearing up everything…"

"Oh no," Abigail said. "What a discovery. When it's all excavated, the baths will be a marvelous draw for tourists."

"Even now," Dolly gestured at their obvious presence.

The disgruntled hotel owner joined them from the back office. "But it's not very picturesque. You'll have to admit to that."

"I will," Abigail said, "but the possibilities are thrilling."

The owner smiled. "They say Bath is where the gods come to die."

"Fitting." Dolly shuddered.

"We do have some of the water bottled from the old Pump Room fountain, if you'd like to try it."

Abigail supposed Grandpa's rules could be set aside this once, since none of the tourists to Bath had ever contracted fever from the waters. After tasting the Pump Room water, Abigail told Dolly, "It is unpleasant enough to prevent any harmful quantities from being swallowed."

In their hotel on Quiet Street, the noise from a street renovation with the use of a new, noisy steam shovel belied the address. Dolly suggested they escape the unpleasant racket by taking a ghost tour of Bath as advertised in the lobby.

The shawl-bedecked matron conducting the walk reminded Abigail of Dolly's mother's hobby. "Here is the perfect career for an out-of-work actress."

The older woman met her eye after hearing the remark, but continued the fantastical journey through Bath. At one point black crows flew from an abandoned house. The tour guide promised. "The house is haunted by the father of a murdered girl."

Abigail denied being as suggestible as Grandpa claimed, but sure enough as the lady described the dire deeds that happened in the next house, A hand grabbed the back of Abigail's neck. She turned expecting Dolly to be the culprit, but Dolly was in front of her. "Time to retreat," she said to Dolly.

"You're quite pale," Dolly said. "Seen a ghost?"

"Felt one. That's close enough for me." Abigail didn't want to talk about the sense of impending doom she experienced.

The touch had come from a long way off, maybe from home.

Chapter Seven

Before they could retire to their rooms, the hotel owner sent Abigail and Dolly back out to the noisy streets with detailed directions to the Bath Museum where they found Thomas Jefferson's 1674 drawing of the King's Bath. Another 1820 drawing by David Cox provided an excellent view of the buildings they had missed by only a year because of the excavations. Abigail purchased several reproduction prints of his Pump Room drawings. "I'll have them framed when I get home," she told Dolly.

Paintings by Edward Gibbon of the Decline and Fall of the Roman Empire furthered the romantic ambience of the site. Relics from the diggings around new foundations for the Pump Room marched across the centuries.

After dinner at the hotel, Abigail agreed with Dolly that the trip to England provided enough stories for more than one season of dinners in Ann Arbor. They both agreed the return trip to New York by way of Portsmouth promised to be easier, because they knew what to expect on board ship.

The next morning, Abigail explained her rush to pack. "I feel like a horse smelling the hay at home."

Dolly laughed at her. "I think Charles might be the fodder."

* * *

Time did fly by on the steamer crossing to America as well as on the trains heading west to Ann Arbor. As the sleeper car from New York passed Jackson, Michigan, Dolly looked up from a fashion magazine. "I didn't see many exceptional dresses in London."

"I think Paris might have been different. We could sketch a few for Mrs. Stone to sew up and declare they are the latest European styles."

Dolly wasn't enamored of the plan. "They'll know as soon as they see the latest drawings in *La Mode Illustrèe.*"

Abigail flipped to a clean page in her account journal. "I wish jackets stopped at the waist instead of the hips."

Dolly leaned over to look at the sketch pad. "No bows or lace ruffles and how about pleats of different materials?"

"We should add a really outrageous hat as a joke, so we'll know who has access to Mrs. Stone's latest fashion gossip."

"Abigail Breckenridge, where do you get this ornery streak?"

"My grandmother, Salome." Abigail busily drew a chapeau to be set on the side of the head with black crows as decorations."

"Stick the wings in the air. How was your grandmother ornery?"

"I don't know about her, but have you ever noticed how often her namesake, the Biblical Salome, the one who asked for John the Baptist's head, is mentioned in the Bible?"

"Did her step-father have an incestuous affair with her after the dance?"

"Grandpa has Josephus's history, which insinuates one woman named Salome gave birth to a child Herod named Bernice. Then her daughter, Bernice, gave Herod another son."

"You are not as innocent as I believed."

Abigail could tell her face was pink with embarrassment. The Biblical Salome was a safer subject than her own story. "Luke's gospel mentions a Salome at the crucifixion and at the empty tomb at the Resurrection."

"Now, that would be some conversion story, saved from the degenerate royal life to be a handmaiden of the Lord?"

As they pulled into Ann Arbor's train station, Abigail said, "Dolly, let's not wear jackets when we get off the train. We'll tell them it's no longer considered stylish in London on warm days."

"All right." Dolly stalled, acting dubious. "What about our hats?"

"We'll have to show them off!" Abigail laughed. "They're brand new."

* * *

Abigail stood at the top of the train steps ready to dismount when she spotted Mrs. Van Aker, Charles and Grandpa. "Dolly, something's gone amiss." She didn't turn around to speak to her companion, who then touched her shoulder.

"What is it?" Dolly's voice lost its happy tone.

Abigail froze on the step. Suddenly, she recalled the grip of the ghost on the back of her neck in Bath. "Grandpa isn't smiling. Perhaps Mrs. Van Aker's mother in Vermont passed away."

Charles wore a new black suit with a black silk armband. "Your grandmother, I'm so sorry," Abigail said, as she gave him her arm to help her down from the train.

"And his father," Grandpa's voice caught on a sob.

Abigail let go of Charles to embrace Mrs. Van Aker. "You shouldn't be here."

"Yes, I should, Abigail." Mrs. Van Aker said. "I wanted you to know directly from me. Benjamin thought the world of you. We've already had the funeral."

Dolly put her arms around Abigail's shoulders. "Take her home, Grandpa. I'll send for my trunk later."

"Won't hear of it." Grandpa had almost regained his natural voice.

Isaac stayed behind to arrange for the draftsmen to deliver the trunks. Charles took his place on the carriage to drive them home, without saying a word to Abigail.

"I'm sorry to ruin your homecoming," Mrs. Van Aker said.

"Ruined," Abigail managed through her tears. "Any day is bankrupt without Mr. Van Aker in it."

She knew Charles was broken hearted, but he avoided meeting her eyes. This trip to England had been ill advised. She should have stayed at his side, helped him get through this somehow. A dull fact edged into her mind. He might not ever embrace her again, never speak to her as the relaxed and confident young man she had left. What would she do without her Charles? He'd never been hers, she remembered thinking she would always be in second place to his family. His father's death only increased Charles's responsibilities to his birth family.

"Benjamin was my closest friend." Grandpa took Mrs. Van Aker's hand. "If you need any help with the children, schooling or anything at all, I'd consider it an honor."

Mrs. Van Aker patted Grandpa's hand. "Benjamin is irreplaceable. My mother always offered to help us but Benjamin wouldn't hear of it. My children never went without. He was a good provider."

Charles's shoulders shook from his emotions.

Abigail's heart lurched. She wanted to stand in the carriage and embrace his back. Was he lost in his own black world with the windows drawn shut against her?

Mrs. Van Aker continued to drone on and on. "Now they're both together in heaven, I'm sure they'll understand my freedom in spending all that money. I've given Charles his portion and the business with John Eric as a partner, when he's old enough. Each child will have a sizable trust for school and more besides. I've bought a lot on Division Street down near Packard and plan to build a new house. After my mother's funeral, her Chinese cook came home with me."

"When did Mr. Van Aker fall ill?" Abigail interrupted. She couldn't help but notice when Charles's back tensed with each financial statement that his mother made. Before she left, Charles said his father was working too hard to keep up with his family's needs. But now it sounded like the family finances had always been secure. Surely Charles was rankled because his father worked himself to death needlessly.

"I was only home a week." Mrs. Van Aker answered the question Abigail had almost forgotten she'd asked. "Benjamin went to bed with what we thought was a chest cold. He didn't last the night. I'd trade all that money to hear his voice, one more time."

Charles drove Abigail and Grandpa home first. Dolly and his mother stayed in the carriage with Charles in the driver's seat. Abigail didn't press to speak with him. Time enough for that.

In the Breckenridge parlor of the hushed house, Abigail sat with Grandpa before dinner. He was smoking but she didn't mind. "It's so good to be home."

"I missed you, especially when…." He couldn't continue.

Abigail said softly, "I'm glad Mrs. Van Aker is taken care of."

Grandpa smiled. "And the children. That Ben was as proud as a mule."

"I think that's a peacock."

"Ever seen a stubborn peacock?" Grandpa asked.

"I've never seen a peacock," Abigail answered, "so I don't know."

"Me either." Grandpa smiled his old sweet smile. "Charles has taken it hard."

"Charles and his father were as close as brothers." Abigail's tears started, her heart tightened. "He didn't say a word to me, Grandpa." She didn't want to upset her grandfather more than he already was. Abigail decided she would go directly to Charles's house. Make him talk to her. "I feel as if he's slapped me, after he kissed me."

"Give him time, Abigail. He'll come around."

Cotton tiptoed into the room. "Miss Colt asks to see you all, if'n it's not inconvenient."

"Dolly?" Abigail rushed to the hall. Dolly leaned against the balustrade, white as a sheet. "Grandpa, help."

Isaac came running too, and they helped Dolly to a sofa in the parlor. "They went through all my belongings," she managed.

"At the boarding house?" Grandpa asked.

"Mrs. Pierce told them she didn't know when I was returning, and they rented my room."

"Oh, Dolly," Abigail exclaimed. "That's awful."

"You'll stay here," Grandpa said. "Isaac, do you have the energy after hauling those trunks around to organize a moving gang to go over to State Street and pick up Miss Colt's things?"

"I'd have to pay you room and board," Dolly said.

"Whatever you think is fair," Grandpa re-seated himself in front of Dolly. "I've always thought Abigail should have a woman in the house with her. Charles is taking his time about putting a family together."

"Grandpa!" Abigail was shocked that he would lay their business out in the open.

"Thank you." Tears slid down Dolly's cheeks before she could find a handkerchief in her purse. "I've been telling Charles the same thing ever since George left."

"Charles has his reasons, I'm sure." Abigail said.

"What are they, I'd like to know?" Grandpa huffed off to his den.

Abigail took Dolly upstairs to the back bedroom's sitting room.

Cotton trailed behind. "I remades dat bed yesterday, laundry day and all. I'll bring up some more face towels. Jest let me fill dis here wash pitcher for yah."

"Ask for tea to be sent up, Cotton," Abigail called after her.

Dolly placed her shaking hands in her lap. "Look at that. I act as if I'm frightened."

"You must feel violated." Abigail patted her friend's cold hands. "Tea will be brought up shortly."

"They stacked my belongings outside my room with the books not even in boxes." Tears started to flow again. "I can't believe I'm this upset over a misunderstanding."

Mrs. McConnell arrived with the tea. "Now, we'll need you to come down to the kitchen tomorrow, Miss Colt. I like to know what my people consider good food."

Dolly smiled weakly. "Thank you."

Abigail asked. "Who gathered up your things?"

"A new purser. It wasn't Mrs. Pierce's fault. She only said she didn't know. They could have checked with your grandfather." Dolly calmed down with her second cup of tea. "Did Charles stop by? How is he doing?"

"Grandpa says he's taking his father's death awfully hard. I thought he would come by. Were any of your possessions harmed?"

"I'm not sure. It is embarrassing to know my personal effects were exposed to scrutiny by strangers."

"There is a lock on your sitting room door to your suite. Grandpa prides himself on everyone's right to privacy. I'll leave you to freshen up for dinner." Abigail stood to leave. "You know, Dolly, you're like the sister I've never had."

"You are all the family I think I'll ever have." Dolly embraced Abigail.

* * *

Five days later, well prepared for ostracism, Abigail entered the side door nearest the Presbyterian Church's cloakroom for the Ladies' Library monthly meeting. Ever since she'd jilted George Lott, Abigail's social standing had altered. Her precarious acceptance into the Ladies Library rested entirely on her grandfather's reputation. The ladies had made sure copies of plans for a new library by Irving Pond, a Chicago architect, passed into Grandpa's generous hands. Grandpa had made a substantial gift for the purchase of the building site on the south corner of Division and Huron and he had insisted Abigail attend their meeting. Abigail declined to disturb Dolly who was busying herself arranging her belongings in the two rooms Grandpa allotted her; so, Abigail faced the rumor-mill alone.

Old Mrs. Hanson spotted Abigail first and took her aside, speaking roughly, "I know the ostrich game is thought a Christian act, but I wanted to apprise you of my late wisdom. The best way to take a man into your heart is to get as far away as possible from him."

Arrant nonsense. Abigail didn't know if the old woman was describing her separation from George's courtship or the state of her affairs with silent Charles. But Abigail understood the desire to flee from eligible men. "Our affairs are in the hands of noodles."

Mrs. Hanson agreed. "My senseless daughter-in-law gave that fool, George Lott, money to invest in Trist. That's the last we'll see of that."

"I'm not sure Grandpa knows." Abigail wondered if anyone ever fainted with shame. The amulet from Grandpa's medicine chest was in her reticule at home. "Tell me the amount, and I'm sure Grandpa will want to return it."

"Won't hear of such nonsense. We hired a detective, though. Would you mind telling him all you know about the man?"

Abigail could feel her face redden. "Please set up a time for him to call on Grandpa and me."

"Watch those ladies out there." Mrs. Hanson turned her toward the meeting room door. "They know the sore and how to hit it every time." Mrs. Hanson wacked Abigail too heartily on the back.

Abigail had a small coughing fit before she joined the poetry reading. People will insist on reading their own rhymes aloud. Many an outstretched hand greeted her. In fact, no one else had the audacity to speak directly to her about the atrocious man. Abigail wanted to explain she was the astounded recipient of the news that George Lott had at least one wife, but she was offered no opportunity to receive sympathy. Instead, Abigail was held in perfect contempt, an abject slave to circumstances she had not foreseen, and given no chance for her defense.

In the new business part of the meeting, Abigail explained Grandpa's gift. A rousing hoopla of approval arose. Abigail gave her tacit endorsement that Grandpa wouldn't mind if they mentioned his gift in the newspaper to inspire other contributors.

* * *

Back home on Moore Street after the ladies meeting at the Presbyterian Church, Abigail struggled to unbutton her dirtied boots. They were caked with spatters of mud. If her button-hook hadn't been all the way upstairs, she wouldn't have ruined her kid gloves. Of course, if she hadn't needed to cross the street quickly to catch Charles, she could have stayed on the plank walk all the way home.

At first Charles was unusually curt. "A lumber delivery is due at the factory in fifteen minutes."

"Come to supper, won't you?" Abigail noted the huge man, her man, took a step back as if she might upset his plans.

"Glad to come." She noticed his mouth watered and then realized he had lost weight. "May I bring Samantha?" Charles asked as an afterthought, over his shoulder, then headed for Madison Street.

"Yes, please," she had to call after him, attracting unwanted notice from shoppers.

He must have thought better of the agreement, turned and nearly ran back to her, giving her a quick peck on the cheek, in public, before leaving on a dead run for the factory. Abigail admitted she still felt unappreciated. Some wife she would make. The poor guy had to take over his father's business before he was ready to man the job, provide for seven siblings, no matter how much money was left for them in a trust, and satisfy her every need.

Abigail only had herself to worry about and she had a fleet of people anticipating her every need. She wondered if Charles would even accept his mother's windfall since the money had failed to save his father. Not that she knew his every thought, but the newly found money must have troubled Charles, since his father wasn't rescued in time.

England had been such a bad idea. She hadn't listened closely enough to Grandpa and Dolly. They'd tried to tell her Charles was under a tremendous amount of pressure to prove himself. It was eating him away. He must have lost ten pounds, if not more. And what had she presented to him for an ideal mate, an impatient princess who could and would go to England without him.

Abigail wondered if she might get him alone for a reassuring hug. Kisses were fine but not if they upset him further. She could love him in her house or his. 'Please, God,' she prayed. 'Help my Charles and poor Dolly.' Abigail did thank the Lord for providing a friend close at hand. The thought of Dolly upstairs in her sitting room comforted her. And Abigail did realize God had not sent the recent rain, dirtied gloves or the factory delivery schedule to personally test her trust in Him. She carried her shoes into the basement for Cornelius to polish.

"It's a chicken you smell roasting," Mrs. McConnell said in answer to Abigail's question about what they might serve Charles and Samantha for supper. The cook sprinkled a fine dust of flour on the pie crust she was rolling out. "Would he be wanting a raspberry or a nice peach pie?"

Picking up the clue, Abigail hugged the cook's shoulder. "Peach. I do love coming down here, if not for the delicious smells alone, I come to hear the music of your voice."

"Go on with you now." Mrs. McConnell's blush confirmed she was pleased.

Abigail headed up the back stairs slowly, eavesdropping as usual.

"Cornelius, did you hear how the lady appreciates me? A Mother, I am, to the girl."

"Yes, ma'am," Cornelius answered in his slow southern drawl.

* * *

Grandpa was delighted to hear about Charles's acceptance of her dinner invitation, but he clearly was disturbed by the news of a detective investigating George Lott, in order to retrieve the money the young Hanson couple gave him to invest in the Trist railway spur. "Young Mrs. Hanson probably knows as much as we do." Grandpa was making the parlor blue with smoke from his pipe. "Both of our families have been foolish. We gave money and affection to a complete stranger."

"Mrs. Hanson, the elder, gave me the detective's card, so that you will receive him." Abigail handed him the card after reading the name, Dredford.

"I'll receive him." Grandpa blew another cloud of scented air into the room. "Bet they'll end up paying this detective more for his fees than they lost in the first place."

"I wouldn't want to discuss the detective in front of Charles," Abigail said.

"Nonsense," Grandpa said. "A future husband needs to know everything about your past. That's how we got in trouble with George, not knowing all of the truth."

* * *

Charles and his fourteen-year-old sister, Samantha, arrived in a brand new buggy. Charles was quite subdued, but he did smile when Abigail divided the bouquet he'd brought with him. "Cotton, put half in Dolly's sitting room and the other half in mine."

"Yes, ma'am," Cotton said, then stopped on her way to the back stairway. "But what if Miss Colt don want dem."

"She will," Abigail and Samantha said together.

Samantha wore a black dress, but Abigail was glad to see her mother had added a broad lace collar.

"Samantha, I'm so sorry about your father." Abigail hugged her and the girl, who had lost weight, clung to her.

"Those were happy days," Samantha said, "the trip to Ohio."

Abigail couldn't help but to ask, "Don't you two like your mother's new cook?"

"Abigail," Grandpa scolded, "Don't be stirring up trouble."

"But Grandpa, look," Abigail insisted, "They're skin and bones."

Grandpa turned an appraising eye on both of them. "Are you well?" He reached for Charles's forehead but Charles stepped back, so Grandpa laid his fingertips on Samantha's. "No fever."

Isaac took a step closer to Charles. "Eyes seem to be clear," he relayed to Grandpa.

"Okay you two," Grandpa said. "Time for confesssions. Isaac, get Samantha a glass of milk and a freshly, buttered roll. One for Charles, too." He pushed Samantha and Charles into the dining room. "Take a seat, right now. What is going on?"

Charles shook his head at Samantha.

"Stop that, Charles." Abigail put her arm around Samantha's shoulder. "Do you want me to take her upstairs?"

Isaac brought the food and Mrs. McConnell with it. "What's this I'm hearing? Are you two being ornery with a new cook?"

Grandpa leaned back to let his cook grill them.

Samantha had started to cry after she devoured the roll and drank the milk. "We can't stand his cooking."

Charles opened up. "Everything is covered in a red-sugary sauce, even the chicken."

"Well now, Charles Van Aker, you and Samantha will continue to eat here, "Grandpa said, "until I get a chance to talk to your mother."

Charles and Samantha smiled at each other as if they'd found treasure.

"What about the rest of the children?" Isaac asked, as Mrs. McConnell nearly pulled him out of the dining room.

"Matilda and John Eric eat it all," Samantha said. "They're so afraid to hurt Mother's feelings. I feed Bea and Cassandra other stuff, because they hate it, too. Mother doesn't mind."

"And Lily and Little Ben," Abigail asked.

"They complain the most, but they eat it." Charles reached for another roll. Some of the tension had left his face. He turned to Abigail and smiled. "But *I* can't go it."

Charles had said it. He used the first person 'I' in her house. Abigail wanted to run around the table and jump into his lap, but she controlled herself. Her big lion of a man had taken his first step toward her since his father's death. Surely she could bring him all the way home to her arms, in time.

Chapter Eight

On an abnormally cool day in late July, Charles helped Samantha into the Van Aker's new buggy. "Try to make yourself scarce when we get to the Breckenridge's."

"How do I do that?"

"Ask Dolly if you can see her new rooms."

"Wait a minute." Little Ben brought out an apple for the horse, his pet now.

The family's friend from Howell, Mr. Smrt, selected the quiet gray mare for the family's conveyance. Flicka, as she was called, stood perfectly still when the children first cavorted around her. The mare did not move one hoof off the ground as if she knew little ones might be in the way. Flicka lowered her head to accept the apple from Little Ben.

Matilda came out to the road to scratch under Flicka's ears. "Mother says to not embarrass us, Samantha."

The mare leaned toward Matilda. All and all, the horse and the Van Aker family made a pleasant marriage. Marriage was on Charles's mind of late. His mother was still in official mourning, so the banns probably shouldn't be announced in church, but Charles missed his Abigail every hour they were apart.

When he first saw Abigail at the train station, he couldn't speak. He'd been managing the factory by himself, comforting the other children and his mother; but at the first sight of Abigail, the loss of his father, so close to his heart, flared past even his initial shock on the morning he had died. Abigail's existence heightened his own bereavement. Her sadness for the death of his father regenerated his own grief.

As his mother went on and on about the awful money that had always been available, Abigail had sensed his anguish and asked for details of his father's illness. His heart broke when he heard her questions, but his anger was his own. He loved his mother, he knew that. All the frustrations his father put up with sat on his shoulders now, intensified, unresolved, and made more horrible with the fact of his father's stubbornness to accept financial help from his mother's family probably hastened his father's death.

Samantha pulled on his jacket sleeve. "Charles don't frown so. You frighten me. I'll cook for you and Bea and Cassandra."

Charles patted her hand. "I'm sorry. I'm off slaying imaginary dragons. Are you looking forward to seeing Abigail?"

"And Dolly." Samantha held a bouquet of flowers intended for Abigail. "I'm glad Abigail has a friend living with her. It must be awful to be born an only child. I bet when she marries she'll want fifteen children."

Charles rolled his eyes at the comment. He certainly hoped not. "Two will do."

"Should we have brought another bunch of flowers for Dolly?"

Charles laughed for the first time since his father had died. "I can only court one girl at a time, Samantha."

Samantha was smiling from ear to ear. "I love to hear you laugh."

They didn't need to mention the cause for the lapse of merriment. They both knew grief intimately. "What if Abigail won't have me, Samantha?"

"Then she's gone crazy in England and you don't need her anyway."

"Sisters tend to be loyal, don't they?"

Samantha smiled. Nevertheless, when Charles arrived at the Breckenridge home, his hands shook as he tied Flicka to the hitching post.

Grandpa came out to inspect the mare. "Did Ben's friend, Mr. Smrt, pick out a good one for you? You were right to turn down your mother's choice of that pair of expensive, high-stepping roans, entirely inappropriate for the carriage."

"Best for the family," Charles said with his mind on other matters as they entered the Breckenridge foyer.

Abigail's appearance immediately calmed him down.

Charles had an odd sensation of time slowing. Perhaps, her unhurried descent down the front hall stairway was deliberate to attract his attention. His buddy from grade school wore the yellow skirt she'd worn to the furniture factory. By the time she reached for the flowers from Samantha, he felt he'd been suspended in a spider's web. Abigail shared the flowers with Dolly. Samantha winked at him. Correct she was, in seeing the need for more.

After the routine snack of milk and warm fresh rolls, Dolly asked Samantha to see her rooms upstairs, and Abigail excused herself to check on dinner. Mr. Breckenridge offered Charles a glass of sherry in the parlor before dinner.

"Come to ask for Abigail's hand," Charles blurted out.

"About time!" Isaac said.

"Never mind," Mr. Breckenridge said. "We'll have to wait a decent interval for your mother's mourning period."

Charles ran his hands through his hair, an old habit he intended to break. "Like to finish the new house on Plymouth, too."

"Sit down, Charles." Grandpa offered him a cigar. "Understand your mother bought land on Division and Packard?"

"Father wanted a bigger house for us all." Charles wondered if grief could kill you. Stop your heart in the midst of planning the future. Grandpa scooted his chair closer and lit Charles's cigar for him. Grandpa's gentle act of solace drove Charles's painful emotions back into their dark cave. "When Mother's house is done, we plan to expand the factory. The export business is doubling our profits."

"Thought it might." Grandpa blew great clouds of cigar smoke toward the fireplace. "Draft takes most of the smoke up the chimney."

The fumes from his own cigar smoke dispelled Charles's worries even further. Tobacco euphoria lifted his eyebrows, out of control again. "Abigail should make the decisions about the Plymouth house layout. Do we need a third floor for the servants?"

"Absolutely not!" Grandpa said.

Charles saw Abigail's face as she entered the parlor. Grandpa heard her gasp and turned around.

"But Grandpa, you know I love my Charles."

"Oh not Charles," Grandpa said as Charles hurried to her. "Of course you can marry. Charles asked me about adding a third floor to your new home."

Charles held both her small hands in his gigantic paws. "He's agreed to let us marry."

"Grandpa! Can I really kiss him?"

"Have at it," Grandpa said.

Charles bent down and Abigail put her arms around his neck, not waiting for him to start the procedure. Her lips were warm and welcoming. He'd missed her so much when she was in England and he needed more than a kiss. He pulled away at the ungentlemanly thought.

"What's wrong?" she asked.

"This isn't very private," Charles said.

Abigail playfully batted at his chest. "Oh no, no liberties before the wedding."

"Never intended to take any liberties." Charles straightened in indignation to his own lie. He looked at Grandpa, who only shrugged his shoulders.

Dolly and Samantha stepped into the parlor to hear Charles's last statement. "Abigail, are you impugning this fine young man's character?"

Abigail bent over Samantha and laughed. "Apparently, I'm quite forward."

"It isn't that, Abigail." Charles sat down too hard on one of the chairs, which immediately broke.

"Are you hurt?" Grandpa and Abigail asked in unison as they rushed to help him up from the floor.

"Just mortified." Charles gingerly arranged himself on a sturdier sofa.

Abigail turned to her friend. "We're engaged, Dolly."

"Not officially, Abigail." Charles held out his arm for Samantha to snuggle close. "Mother is still in mourning, but with your help, Abigail, we could start building our house."

"Well early congratulations to both of you." Dolly kissed Abigail's cheek and shook Charles's hand.

Samantha clapped her hands.

Grandpa asked the girls to excuse them and motioned for Charles to follow him into the library. He pointed to a chair for Charles. "I want to mention your father's death only to say not to try to make sense of fate. Poor old Abraham thought Jehovah might be jealous of his love for his first born son, Isaac. Abraham tried to kill him to please God."

"Doubt he could have made sense of that." Charles wondered what Mr. Breckenridge needed to talk to him about, in private.

Grandpa continued, "I don't think only Christians know how to forgive. Joseph forgave his brothers after they sold him into slavery." Charles could add nothing. "Sometimes." Grandpa looked Charles straight in the eye. "We have to forgive God when things don't make sense."

"Like my father's death?"

"We need to love a perfect being," Grandpa said as if he hadn't heard Charles.

So, Charles made his statement as clear as he could. "No reason for my dad to die of hard work with all that money available."

Grandpa hung his head. "Reason and order are great bugaboos. Give up trying to fathom fate. Put meanings on what you deem meaningful, and let the rest of chaos alone."

Charles wondered if he could be honest. He sometimes wondered if asking for Abigail's hand was prompted by the fact that he couldn't get a decent meal in his mother's home. He could show up for supper every evening at the Breckenridge's now, with Samantha. He did love Abigail, but he would have waited a few more months if the cook hadn't insisted on so much sweet red sauces.

"And Charles." Grandpa laid a heavy hand on his shoulder. "Benjamin and I were friends for years. He told me how the school kids bedeviled you into changing the way you speak."

"My stutter."

"You never stuttered. You outgrew the rascals, that's all, heart and body." Grandpa finished his cigar, fixing his watery eyes on Charles. "You have an obligation to convince Abigail you accept her uniqueness, as she accepts yours. Do you understand?" Charles shook his head to clear his thinking. "You must unlearn your own censorship," Grandpa said. "My granddaughter deserves your best, and the use of 'I.'"

Charles took a moment. "I love the girl, Sir."

"Good. Let her hear it often. The years go by too fast."

As they headed for the doorway, Grandpa stopped. "One more thing, I like Abigail just the way she is. I expect you to not want to change a single hair on her head."

"Yes, Sir."

Grandpa said, "She's a modern woman invested with psychic powers, adroit with magic."

Charles added, truthfully, "Highly educated, widely read, smart, and full of independent sass."

Grandpa allowed Charles to pass into the hall. "See to it that you keep her that way."

They heard the knocker on the front door. Isaac rushed past them to answer it. Callers were rare at dinner time, unless they needed a meal, and that invitation was usually offered at the Breckenridge's backdoor. Isaac announced to those assembled in the hall and parlor. "Mr. Joseph Veltman, Mr. Samuel Dredford and Mr. and Mrs. Darrel Hanson."

"Oh, Grandpa," Abigail said, as if recognizing the strangers' names.

"Isaac, please add four more places for dinner." Grandpa pulled the ragged, potbellied older man into the parlor. "Abigail, this is the best man you'd ever want to fight next to in a war."

"Mr. Veltman," Abigail took his rather unclean hand. "Grandpa says you saved his hide…life more than once."

"Couldn't save his brother, Denzle." The old man bowed and sat next to Dolly, who Charles was sure wrinkled her nose at the man's earthy odor.

Mr. Hanson offered his hand to Grandpa Breckenridge. "I was informed you would receive Mr. Dredford. Since I'm vitally interested in these proceedings, I've taken the liberty of joining him."

Grandpa shook his hand for the shortest possible minute, then addressed Mrs. Hanson. "Dorothy, I haven't seen you since you were in school with Abigail. We all adored your mother's beauty, but you are far lovelier."

"Who was her mother?" Joseph Veltman asked. "That skinny English teacher?"

"Lithe, Joe. Yes, Antoinette Kerner owned a lovely heart," Grandpa said.

Mrs. Hanson recovered somewhat from a bit of shyness or embarrassment. "You needn't invite us to dinner, Mr. Breckenridge. We shouldn't take but a minute."

"Won't hear of it. I love company. Abigail, make sure Dorothy sits between you and Dolly. Samantha, you sit between the newly engaged couple, Abigail and Charles. Be their chaperone."

Fourteen-year-old Samantha giggled at the task. The Hansons offered their congratulations to Abigail and Charles.

Grandpa approached the short detective. "And Mr. Dredford."

Dredford looked up at Grandpa and they shook hands. "I hate to impose. I can return at your convenience."

"Nonsense." Mr. Hanson and Grandpa shared one opinion.

Isaac announced, "Dinner is served."

As Charles helped Abigail with her chair, he whispered. "How does the famous Mrs. McConnell feed eight when four were expected?"

Abigail blushed as she revealed the family's secret. "The staff will eat leftovers from yesterday."

After everyone was seated, Grandpa directed the conversation. "Let's get this dreaded Lott situation off the table so our stomachs can enjoy supper."

Mr. Dredford asked, "Do you know his whereabouts or background?"

"Neither," Grandpa said. To Mr. Hanson he added, "We did hear him praise the benefits of buying property along the railroad to Trist. I suspect that's why you invested money with him?"

Mr. Hanson motioned toward his wife, Dorothy, across the table from him. "Yes. We thought the idea reasonable at the time. We gave him money to buy bonds for us."

"I wasn't taken in," Grandpa said. "Thet North-South spur to Toledo still hasn't paid back my investment."

"Unfortunately," Dorothy Hanson said calmly, "we never received any bonds for the payment I unwisely made."

"I'd be happy to reimburse you," Grandpa said even without hearing the amount.

"My mother won't hear of it." Mr. Hanson turned a bright crimson. "I saw his dark menace. The devil can pass as high society. As a good Christian I intend to pray for his death."

Mr. Dredford shook his head. "I think we've finished any need for further discussion of the dreaded Lott."

"Good," Joe Veltman said. "Cause I want to introduce myself to the ladies. Israel, his brother, Denzle, and I joined the First Michigan under Captain Mann."

"I remember Major C. B. Grant was the recruiting officer at the Cook Hotel," Grandpa said. "Thirteen dollars per month for what Grant himself claimed would be 'a prolonged sanguine struggle."

"August 17th, 1864," Veltman said.

Taffy had sneaked into the room, and Abigail picked her up.

Veltman continued, "We was switched to Lt-Col. Copeland's group, the 5th Michigan artillery, after Israel mustered out. We were known as Danie's Battery, 1,400 men. How is Kingsley?"

Grandpa sliced and passed dishes of the ham. "Gone. Remember he was too feeble to give a speech for the July 4th celebration."

"1875," Veltman said.

Grandpa cautioned. "Gory stories are hardly dinner fare."

"Tough," Veltman said, and launched away. "I shot horses, wounded ones." He scratched his white head, as if a thought struggled to get out. "Israel, who was that boy, his name, the one who helped me with the horses?"

"Clayton?" Grandpa offered.

"No. That warn't it. Clayton was the drummer boy. This other kid came right off his Daddy's farm. Told me hair-raising tales of getting beat up by his pa. He was one of nine children."

How many children did Abigail want? Charles wondered. Abigail smiled at him over the waif's head. 'Lord,' he sincerely prayed in silence, 'why did I wait so long to ask for her hand?' Charles spoke softly to Taffy, whose eyes were getting pretty big with the talk of hitting, "Men were mean in the old days without anyone getting after them."

Taffy was not consoled and skidded off Abigail's lap to rejoin her mother through the swinging doors to the serving room. Charles saw the child cling to her mother's knees. Cotton swung Taffy up in her arms, taking the delighted child around to the large side yard. Abigail turned in her seat to see what was amusing Charles.

"...digging a new outhouse." Veltman was saying. Charles turned back to the mean farmer story. "Kid said his dad looked right at him when he threw a shovel of dirt on him, twice."

"Dirty bugger," Grandpa winked at Abigail.

"They shot him," the old soldier said.

"His father?" Samantha asked.

"No. The boy," Veltman said.

Dolly gasped. Mr. Dredford rose to join her side of the table. "Are you all right, ma'am?"

Charles had never seen Dolly so flustered. "Yes," she said, "Quite all right."

Mr. Dredford returned to his seat. Charles couldn't help but notice the antics of the two of them. Dolly Colt and Samuel Dredford only had eyes for each other. Remarkable. He might be witnessing his first experience with love at first sight. Charles cocked his head for Abigail to notice. Abigail winked at Charles in appreciation of the phenomena, so unlike their affection which grew up with them -- in spite of them, in fact. Charles asked. "Why on earth did they shoot a boy?"

"Well," Veltman bowed in his seat as he accepted a plate of ham, mashed potatoes and peas from Isaac. "He used to shoot the wounded horses, like me."

Samantha had already devoured her serving. Abigail signaled to Isaac to replenish Samantha's plate and Charles's. The food was so good. Charles wondered if he'd ever get enough of the mashed potatoes and gravy. Thank God, nothing was the least bit red, not even pink. And thank the Lord, he added, the conversation kept attention away from their ravenous appetites. Thank God too, because he and Samantha had been saved from the Chinese cook. Grandpa would do something to permanently solve the problem, without hurting Mother's feelings. Listening to his chatter, Charles wondered how Joe Veltman had time to eat.

He was still talking. "But the day after Gettysburg, the young chap lost it, I guess. Started shooting the wounded men out there in the field. For some, it was a blessing. But then he came in and started killing the horses that only needed washing. First, we thought he misunderstood, the blood on them, and all. Maybe thought they were wounded. We soon saw that was wrong. Captain Warner pointed his pistol right at the boy's forehead but he wouldn't stop firing. I do remember his name. It was J. D. At the funeral, Captain Warner said maybe J. D. was trying to save the horse from the carnage."

"We all would have voted for that," Grandpa said.

Charles's plate was empty again.

Abigail stood and rubbed her hands. "Isaac is serving dessert in the parlor. I feel like a field of cold dead men marched through my soul."

Grandpa followed Abigail into the parlor with the rest of the guests. Still lost in an old landscape of war, Grandpa said, "I was at Denzle's side when he fell. Breckenridge's name their second sons Orlando or Israel, because the first son usually dies in war. My first son, Joseph, didn't reach the age of two. Orlando brought home typhoid from the gold fields. Fool wiped out my wife and his."

"Israel, remember Bolthan in Grand Rapids?" Joe pounded the slate fireplace mantle. "Oh stupid, stupid! Even an ox knows right from left, but ye will never learn."

Grandpa smiled, sadly. "They promised us an ephemeral frolic."

Mr. Dredford informed Dolly, "Eighty local men were lost, one-half from the Fifth Ward."

Charles bent close to Abigail. "Men talk. Let's go into the library. We can find something to alleviate the chill of death by printed words of affection."

"Who said that?" Abigail rose, excusing herself. Her frown showed she had tired of asking.

"Me," Charles said. "Just me."

"Well, I agree with it." Abigail took his arm as they crossed the hall to the library. She picked out *'Daisy Miller,'* the new novel by Henry James. "I've tried reading this, but the innocent girl keeps being accused of improper manners."

There it was again, George Lott's actions staring them in the face. Charles closed the door.

Abigail instantly took a step closer and turned her eyes up to him. "They think I let George make improper advances, don't they?"

"Who knows?" Charles wished he had had the courage to say, 'I don't know.' They had to talk about Lott to clear the air. "You thought you were to be married."

Abigail turned back to the shelves of books and waved her hand as if dismissing the subject. "I wonder if the Virgin Mary experienced anything at all. Of course she didn't have to worry about original sin." Without turning around, she continued, "I need to tell you how excited George made me feel, physically."

Charles did not want to listen. "We do not need to know."

"Who can I tell?" Abigail turned again to him, her eyes pleading. "Dolly has never been married. I doubt she's allowed herself to encourage flirtations, like Mr. Dredford's before tonight."

"Mrs. McConnell then," Charles ventured.

Abigail stamped her foot, as if she was his childhood friend, again. "You listen. If we are ever going to marry and be good friends, you need to understand."

Charles sat down at the library table, more comfortable with his knees hidden. "You go ahead, if you think you should."

"First of all, it wasn't like us." Abigail's face colored with her effort at honesty. "I look forward to seeing you. I dress meticulously, hoping you'll like the colors or my attempt at being stylish. I always dreaded getting dressed for George's call. I had to think of where the buttons were. In the back was best, because he could not quickly undo them."

Charles could feel heat rising from a central source of his own. "Perhaps we shouldn't…."

Abigail acted as if he hadn't spoken. "My heart seems to swell when I think of you. With George it seemed to shrink."

Charles was on his feet in a minute. "Abigail." He stretched out his arms to embrace her.

She stepped back. "Go sit down. I'm just getting started."

Charles did as he was told.

"Something happened to me," Abigail went on, as if listening to the inside of her body. "My blood would rush around, down to my toes, up to my head. With you I feel warm all over, as if expecting a pleasant thing to happen, some engrossing action on your part that will completely focus my attention on my love for you." They smiled at each other. Abigail continued, "The married women I know told me it was natural to pull away. I asked Dorothy Hanson about it, she's only nineteen, you know, even though she's been married for three whole years. She said men were grabbing beasts." Charles interrupted her with a protest. "And a woman has to bear some things with courage." Abigail appealed to him.

"Abigail," As he spoke, Charles experienced an infusion of courage. "No real man would ever injure or take advantage of a woman."

"Oh, he didn't hurt me," Abigail stated matter-of-factly. "I would never have allowed that, but it was the pulling and pushing I didn't like. I look forward to touching your shoulder, kissing your face. I look forward to more…." She stopped.

Charles reached out his arm toward her. "You're saying you love me."

Abigail came close to his side. "Yes."

"I love you, too." Charles did not choke on the word. He wanted to marry her right then. But the truth was he could not, not yet. "I always will."

Abigail leaned against his side and he wound his arm around her waist. "Let's join Grandpa; hopefully they've stopped reminiscing about the War."

Bless her heart. Abigail knew he was in trouble, unable to say more on the subject of her physical reaction to George. Charles stopped her at the door. "Swinburne says, 'The time of lovers is brief; from the fair first joy to the grief. That tells when love is grown old, from the warm milk kiss to the cold, from the red to the white rose leaf. They have but a season to seem as rose leaves lost on a stream that part not and pass not apart as a spirit from dream to dream, as a sorrow from heart to heart.'" Abigail's eyes shone with unshed tears. He kissed her then, without restraint. She pressed herself against him. Before he let her go, he had kissed her long neck down to the start of her sweet warm bosom. What joy marriage would be with his Abigail!

* * *

Charles became accustomed to heading up to Broadway each night with Samantha. They told their mother Grandpa was intent on having Dolly teach the piano to Samantha and it was the only time the professor had free. Most evenings, Abigail, Dolly, Samantha, Grandpa and Charles were the only ones at dinner. Mr. Dredford joined them, on occasion. Nearly every Sunday the previous minister's widow, Mrs. Earl, and her retinue came to re-taste Mrs. McConnell's cooking.

Mrs. Earl was always ready to wage war between the sexes. "Generations of relentless hostility, battles to face as women for the rest of our lives." At the piano, Samantha gasped. Mrs. Earl continued without pause, shaking her finger at the younger women in the parlor. "Remember, the woman always wins."

"Mr. Van Aker lost," Robert Koelz said quietly to Grandpa.

"The suit," Grandpa said.

"What happened?" Abigail turned a page for Samantha's half-hearted attempt at practicing.

"Mother," Charles said. "She put the suit on Father that he refused to wear to church."

"In the coffin?" Dolly whispered.

Charles and Samantha gave affirmative nods.

"I'm not against religion," Mr. Dredford said, "but if a man sees an ethical issue, I think it would be begging perdition to go against it."

Samantha started to cry softly.

Dolly scolded Dredford. "Samuel, how could you say such a thing in front of the child?"

"It is getting late," Charles said, lacking anything to say in defense of his mother. "We need to be on our way."

"Oh, you can't," Miriam Pettibone, Mrs. Earl's crony, gushed. "Abigail promised we would pick out any furniture you might want of Grandpa's. I'm here especially to tell you its worth."

"Charles." Grandpa motioned for Charles to sit back down. "The women have been planning to inventory the value of the furniture for a week. They have tags they're going to tie to anything you want once you and Abigail set up housekeeping." Grandpa got up to sit next Samantha on the piano stool. "Besides, your sister here needs at least another half-hour of Dolly's time, if Mr. Dredford will agree to watch instead of talk."

Charles gave in, and a parade began through Grandpa's home. Miriam, Mrs. Earl, Abigail, and he marched through each of the rooms. Four decades of furniture fashion filled the house.

"We're going to store whatever we agree on in Grandmother's room," Abigail explained.

Miriam Pettibone began writing on the color-coded tags. "Yellow is for Abigail."

To Charles the travesty of pricing Grandpa's belongings appeared ghoulish. He couldn't forget the wagon of furniture his mother had shipped home from her dead family's estate. "The timing seems wrong," he said.

"Nonsense," Miriam chatted away. "Best know what you have before you *need* to part with it. I've seen people practically throw their furniture out of the windows when they should have wrapped it in lamb's wool and stored it in a bank."

Salome's bedroom suite of the Gothic Revival period was unusual. Charles pointed at the 'sanctified' bed, "Looks like it could float in a flood."

"It won't diminish in value," Miriam said.

"Do you like it?" Abigail asked.

"Don't you?" Charles fished for safe ground.

"Well, we won't have to have it moved into Grandmother's room." Abigail kicked at one of the bed's sturdy legs. "It's already here."

Mrs. Earl contributed, "It looks like a bed you could take comfort dying in."

"We're looking forward to creating life…," Abigail handed the price tag back to Miriam Pettibone, "…not seeing it snuffed out."

Chapter Nine

For the first dawning of October, a full regalia of red, orange, and yellow rolled out their leafy splendor. On his fifth trip to the open carriage, Charles stopped to enjoy the maples, elms and ash trees lining his street. Abigail promised to spend a day away from her law studies to attend the Farmers' Picnic at Whitmore Lake. His heart gave a great thud against his chest. Mercy he was stricken with the girl.

During his daily courtship rides across town with his sister, Samantha, he had contemplated the shortness of the dinner time with Abigail, wanting her all to himself. Abigail's mind was occupied with new worlds, school, texts, and ideas. Charles loved her even more for her lack of attention to his presence, which only helped to kindle his pursuit. Her smile of welcome was enough to vouch for his importance in her world. The ritual of saying good-bye each evening afforded him the sweet opportunity of a lingering kiss, enough to dream on all the way home and through the lonely night. Any pangs of remorse for not yet living together were almost assuaged by the promise of dinner the next evening.

Stone foundations and the first beams of their new house on Plymouth Road further attested to their private troth. By Christmas or New Year's Eve they could be husband and wife, living in the hilltop house! The concerns Charles harbored about providing for both families, his father's and his own, had lessened with the infusion of capital from Vermont.

At the Whitmore picnic Charles planned to ask Abigail when she wanted the banns read at St. Andrew's. He hoped she'd agree to the first day of November.

"And what are you smiling at, Charles Van Aker?" Matilda, his oldest sister, called him back to the business of loading the carriage. "Happy to see the cook stay away from your food?"

"Abigail," he answered truthfully, although the cook's absence from the picnic was a blessing. "Glad to see Mother has allowed you to take off part of the mourning garb."

"Mother said a black skirt was pain enough for a 16-year-old to wear to a picnic. And my black curls were apt homage." Matilda straightened the black-edged collar of her sailor blouse. "Do you think it's all right?"

Charles's throat constricted as he noticed the tears on her dark lashes. Matilda had been Father's favorite among the children. He put his arm around her shoulder for a brief hug. "Father would want to see you happy."

John Eric hauled the last basket of food over to the carriage. "Are you sure Mother is well enough to go? I can stay with her."

Charles didn't know what to do. Mother had insisted on coming to the picnic.

Doctor Vaughan had come to the house twice in the last week. "A vague emotional malady," Doctor Vaughan had explained. "Widows often complain of stomach problems."

Dr. Wells had been more concerned, asked to see a stool sample and ordered a liquid diet.

"If Mother wants to come home early, John Eric," Charles decided, "we'll leave the younger children in Abigail's care, and take you and Matilda home to be with Mother. We can go back for the rest of the family when the picnic is over."

John Eric's face registered no relief until Samantha piloted a laughing crew, Lily and Beatrice, from the house to the carriage in the street. The little ones wore striped-lime green dresses made from the material Abigail helped choose in Ohio. The dresses' perfect color complemented their red hair. Little Ben produced the standard apple for Flicka. Cassandra toddled out, pulling at her mother's hand. Charles caught up the tyke, and lent an arm for his mother. "Are you sure you're strong enough for the long ride?"

"I don't know, but I'm going." She gave Charles a brave smile. "John Eric, Did you pack enough lemonade?"

"Yes, ma'am. And I brought extra lemons and sugar to make more, if we run out." John Eric placed a pillow behind their mother. "Should we put up the top?"

"The sun will do us all good," Mother said.

Charles noticed the effort her smile cost. Something *was* wrong, more than grief. He pocketed his fears. The anticipation of seeing Abigail overwhelmed his good sense. Before he mounted the driver's bench, he whispered to his mother. "Going to encourage Abigail to announce the banns in November."

His mother's open smile warmed his heart. "Then, let's get started."

The roads to Whitmore Lake were rutted from the rains of a sodden September. Every bump made Charles wonder if they should have stayed home. He drove slowly; arriving on East Shore Drive after most of the places had been taken along the road for the Farmer's Picnic. Spotting Grandpa and Isaac, Charles reined in Flicka at the picnic tables. The Breckenridge household rushed over to help his family dismount. Charles planned to leave the carriage right where it was to be handy if Mother wanted to leave.

"Cornelius will run for the carriage, when it's needed," Grandpa said. "Go join Abigail while her nose is out of her books for five minutes."

Charles did not have to be told twice. Acting as young as his brother, he ran to Abigail, picking her up and swinging her in a wide circle.

"Now, Charles, behave yourself," Abigail scolded. He sat her down under the boughs of a willow tree. Its small leaves created a bright yellow dome. Could summer fade when there was so much to do? Abigail tucked her hair under her wide-brimmed hat. "What will people think?"

Charles righted the brim of her hat. "We can marry before Christmas. You can announce the banns at St. Andrew's whenever you want."

A slow smile of sensuous pleasure spread a blush down her throat. "Charles," was all she needed to say. They kissed again. His life, blessed with Abigail Breckenridge, stretched out into the future. As if reading his mind, Abigail said, "Every day is going to be this glorious."

For so many years they'd known each other's mind Abigail knew the first sway of his thoughts. "I might have to hold an umbrella over your head, eventually." No thought of the pesky pronoun limited its use when Charles was comfortably situated in Abigail's world.

"Rain?" Abigail tugged on his ears. "How dare the fates allow dark clouds."

To hold her again he lifted Abigail up into the yellow leaves of the weeping willow briefly while the rest of the family caught up. The group's chatter and picnic clutter interrupted any further intimacy. Abigail and Mrs. McConnell helped Mrs. Van Aker place a folding chair in the shade facing the shimmering lake. Everyone joined in the task of emptying the carriage.

"Your mother is not feeling very well, is she?" Abigail inquired.

"No, but she wanted to come." Charles added, "Dr. Wells seems to think it's more serious than Vaughan does."

"Vaughan's more interested in himself than his patients," Grandpa said.

"He asked for a water sample from our well," Charles said, "I paid a week's wage for him to analyze it."

Grandpa grumbled to himself. "Asked for payment in advance, no doubt."

Charles absent-mindedly surveyed his colorful clan under the turning leaves of the picnic-area trees. Matilda and Samantha assisted the younger girls in getting their toes comfortable in the bright lake. Cassandra was busy teasing the kitten that she usually kept hidden in her apron pocket. Abigail took a blue ribbon from her hat and tied it carefully around the prancing ball of white fluff. Cassandra ran in the direction of her mother to show it off. Abigail caught up the cat before it was strangled, running with the child toward Mrs. Van Aker's side.

"Oh, Abigail, be off with you," Mrs. Van Aker called out. "My eyes will swell shut if I'm within a foot of that creature."

Abigail dutifully withdrew with the offending kitten and the crestfallen Cassandra. Summer couldn't last forever. Ninety degrees was unusual for October. The mosquitoes had been slowed down by old age, but the flies were still busy.

"Use'ta burn rags down South," Cotton told Mrs. McConnell as they fanned the table. "Kept dem off da plates."

Samantha came up to Cotton with Taffy in tow. "Taffy says she cannot take off her shoes for the lake."

"Caint be swimming where white folks can see her." Cotton shook her head.

Grandpa heard the comment. "Samantha!" He yelled, "You take that child in with your sisters this minute. I'll be jiggered if I'll see my brother die in vain!"

Abigail rushed to his side. "Grandpa, calm yourself."

"Let him yell," Mrs. Van Aker called from her chair. "If we didn't lose our menfolk for equality, why did they perish?"

"Good people," Isaac commented to Cornelius, as they finished laying the tables.

When all was ready the families assembled. Grandpa said grace and the children dove into the food. "They're all so young," Grandpa remarked as he brought Mrs. Van Aker a plate of food.

"I think I'll just stick to lemonade," she said. "Doctor Wells thinks a liquid diet might help."

Charles wandered over, even though he'd rather hold Abigail's hand.

"Do you find it easier to lie on your back than your side?" Grandpa asked. "Any hemorrhaging?"

"Yes," she said. "And the skin on my stomach is tender to the touch." Charles watched his mother blush deeply. "Israel, I'm sorry."

"Aren't we old enough friends for solicitous concern?" Grandpa bowed to Charles's mother.

"We are." She spotted Charles. "Charles, perhaps John Eric should take me home. You stay here with the children and Abigail."

"Mother, we've arranged for me to drive you home. John Eric and Matilda will stay with you. Then I'll come back."

Ignoring Charles's arrangements, Grandpa looked as if a musket ball had churned up the picnic in his stomach. "Cornelius," he called, "get the carriage. Charles, when your mother is settled, get Dr. Wells to attend to her."

Grandpa marshaled Charles away from his mother to the far side of a nearby ancient oak. Charles bent down to hear the whispered bad news. "Dr. Wells knows." Grandpa wiped his brow. "It's typhoid."

"No," Charles said. Typhoid had taken Abigail's parents and her grandmother.

"She can beat it with rest." Grandpa shook Charles's arm. "Listen to me. Boil all the water she drinks. Pour hot water over your hands before and after touching her. Burn her soiled linens. Dig a new outhouse immediately. Board up the old one. Can you remember all that?"

"Yes," Charles's knees weakened. "The children?"

"Matilda, Cotton," Grandpa hailed them and they rushed over. Charles couldn't move, as if rooted to the spot. "Mrs. Van Aker might have typhoid. Cotton, you know how I keep a clean house. I want you to nurse Mrs. Van Aker with Matilda's help. You can tell me no, girl. You have a baby to consider."

"S'all right, Sir." Cotton tightened the cloth around her hair. "My baby will be safe with Cornelius and Mrs. McConnell. "I knows how to boil the linens."

"Burn them, Cotton. Isaac will bring you clean supplies."

Charles put his arm around Matilda's thin shoulders as Grandpa instructed them. "You two need to make some hard decisions. Right now. The babies, Beatrice and Cassandra, won't come down with it, for some reason. Will you let Samantha and Abigail care for them at our house?"

"Yes," Charles and Matilda said, clasping each other's hands. Charles moved like a zombie. Mother was safely in the carriage with John Eric, Lily, and Little Ben.

Grandpa continued, "You both know I saw a lot of this in the army. Half of the men we lost were never felled by bullets. This or some other godless fever got them. I recognized the odor on your mother's skin. She has a fever now. Only give her hot lemon tea or lemonade. Charles you'll have to arrange a cold bath at night when the fever is the highest. Pick her up in her bed clothes and gently lower her into the bath. It will keep her fever down."

"Matilda, she'll want to lie only on her back. It's too painful for her to sit or recline on her side. Bed sores will develop if you don't keep the sheets dry and clean. Charles is strong enough to lift her once a day when you change the bedding. I'll send over the rubber mats I used for my family. Things will get frightening, and Dr. Wells will leave you a supply of medication for her pain. Keep the food very simple for yourselves now. No sauces. I'll have Mrs. McConnell send over food for the children. Can you two handle this?"

Charles and Matilda looked at each other and nodded dully.

"Charles." Grandpa caught a sob before it erupted. "Please don't kiss my granddaughter good-bye. The disease is highly contagious, and I've lost so many." Grandpa stopped speaking for a moment then said, "Come sit on the front porch every night, while you're able. Abigail can talk to you from the parlor window. Promise?"

Charles aged ten years in ten minutes. "Yes," he replied. He'd been stuffed back into the role of caretaker of his father's family when he'd only begun to experience the first excitement of starting his own life, a world with Abigail in it.

Grandpa leaned against the oak, clearly stricken with the realization of the ramifications of the disease.

Charles had trouble concentrating on the rest of Grandpa's speech. Instead, he fixated on Abigail and Cassandra running in a circle with the white kitten. The blue ribbon, Cassandra's pretty lace trimmed frock, and Abigail's dusty pink pinafore held him captive. They looked like china dolls turning and turning on top of a delicate music box.

"Bring Cotton home every evening so I can give her instructions." Grandpa's voice sounded lethargic, hopeless. "Dr. Wells is a good doctor. I wouldn't waste time on Vaughan. Isaac and Cornelius can dig the new outhouse. Show them where to place it downhill from your well."

Matilda tried to control her sobbing.

"I can't remember anything else." Grandpa sighed. "Did I tell you to boil the drinking water, to wash your hands every time you touch anything?"

As if looking for Charles or Grandpa, Abigail stopped the kitten chase. Cassandra ran into her skirt. Abigail handed the ribbon to Samantha. Charles wanted to shout to her to keep playing, but instead she started toward the group.

"What is it, Grandpa?"

Grandpa righted himself, taking fast strides toward her. "I'll explain at home, Abigail. I'm feeling rather tired. Charles will be over this evening."

Abigail stepped around Grandpa's arm quickly reaching Charles.

Charles had to back away, with his hands raised above his head. "Abigail," he groaned.

"Charles," Grandpa scolded. "Abigail, come with me."

Charles kept eye contact with her questioning face. He wanted to speak but there was so much to say. He watched as Isaac pulled her away from him.

Grandpa revealed the reason for their actions. "Typhoid."

Abigail stopped, turned to him, unable to move further, even when Mrs. McConnell tugged on her arm. "Charles," she called. "I understand."

Isaac picked Abigail up physically removing her to the edge of the lake shore. Abigail raised both her arms as if drowning while she stood on the safe ground. "Take care," Charles heard her cry.

Then Charles was alone in the long nightmare of beating off death.

Chapter Ten

"But how did Mother get typhoid?" At sunset Charles was stationed on the Breckenridge front porch with his back to the street. He asked Grandpa, who was sitting at the parlor window, "But how did Mother get typhoid?"

"Traveling." Grandpa pulled at wisps of hair behind his ears. "Boys usually got it a month after they reached camp."

"Why do you think Cassandra, Bea, and Samantha won't come down with it?" Charles pushed the food around on his plate.

"I don't know." Grandpa pulled at his ears, letting the remaining strands of white fluff alone. "Cassandra and Bea complained to our Taffy that they're bathed by Samantha every night. I doubt John Eric and Matilda bathe more than once a week like the rest of us; and Little Ben and Lily probably think they're too old for nightly immersion."

"That makes a difference?" Charles rubbed his damp hands on his dinner napkin.

"And you are in a courting mode," Grandpa said, "so you're careful about your appearance."

"Yes, Sir."

"Boiling water from now on, inside and outside. Even from the porch we might contract it. Trust all of Cotton's rules."

Sterile, that's what everything must be. Charles didn't like this cleaner world, especially because he wasn't sharing his meal with Abigail. Mrs. McConnell's cooking lost its flavor when tasted without Abigail in view. The pots of geraniums and yellow mums on the porch offered no scent. The birds had ceased their evening calls. The world had turned cold and empty in the space of one afternoon.

* * *

Sitting on the piano bench, waiting for her turn at the parlor window, Abigail suffered, wrapped in a dark prison of her thoughts. For all of September, law school had increased her confidence. She hadn't realized how far George's misadventure had undermined her. The ease with which she comprehended the stuffy text books reassured her of the powers locked in her mind. Now, knowledge of the law seemed like useless rubbish.

Her emotions choked her, cutting off any desire to think rationally. Swinging around in Charles's arms at the picnic, she imagined if he let go she could flap her wings and fly. How infantile! She was an emotional midget. She couldn't sustain joy or even sort out the injuries caused by their latest separation. Isaac, Mrs. McConnell, even Grandpa were aligned against her. Of course, they were not. The thought was illogical, but they did all conspire to remove her from Charles, when he needed her the most.

Charles looked so lost as he sat in the small wicker arm chair. Six-foot-five inches of legs and arms sprawled on the porch.

"Charles, Charles," she called.

"Survive," he said.

One command? "I miss you, Charles." She couldn't control her sobs.

"Not now," he said.

Did he mean he couldn't bear to hear her cry? "Sorry, sorry. I'm going to announce the banns anyway."

"Don't"

The word sounded like rejection. The minuscule portion of her functioning mind assessed that as false. "What shall I do?"

He only shook his head. "Need you alive," he managed before a great heaving in his chest completely cut off his flow of words.

"I want to help you." Abigail couldn't find the words to woo him, rouse him from his lethargic trance.

Charles turned his face away. The setting rose of the sun or anger flared on his face. "Vaughan. Xing." The words emitted through clenched teeth. His slack fingers balled into gigantic fists.

Abigail instinctively drew back from the window. A monster had awakened in her gentle poet. "Charles, Charles," she cried, brokenhearted.

Grandpa entered the parlor, squeezed past her at the window. "Charles Van Aker, my granddaughter doesn't need to be tortured. Keep your decency about you in her presence."

"Yes, Sir," she heard Charles say.

Grandpa retreated again.

"Sorry," they said to each other in unison.

"Got you in trouble again," Abigail said, retreating to their childhood years. She thought she saw him smile.

"Own fault," he said. "Love you more than I can say. My tongue is stuck to the roof of my mouth, no matter what I swallow."

"Fear," Abigail said. "Fear always fills my mouth with cotton. I should have stayed with you, gone with you to help with your mother."

"No!" Charles shouted.

Grandpa pushed past again. Charles was already deflated, tears streaming down his face. Grandpa said not a word, only patted Abigail's shoulder. "Calm him down, girl."

Calm him down? What about her ranting soul? "Get mad," Abigail said. "Shake your fists at whoever you must. I understand. But, Charles, don't shut me out."

"Safe," he muttered. "Have to be about my father's business. Wait for me?"

"I'm here, Charles. I'm never going anywhere without you, ever again. Even England was a mistake. I wish we'd married immediately. School is ridiculous with you facing this monster."

"Abigail," her name sounded best from his mouth. "Keep studying. Glad you went to England, saw everything. We'll see it together again." He lifted his hands to his throat as if to push out the reluctant words. "I love you, Abigail."

"That's better!" Grandpa announced from the library.

A smile briefly played at the corners of Charles's mouth. "I do love you, but other matters will occupy me just when we had lifted the reins to start our own journey."

"I haven't left the buggy," Abigail said. "Let me announce the banns."

"Can not in good conscience." Charles coughed. "We are a brief candle in a strong hurricane. Pray for us, all."

Abigail's fury mounted against the inevitability of their continued separation. "I am a lighthouse for you in this brief storm."

"I may misplace hope. Keep it for me." With that he thundered down the steps, not as a light-footed gentleman suitor, but as a raging animal. He yelled for Cotton and whipped poor Flicka down Broadway to the horror waiting on Madison Street.

* * *

At the introduction of Cotton to Xing, Charles noticed a certain cold stiffness permeated the house. Cotton fluffed her apron at the dark corners of the fragrant kitchen. Pointing to the cluttered cabinet counters, the dirty dishes in the sink, and the bread on the center table, she demanded, "Clean dat with lye and hot water. Put all dis away after yous boils them. A sitting fly carries no good."

"A roll of screening planned for Abigail's house might be put to good use," Charles tried to ameliorate the situation.

"Too late now," Cotton used her apron to lift a cold teakettle to the sink."

"Not hot," Xing said.

"Should stay hot, all da time. Give me dat big pot."

Charles pulled down the pot from its hook over the stove.

"Keep dem both cookin."

"Make kitchen too hot," Xing complained.

"Step outside, if it's too much for you." Charles contained his anger and fear, leaving Cotton in charge.

"Make a nice beef soup for da children." Charles could hear Cotton, as he stood in the hall before his parents' bedroom door. "Liquids only til it passes."

"What pass?" Xing asked.

"Typhoid," Cotton said, pumping water at the kitchen sink pump.

"Wiped out Mrs. Van Akers's Vermont family," Xing said.

* * *

The sick room was dark and fetid. Charles whispered, "Open the widows."

"Mother needs to sleep," Matilda argued, but John Eric opened both.

"Don't close the door anymore." Charles caressed his mother's hot hand. "The parlor windows too, John Eric."

Elizabeth turned her red-rimmed eyes to her eldest son. "The children?" she asked.

"Cassandra, Bea, and Samantha are at the Breckenridge's. Grandpa says they'll be fine."

"Abigail?"

He knew what she meant. Was his courtship ended by her illness? Charles lifted her shoulders as he held a glass of lemonade to her parched lips. "Relegated to discourse from the front porch."

Elizabeth coughed and then groaned from the pain. "Trust Grandpa. He kept Abigail safe when his son brought typhoid home."

Charles wiped her damp forehead with a clean handkerchief. "Rest now." Her skin gave off a vinegary smell. "We'll see this through."

"No." Elizabeth waved him out the door. "Matilda is already exposed. You keep to the hall. The children will need you."

Charles left, not in agreement, but to heed Matilda's remonstrations to let Mother rest. He sat in the parlor staring at his mother's desk until late into the night. What had she written to all those relatives, now buried in Vermont?

* * *

"We're losing her," John Eric fell against the door frame.

"No, we're not." Charles rushed to the bedroom throwing the bedclothes to the floor.

Cotton had a canvas sling bath prepared at the end of the bed. The cooled water brought down his mother's raging fever. Placed in the clean, dry bed, Elizabeth rested after her fitful delirium. "Thank you," she weakly smiled at Charles.

His heart ripped in half, bleeding hotly as it beat in an outcry of devotion, "Mother."

Cotton pulled on his sleeve. "Time to call on the Breckenridges."

"It's too late," Charles said, exhausted from spent emotions.

"Get yourself cleaned up, boy. I need to hear 'bout my baby, and I ain't walkin cross town without no escort."

"Yes, ma'am." Charles headed for the kitchen for a kettle of hot water to wash up.

The fresh air on the buggy ride revived his senses. Surely this would pass, and his mother would be restored. "Were you there when Abigail's parents passed?"

"Not me," Cotton said. "Not til Mrs. McConnell demanded Miss Abigail have a maid. She taught me most of Master Breckenridge's army rules, but he watched, careful like, too."

"Is the cook going to work with you?"

"Might." Cotton tied and retied a fresh apron around her middle, as if deciding how to be diplomatic. "He's not near clean 'nuff."

"There is a room over the carriage house. He could stay there."

"Best place for him. Den I can cook my soup without him throwin stuff in."

"He'll be moved out in the morning."

"Told me Mrs. Van Aker folks died from typhoid up in Vermont."

"It's true." His mother's relief at securing a cook might have brought the destructive typhoid home. Charles stopped before walking up the short plank walk to the Breckenridges. "Might bring it here."

"No, Sir. I wouldn't let you near dis place if'in I hadn't seen you wash up."

"Will that make us safe?"

"Can't be safer." Cotton knocked.

At the door Isaac inspected them before rousting out Grandpa and then Abigail for the midnight call.

"Your well is probably tainted since he came." Grandpa agreed with Charles's blame for the sickness on Xing's arrival.

"Dig a new well?"

"No." Grandpa sounded tired. "The new outhouse will help. Remember to pour lye down both of them, regular like. But if you don't boil even laundry water, you're contaminating everything."

"But Xing will use the new outhouse."

"Tell the children to wash before coming back into the house. It's too late to keep them from it, but you have eaten very little at home since George left."

Charles ran his hands through his hair hooking a hangnail into one of his curls. "Mr. Breckenridge, Samantha copies nearly everything I do. She picked up my habit of complaining and avoiding Xing's cooking, and the babies never did eat it. Will that help?"

"Absolutely, Might have saved them."

"It's a horrible illness," Charles said.

"Hemorrhaging is the last stage."

Charles understood. "I'd hoped...."

"Did Ebenzer leave morphine?" Grandpa asked.

"Dr. Wells said the children will need less," Charles's voice broke, "if they become infected."

Grandpa sighed, before letting Abigail have her turn at the window. "Tell him about the meeting at tomorrow night."

Abigail's sweet voice met his eager ears. "Charles."

He asked to see her better. "Could you move back from the window? Your face is in the lamp's shadow."

Abigail moved. Her face and the sight of her blue silk robe with lace from the nightdress showing at her throat settled his nerves. There she was, safe and sound. That's what he wanted...her alive and well. Even if he couldn't smell her sweet perfume, even if he couldn't hold onto her.

Isaac made a horrible racket as if to stop imagined intimacy from the silence they were sharing. He lit the largest table lamp and carried it out to the wicker table on the porch.

"Thank you," they both whispered.

"Do you get any sleep? Abigail must have recognized signs of his weariness with the increased lighting. "The City Hall meeting was called to stop the panic. Several cases are downhill from your property according to Vaughan."

"Oh, God," Charles said. "That sewage and water contract will not get enough pipes laid. My family...."

"Charles, protect your family by fighting for the treated water you and Grandpa lobbied for. They'll listen to you now. People are so incensed; there are meetings every night at City Hall."

"Don't let's talk anymore about it. Abigail, the plans for our house need to be in your hands." Charles slipped the roll of architectural drawings through the window. He could hear Isaac cough and Grandpa swear to him paper wouldn't carry the pestilence. "Here are stove catalogues from Rison and one from Christonmon. Mrs. McConnell will help you pick the best one. You'll have screens on all the windows, even in the basement. Cotton says she *caint* stand house flies or what she calls *eve gnats*. Planning the house...." He couldn't go on. 'I miss you!' is what he wanted to shout.

"Of course, Charles." Abigail knew how his breath alone depended on her. He was sure she understood his plight, his longing. She did reassure him. "We'll be together soon."

Unable to control himself, he said hotly, "Tonight would be soon enough."

Abigail laughed, but then a sob stopped the carefree release. "For me, too," he thought he heard Abigail whisper.

* * *

The next evening, Charles arrived early for the City Hall Meeting. He took a back row seat in the corner to watch the doorway for Grandpa. The room filled with worried citizens who acknowledged Charles in the general direction of his black morning suit, but never met his eyes. Charles was about to abandon ship when he spotted Grandpa's shoulder pushing open the door for his granddaughter.

Abigail wore the red-and-white striped dress with the rick-rack trim which showed off her petticoat, the dress she'd worn on their trip to Amish country. The room took in a common breath at her beauty, maybe from the surprise because she attended, but all talking stopped. Grandpa seated Abigail in the row opposite Charles and marched up to the front.

"You all want to hear from young Van Aker, but you'll listen to me first. Professor Vaughan has delayed the formation of a State Board of Health long enough. This city is a disgrace. We'll have electric lights on Main Street before a drop of safe water ever reaches one home. Typhoid isn't the only plague that has hit us in the past. I remember the 1849 cholera outbreak. I want you to remember something else too. Most of you know C. A. Sauer. He had typhoid for three weeks. The silly fool's still alive. Sorry, Abigail."

Charles stood up, and everyone acted as if they had eyes in the back of their heads. They all turned in his direction. "New York City has had a metropolitan Board of Health since 1849 when Charles Rosenberg linked typhoid to the water supply. You ask yourselves who is profiting by us not having clean water. Who do we pay to test our well water? Vaughan, that's who. He's been to Europe and knows how this disease is spread, but he is more interested in building a new university laboratory than in saving lives. And who is charging us hours of labor for laying the pipe he manufactures? A member of the Board of Public Works, Christian Schlenker. We've got to fund another bond issue, change the contractor and get our water made safe before more families are destroyed."

Abigail stood and applauded him. The rest of the crowd joined in.

* * *

As death drew near and his mother worsened by the hour, Charles sat with her through the long nights to let Matilda and John Eric rest. Matilda already had a feverish glow about her, and John Eric admitted his bowels had turned to water a week earlier.

Charles held his mother Elizabeth's claw-like hand. Matilda had removed her wedding ring after it kept slipping off. Charles wasn't sure his mother even knew the ring was missing.

Elizabeth would act as if she recognized him, only to ask if he'd ordered his suit for church yet. Was it ironic that his dad did wear the hated suit in his coffin for viewing at the St. Andrew's funeral mass? Now Charles needed to arrange for his mother's burial. Soon he thought. She didn't suffer anymore. Dr. Wells had doubled the morphine twice. They waited for her to ask before giving each dose.

His father had only left him four months earlier and now this. He couldn't face visiting the factory. Earl Henry, the shop manager, assured him he could run the company until Charles could resume his duties. Not now. Not with his family disappearing before his eyes.

Charles wanted to stop time yet he wished away the hours of his mother's suffering.

At first, seeing Abigail each evening held a promise of tomorrow. Then at some turn for the worse in Elizabeth's stamina, the trip up Broadway to the corner of Wright and Moore to see her became an added toil, a duty call where loving solace had flourished.

His family's bout with the epidemic was snuffing out his chance for affection. Cotton could just as well tell them the pathways death had made in the Van Aker family, of the condition of his cold and dying heart.

Chapter Eleven

The day after the picnic, Grandpa gave his suite of rooms to Samantha and the girls. Abigail helped supervise the move of his personal belongings downstairs into the study. Abigail heard him explain to Isaac. "The daybed served up plenty of good naps. We'll see how it behaves at night."

"Yes, Sir." Isaac didn't sound confident in a good result. "Although, I'm not sure you'll enjoy sharing the servants bathing arrangements."

"Better than when I served in the army," Grandpa said.

Abigail took the opportunity to discard most of Grandpa's stash of home remedies. After all, the labels on the top shelf of his shaving cabinet were turning brown with age, the lids rusted. Mother's old medicines, maybe even those of Abigail's grandmother, were stored on the top shelf, too. A box of Lydia E. Pinkham's vegetable compound pills sat next to six bottles of the blood purifier. A large bottle of Merchant's Gargling Oil had turned a murky brown. St. Jacob's Oil container for rheumatism, neuralgia, sciatica, lumbago, gout, quinsy, and tooth aches was nearly empty. All were thrown out with Isaac's tacit approval.

As Abigail inspected the hall outside the girls new lodgings, she noticed the dusty, second-floor wood moldings as if seeing the dirt through her young guests' eyes. Pictures of Union Generals littered the walls. White would be a better color for the walls with paintings of flowers to replace the sour, battle-scarred faces. Could she remember plants up here? Not much light to grow anything, yet she recalled a happier place. Maybe Isaac had moved all the plants into the parlor to cut down on the work of watering, which might explain the profusion in the parlor. She'd ask him and offer to water the ones upstairs. A few of the flowering violets would be nice in the Van Aker girls' rooms.

Dolly and Abigail reassured the girls Grandpa could purchase all the clothes they needed until they could return to their Madison Street home.

Samantha gathered Cassandra and Beatrice under her arms. "We'll pretend we're on vacation and all our luggage has been stolen." After the younger girls went off to explore the house with Taffy, Samantha touched Abigail's arm to get her attention away from shoving Grandpa's clothing into boxes. "Will you thank your grandfather? I'm not sure my words will be adequate to the task."

Abigail promised. "Grandpa loved your father as much as you did, Samantha. And, Benjamin would have taken me in under similar circumstances. Don't fret about anything now. We need you to keep up your sisters' spirits, since they've never been away from their mother or their home."

Mrs. McConnell managed the extra work with her usual good humor. "Oh, it's fine, it is, to have this old house filled to the rafters with pretty faces." The loyal cook prepared, without complaint, the extra dinners for Cotton and Charles. They were served on the wicker table on the front porch. Grandpa supervised the napkins and dishes making sure they were boiled after each use and no other member of the household was allowed to use them. Grandpa also hired a cleaning woman to fulfill Cotton's work load. The laundry alone kept Jessie, the young Irish girl, busy most of two days.

Dolly and Abigail shopped with the girls constantly, replacing the contaminated wardrobes Grandpa thought best left at the Madison address. Samantha helped with Taffy and Cassandra while six-year-old Beatrice pretty much looked after herself. Cassandra's happy disposition only lasted for the first two days, but the second night without her mother at bedtime, left the four-year-old screaming at the overwhelming terrors of babyhood. Samantha's entreaties for quiet failed, Mrs. McConnell's lullaby flopped, and Grandpa's gruff inquiry added to the reasons to wail. Ultimately, Taffy climbed into the bed and cried with the distraught child. Cassandra petted Taffy's face wiping away *her* tears. "There, there, baby," she crooned, "Mommy be back soon."

Abigail attempted to keep the household clinging to a studied cheerfulness, which became stiffly entrenched as each day of Mrs. Van Aker's illness progressed. The adults knew the horrors happening in the Van Aker family. Except for Abigail and Dolly, they had seen death first hand in the Breckenridge home, because of Orlando's defeated trip home from the gold fields. Orlando's wife, Bernice, was worn down from caring for Salome and succumbed to typhoid after weeks of meeting the nursing demands of her husband. Abigail, their child, had been orphaned at two, younger than Cassandra and Taffy.

Late into the evenings, seated at the piano bench, Abigail had listened to the two men she loved the most. Charles's voice had deepened while relating details of the tragedy occurring in his house. She remembered he had said once, "A poet should be clever enough to devise a re-imaging of these unacceptable scenes at home."

Grandpa patiently questioned Charles, before Abigail was allowed to change places with him at the parlor window. Charles's tones of sadness resonated through Abigail. His ascetic life had not trained him for the stark realities of the quotidian nursing of his dying family.

The unrelieved passion he had awakened in Abigail at the picnic promise, fed on Abigail's raw nerves. Her stomach never stopped hurting. Wasn't one of the first symptoms of typhoid, stomach pains? Diarrhea would be green if she developed the disease. Nothing like that yet, but she avoided green vegetables. She resolved to drink pitchers of iced tea and pink lemonade to prepare for any onslaught. Life with Charles had been promised with peace and literary leisure, unbroken by care and anxiety. Where had she read that roseate view of the future? Surely God wouldn't snuff them out.

The sofa had been moved as close as possible to the parlor's window ledge. Abigail extended her hand onto the sill as if Charles waited outside. She remembered when he had draped a clean napkin over her hand, before squeezing it. Had Cornelius and Cotton held hands through a napkin on the back porch, too?

When Charles didn't arrive with Cotton each evening, a deeper pall was cast over the Breckenridge house.

* * *

One morning Abigail awakened to the sounds of hammering. Grandpa was nailing together a Sears and Roebuck gazebo-office for her at the back corner of their lawn. The free-standing office structure promised to provide sufficient room to spread out research and text books and write required assignments. Her grandfather had decided Abigail needed a place to study away from the hubbub of the Breckenridges' growing household. Dolly, Samantha, Bea, and Cassandra constantly found desperate reasons to interrupt her book time in the library. Abigail didn't have the heart to scold any of them. Her grades hadn't suffered because she spent midnight hours under the gas lamps in her sitting room. The drawings for the gazebo sported a story-and-a-half library with a gallery of bookshelves and a ladder for speedy access to the law books. Intricately mullioned side windows with dark wooden groins mimicked gothic forms for the vaulted, stately ceiling.

"Room enough to receive clients; collect a bigger law library, with room left over for your own law clerk and receptionist."

"The neighbors will complain," Abigail said when he first showed her the plans.

"Let them." Grandpa had laughed. "You can sue the pants off them."

Abigail loved the design of her office, fashioned of light and shadow but feared the reckless extravagance might draw reproach, as if she were un-heedful of the community's suffering. Although the busy new domestic arrangement took more time away from Abigail's studies than she would have imagined, law school remained one of her priorities.

She had not been visited by Charles for a week of lonely nights. Knowing the reasons for Charles's reluctance to actively court her didn't relieve her anguish. Marriage remained an airy goal, unlike the finite law decisions building their labyrinths in her mind. Abigail did experience momentary relief from her longings to touch the man she loved by bending over the dry volumes of law.

Abigail nearly knocked into Isaac as she barged out of her sitting room for breakfast. Ten boxes of books were stacked in the hall. "Dolly's things?"

"Yours." Isaac bowed. "From Master Koelz's library."

"The Justin estate books." Abigail started to scoot one of the boxes into her room.

"Leave that to me, Miss Abigail." Isaac indicated she should descend the staircase. "Your grandfather needs a break."

Abigail touched Isaac's sleeve to stop his work on the boxes. "Have you noticed Grandpa has trouble breathing?"

"At times." Isaac shook his head, then turned back to add. "How can he keep hammering with his head aching so badly? And, Miss Abigail, Mr. Dredford is expected for lunch, Miss Dolly informed us."

Mr. Dredford had been showing up regularly to court Dolly. Abigail checked her morning outfit in the hall mirror. She missed Cotton's dictates. "Do I look all right, Isaac?"

"Of course." Isaac wasn't attuned to complimenting his young mistress. "You'll change for afternoon callers?"

These clothing regimens would be the death of her study schedule. Abigail decided to give her morning dresses to Dolly, if she wanted them. Dressing once for school would have to be acceptable for afternoon callers. Not enough time in a given day to bother about such things, especially without Cotton at hand.

Abigail could see Cornelius through the dining room windows as he wheedled her grandfather into laying down his hammer.

"Up for all day?" Grandpa hugged Abigail's shoulders as he passed heading for the basement kitchen to wash up.

When he returned, Abigail said, "Isaac says you have another headache."

"Couple days now." Grandpa frowned, moved his plate to the side and put his head down on the table cloth. "Hurts like crazy."

"Should you *not* see Dr. Wells?"

"Ebenezer Wells has his hands full with all those typhoid cases. I can't go to him about my absurd head. I did buy more calomel powders from Eberbach to quiet down this siege."

Later that afternoon Abigail paused outside the parlor where Bea, Cassandra and Cassandra's kitten listened to Samantha's piano lesson with Dolly. Abigail observed how closely the Van Aker children's hair coloring matched Dolly's. Feeling like an intruder to a family gathering in her own house, Abigail was reluctant to join them.

Cotton's daughter, Taffy, crept down the hall from the dining room door. She startled Abigail when she took her hand to pull Abigail into the parlor. "It's all right."

The sagacious child sensed the intimate group of four redheads excluded her and, like Abigail, needed permission to disturb the close assemblage. Abigail had put off her own piano lessons until her law degree was completed.

Cassandra's kitten swatted at Samantha's fingers. Fluffy had them all laughing with the resonating music by the time Samuel Dredford tethered his horse out front. Samantha scooted the children off for their lunch and naps.

Dolly randomly sampled the luncheon buffet. She definitely showed signs of attraction to the detective as he gave the latest news.

"I ran across a paroled thief who hadn't learned to work for wages." Samuel served himself another ham sandwich to go with the heaps of cheese and potatoes and Mrs. McConnell's corn relish. "When we arrested him in the bank, he said he had enough information on the shenanigans of the Jackson prison warden to make a deal."

"Who is the man?" Grandpa busied himself with cold chicken and sliced onions from the buffet.

Abigail considered his appetite a good indication that his headache might have ceased bothering him.

"I thought you'd like to know." Samuel stood with his back to the fireplace. "It's George Lott."

Abigail stopped sipping her tea. Dolly took her hand.

"Seems this goniff was able to buy opium in prison. The bank job would finance his habit. He said he could name names and worse injustices for a lighter sentence."

"What did Hanson say when you told him?" Grandpa asked.

"You know Hanson." Samuel looked embarrassed. "He's still praying for Lott's death."

"Not very Christian," Abigail managed. Even she had not wished the man ill.

"What will happen to him?" Dolly asked Samuel in a voice Abigail didn't associate with her straight-forward friend. Nearly cloying turgid it was.

Grandpa noticed his boarder's soughing, too. He cocked an eyebrow at Abigail, who tried to answer his question by rolling her eyes and touching her heart. Grandpa inclined his head, understanding follies of the heart were in progress.

"Federal Marshals will decide what to accuse him of," Samuel said, smiling with every one of his beautiful teeth in Dolly's direction. Conversation lagged as the two lovers traded affectionate glances. Samuel collected himself. "Sorry to hear of Charles Van Aker's problems. Nice young man," he said to Abigail.

"Who is the Federal judge?" Grandpa asked, as if to guide the talk away from typhoid. "Elihu Pond is all set to take over at the prison. He's been promising reform of that Cooper Street horror in Jackson for years."

"Senator Pond wrote a fine editorial yesterday," Samuel said. "Called George Lott a permanent shade in the underworld."

Abigail touched her throat. And to think she had considered being the man's wife.

Dolly blushed, and Samuel took note, changing the subject again. "The marshal's asked me about another citizen of Ann Arbor. Professor Maynard's nephew is a perennial trouble-maker in Washington, proselytizing people in bawdy houses. Can't keep a job.

He's in his late 30's. Chap ought to grab hold of something established by that age."

"Ever hear about the newspaper man who gave out all the secrets of the Masons here in Ann Arbor? They were banned at the time. John Allen, Ann Arbor's founder was certainly against them. The editor disappeared and was said to have been held illegally in the Milan prison."

"Can't say I have, Sir." Samuel's eyes were not able to leave Dolly's face for more than a second.

Grandpa tried again. "City used to be against fraternities, too." Abigail shrugged her shoulders. There was not a graceful way to break into the couples' reverie. But, Grandpa kept at it. "Now the Psi Upsilon house is going to be built on the corner of State and South University."

"Which corner is it?" Abigail asked. Samuel and Dolly stayed locked in their own private world. "I hear President Tappan is having plans drawn up to build a home on campus."

The silent conversation of Samuel Dredford and Dolly Colt ended. "Sir," Samuel said. "You're the closest family to Dolly in Ann Arbor, I was wondering if it would be proper to speak for her hand?"

Grandpa's mouth dropped open. "Dolly, is this in keeping with your wishes?"

"Yes, but I haven't said yes." Dolly looked down at her plate. "I'll lose my position at the University."

"You can give lessons here," Grandpa offered. "When you and Samuel set the date, I'd be honored to walk you down the aisle."

Abigail got up to embrace Dolly and then Samuel. How quickly the world moved on even while other people were in the midst of anguish. "Would you like to be married at St. Andrew's or here?"

"Oh, here," Dolly said. "I love this house so."

Samuel cleared his throat. "I've purchased a small place in Ypsilanti."

"It is very nice with a beautifully kept garden lot." Dolly smiled into her man's eyes.

Abigail's envy increased her longing for Charles and their postponed happiness. Charles's eyes no longer met hers with anticipation. His desperation had snuffed out any glimmer of the boundless love she'd once seen. She prayed for Charles's restoration to her arms. Her affection could knead him into shape; push out all the resentful bubbles from what fate had dealt them. Their love would rise with the heat of her devotion until the glow returned to his sweet eyes.

* * *

Cotton pounded on the front entrance the following morning. Abigail opened the door, but Isaac picked her up and sat her down in the parlor. "Use the window, Miss Abigail."

"Cotton needs me," Abigail persisted, struggling against Isaac's strong arms.

"We need you safe," Grandpa rushed to the door. "What news?"

Cotton collapsed on one of the wicker chairs on the porch. Abigail heard the chair squeak with her weight. "She gone, Master Breckenridge. Mercy, it is, too."

"Tell Charles," Grandpa coughed instead of sobbing. "I'll make all the arrangements for the funeral."

"Dr. Wells is there now." Cotton started to weep.

"Mamma, Mamma," Taffy hurried to the parlor window, climbing onto Abigail's lap. "Are you home?"

Cotton muffled her cries. "Not yet, baby girl, not yet. You be'in a good girl, ain't you?"

"I sleeps with Sandra."

"Cassandra," Abigail explained. "Yes, baby," Abigail petted the child. "Run go get Cassandra, now. She'll miss her breakfast."

Taffy went scampering out of the room to find her newly orphaned friend.

"Abigail will take Samantha to the funeral," Grandpa said quietly, "but the other girls are too young to understand."

"What will you tell dem?" Cotton sobbed.

"Heaven is a comfort for the young," Grandpa sniffed.

"I found her, but John Eric had done got dar first. He'd climbed onto da sick bed and he being feverish."

Grandpa moaned.

"And Matilda draggin around, feeble like."

"Little Ben and Lily?" Abigail asked. "Could Lily come here?"

"No, Miss Abigail," Cotton said. "She's already abed, poor baby. Ben too."

"Cotton," Grandpa demanded. "Are you keeping clean?"

"Yes, Sir, I is. Ever time I'm hurried, I always keeps a pot boiling, so's I kin wash up proper like between each child."

"Good girl." Grandpa said. "You keep Taffy in mind each time you leave a sick room. We all need you healthy."

Abigail crept through her upstairs sitting room to lay her heavy head on the uncomforting bed pillows. Even Lily had typhoid. Would Charles outlast it? She tried to reason with God, bargain to no avail.

* * *

The bright November day of Elizabeth Van Aker's funeral refused to allow one cloud to grace the sky. St. Andrew's was filled to capacity and the altar held more flower arrangements than the number of people who paid their respects. Reverend Tatlock repeated his sermon at the grave site. "Elizabeth Van Aker was a precious jewel in the temple of the Lord."

The Van Aker children attended their mother's funeral, those who were still ambulatory. John Eric and Matilda remained bedridden. Little Ben, all of eight, held tightly to Charles's left hand while Lily, a wan ten-year-old, nestled under his right arm. Grandpa and Cotton stood next to them.

Abigail, Dolly, and Samantha stood on the far side of the casket. Grandpa said waving was fine, but hugging too dangerous even for the comfort it might bring to the grieving children. Seeing Lily dressed in black deeply affected Abigail. She'd hoped to remain in control to provide the children some measure of normalcy, but the black-clad orphans undid her resolve. She wept openly and to her own horror, loudly.

Charles could not come to her side. The open grave gaped between them. Gazing at Grandpa's frown of disapproval restored Abigail's sense of propriety, but by then Samantha, Little Ben and Lily were howling too.

Cotton tsk'd, "Fine spectacle you all are makin. What would your mother say?"

That stopped all the noise, except for Lily, who let her voice soar to the heavens in an unbroken wail. Charles met Abigail's gaze only once. His look of fearful hopelessness seared into her mind. She touched Samantha's arm in her panic. Samantha broke down again, at Abigail's touch. Isaac carried the distraught girl back to the carriage.

"I'm sorry." Samantha tried to calm herself. "I'm so afraid I'll lose them all."

* * *

Cotton came the night after the funeral to the Breckenridge porch without Charles. "He's changin, Mas'ser."

"Mister Breckenridge," Grandpa corrected quietly. "How has he changed?"

Abigail listened from her perch on the piano bench.

"You know how gentle he is, for a big man. After Dr. Wells cut Matilda's hair so da fever don't use it for food, dat young man banged da furniture against da walls. Scart dem little ones near to death, making dem worst sick."

Abigail couldn't believe her poet, Charles was angry enough to smash furniture.

"It's the fates he's angry with," Grandpa turned to Abigail.

"Don't know nothing 'bout such." Cotton got up and took hold of her chair and thumped it down on the porch. "He's mad at God for takin his mamma!"

"Yes, he is." Grandpa tried to temper Cotton's outburst by agreeing with her.

"He tore out all his mamma's papers from dat desk of her'ins and tossed dem into a suitcase. Told me, have Isaac give it't Miss Abigail. Dat's what his mamma tolds him to do. A box too. Den he took dat desk out behind the chicken coop and banged it against dat rock wall until dar warn't but splinters of wood and slivers of glass."

Abigail got up to fetch Isaac, bumping into him in the hall.

"Excuse me," he said, bowing. "I'll just drive Cotton back down to Madison Street. Make sure young Mister Van Aker knows Grandpa don't expect this kind of behavior."

"Wait a minute," Grandpa said. "I'll go with you. I need to speak to the boy, too."

Abigail followed them out to the road. "Grandpa, he has too much to bear to have you lay into him."

"Not my intention. Love that boy. Don't know what I plan to say. Maybe just listen."

How could she doubt her grandfather's motives? Of course he'd take care of Charles's feelings. She noticed Grandpa rubbed his forehead as if his headache had returned.

Cotton whispered to Abigail. "Might want to reconsider dat husband material. Dat boy's growin inta a dangerous creature."

"Nonsense," Abigail said. "Not Charles."

"You best rein him in." Cotton warned.

Chapter Twelve

Abigail prayed as soon as she woke in the morning, "Please Lord, listen to my plea. Charles is not Job. Relieve his suffering. He's just a boy really. Eighteen going on nineteen isn't near enough time to know how to deal with all the trouble he's seen. Please, if it be your will, lighten his load. And Lord, forgive my selfish desire to see him relieved of all pain. I want him for my husband, undamaged. Thank you for Grandpa and his unending hospitality. Keep us safe and close to your heart."

After breakfast, Isaac explained Grandpa had brought home Charles's mother's bequest. Abigail dragged the suitcase which contained her letters into the middle of the sitting room. Isaac carried in another box, postmarked from Vermont which held Elizabeth's letters to her relatives.

A note to Charles lay on the top of the jumbled letters in the suitcase. "Make sure Abigail is given these and my letters. She hasn't had a mother since she was two. She'll need any wisdom I might have gained from the Lord's gift of many children." The shaky handwriting revealed typhoid's presence and the tenacity of the writer. "Mothering is not a self-taught art. It is best learned by example, and these letters may give her a chance to experience my realities of motherhood."

In the cardboard box on top of the letters, a blue ribbon was wound around a black cluster of long ringlets. Matilda's curls must have been placed there by Charles before his disgraceful temper tantrum. Abigail pictured the young sixteen-year-old skipping down the Amish country road, holding hands with her sister, Samantha. How sweet the sisters had been to leave Charles alone with her. Abigail held the curls to her nose and smelled the clean, rose water scented hair. Her spirits quailed. "Please God, let Matilda survive."

Hope seemed as black as the shiny hair.

Abigail read the first letter in the box, expecting dictates on various issues. Instead, she found praise for the children, small details of actions, milestones on the pathway to human kindness: "Charles follows his father around the house like a puppy. When Benjamin is off to work, Charles sits at the window as if he could wish him home. I don't discourage the devotion. When it is time for dinner, I tell Charles to open the door to see if his father is on the way. It warms my heart to see Benjamin smile at the ecstatic welcome he receives from his firstborn."

As if he heard his friend's name read aloud, Israel Breckenridge knocked on his granddaughter's open door. "Is the law bogging down your spirits this morning, Abigail?"

"No, Grandpa. I miss touching Charles."

Grandpa looked around the female domain for a place to sit near her.

"Try Mother's rocking chair," Abigail said.

"Bernice," he said rubbing the white paint on the arms of the rocker. Grandpa's face softened with his sweet memories of Abigail's mother.

"These are Elizabeth's letters. Charles thought she hated being married, I think, he even believed she disliked having children."

"Not Elizabeth! Benjamin often tried to talk her out of making more children."

"Eight is a lot." Abigail imagined mothering such a large brood. "How many are in our house now?"

"Five servants, four boarders, and you and me." Grandpa smiled, then rubbed his forehead.

"Headache?"

"I'm almost getting used to the pain." He leaned forward picking up the top letter in the box. "Has Charles read these? Looks like he just jammed them back into the box."

Abigail held up Matilda's curls.

"Mercy." Grandpa sighed as he rubbed his aching head.

Abigail read the rest of the letters containing similar notes of the pleasures of motherhood. "His first step happened at two o'clock in the afternoon. I propped Charles up against the wall, holding a cookie just out of his reach. Charles knew he had accomplished something grand. He looked at his feet and sat down hard."

"Matilda pulls at Charles's hair, but he doesn't mind. He worries about her every move, following the crawling infant as if she will drop off the earth if he doesn't keep an eye on her."

Dolly peeked in the open door. "Do you have room for me?"

Grandpa started to rise to offer his chair, lifting his hand quickly to his ailing head.

"Sit, sit." Dolly gently pushed him back into the rocker and sat on the floor next to Abigail.

"Charles's mother wrote to her Vermont family at least once a week." Abigail poured over the precious tangible records of the Van Aker family.

"Did I hear Charles's name?" Samantha joined the group. "Remember when Charles broke one of your chairs, the day he asked you to marry him?"

"Samantha," Grandpa held out his hand for the young girl before saying, "These letters of your mother's might be difficult to hear."

"Nothing's as bad as the silence without her words." Samantha snuggled close to Dolly, who put her arm around the slim girl. Abigail handed Matilda's bundle of hair to Samantha. Samantha didn't cry. "Little Ben's is dark and curly, too."

"Like your father's," Grandpa said. "Before the sun turned it white."

"It wasn't the sun," Samantha said quietly. "It was hard work."

The happenings detailed in Elizabeth's letters followed each Van Aker child. Abigail read the next letter to those gathered. "John Eric found his hand today while he was nursing. First he opened and closed his little fist and then he pulled away from my breast to concentrate entirely on the movement of his hand. He looked down his arm to his elbow then up to his shoulder, and knew his hand belonged to him. How did I miss the older children discovering they owned hands?"

Abigail looked over to Grandpa who surely must have been thinking about John Eric climbing into Elizabeth's bed as she lay dying. "Oh, here's one about you," Abigail handed the letter to Samantha.

"Samantha is quite the little mother to Little Ben and Lily." Samantha stopped reading. Her eyes were brimming with tears.

"And now with Cassandra and Taffy," Grandpa read the rest of the epistle. "Lily doesn't appreciate the interference, but Little Ben doesn't mind being hugged."

Beatrice with Cassandra and Taffy popped their heads in the door and quietly added to the group on the braided rug.

"Mrs. Van Aker never lost a beat of love for any of her offspring," Dolly said.

Abigail read from another letter. "Beatrice has been nicknamed 'Bea.' It doesn't matter. She is as sweet as honey, smiling with those giant green eyes of hers." Abigail folded the letter carefully and picked up the next. "Cassandra has a kitten hidden. The others call her Sandra behind my back and know I'm allergic to cat fur. I hide my sneezes and red eyes. I can't bear to see a tear in the baby's eyes."

Grandpa read the next letter. "They are all so beautiful. I do not think it is just because I am their mother. When all eight are assembled at the table, it is quite breathtaking. Benjamin says we must gather at the photographer's to get our family picture taken. He thinks we are pretty special, too. I'll send you copies."

Sure enough, a print of the Van Aker clan showed both of Charles's proud, beaming parents with all their children. Abigail passed it around. "We'll have it framed for the mantle. Charles can see it on his next visit."

"May we keep it in our rooms," Samantha asked. Cassandra had crawled into her lap and Beatrice hung over her shoulder stroking the locks of Matilda's shorn hair.

"Absolutely." Grandpa coughed into his huge white handkerchief, a sure sign his tears were at hand. He escorted the Van Akers across the hall with the picture and the ribboned locks of their sister's hair.

Dolly quietly shut Abigail's sitting-room door behind them. "They rend my heart."

Abigail tried to stifle her tears. "Pray with me for Charles. I might be able to help his grief if I could be with him."

"He won't avoid you after the typhoid has had its sway," Dolly said.

"Dear Lord," Abigail prayed. "Help the Van Akers bear their grief nestled in your caring arms."

* * *

In November of the worst year of his life, Charles bent over to listen to the ravings of his feverish oldest sister.

"It's coming for me." The last day Matilda Van Aker spent on earth, her typhoid delirium convinced her the pounding in her ears was death approaching in black, hob-nailed boots. Her ashen face and tilted bald head with its distorting neck tumor bore no resemblance to the frisky colt of a girl Matilda had been at the Farmers' Picnic. She lay in her mother's bed, thrashing from side to side in agony, trying to escape the oncoming inevitability. Charles's mother had passed more peacefully, without torment.

"She hears something," Charles said to a distracted Cotton, just then running up the stairs with a tray filled with a pitcher and three glasses of snow.

"Dey's a racket somewhere."

"When you're done upstairs, could you fan her until I get back?"

"Has ta get my shawl. Colder den a witch's nose in dat room."

Charles checked the front room. He could hear a noise too, a dragging sound of wood on wood, like a coffin across an un-carpeted floor. The darker wallpaper behind where his mother's stately, cherry secretary had stood pointed to his earlier crime. Smashing the poor, beautiful thing solved nothing. Typhoid couldn't be beaten.

"Lord," Charles prayed. "I'm beaten. Come to our aid. Help me be strong for my sisters and brothers. Please, Lord, in your name I pray for these children. Bless them with health to fight this awful disease. Help me control myself when I can't find a way to help them."

Charles wandered into the immaculate kitchen. Warm and inviting, the room smelled of cornbread in the oven, a vegetable soup on the stove and a pot of freshly brewing coffee. He passed through without stopping even for coffee. A sharp pain in his stomach reminded him he hadn't eaten since the night before, or maybe typhoid had arrived to smite him down, too. Maybe not, Grandpa and Cotton promised to keep him safe once the cook, Xing, was quarantined to the carriage house.

Flicka. Maybe the cook was bedeviling the poor beast. The noise was louder outside the house. As he swung the carriage house door open, Flicka whinnied. Charles hadn't washed his hands after leaving Matilda's room. Not wanting to touch any living thing, he crooned to the lonely beast. "You miss Little Ben, don't you?"

Charles pitchforked a fresh pile of hay into Flicka's stall. He told himself to take the rake back to the kitchen door to pour scalding water on its handle. He continued to trace the noise out behind the furniture factory. He brushed the snow from his warm shirt. A new winter storm was piling up the white stuff on the plank walk. The pitchfork remained in his hand and the noise increased.

At the edge of the Madison Street lot, factory workers loading crates of furniture headed for export markets hadn't considered part of the job was to work silently.

Charles harangued the men loudly, brandishing the pitchfork to get their attention. "Stop. Be quiet. There's a dying girl in the house."

Behind Charles, at the factory door, a sympathetic Earl Henry protested. "You have no quarrel with these men, Mr. Van Aker."

The men continued to load the wagons. Charles tore at his hair. "The lot of you are fired!"

Again Earl Henry tried. "These men have families, Charles, and the holidays are just around the corner."

"Get off my property!" Charles touched his own forehead to see if his fever had started.

Earl Henry waved his hands. The men watched him rather than Charles. "Go home, boys. Come back in the morning."

Matilda would be dead by then, Charles thought. "Shut the whole thing down." The foreman's hands dropped to his side. Charles yelled after him as he retreated into the factory. "I don't want to make money." Exhausted, he ineffectively threw the pitchfork at the men.

They turned and walked back into the factory where Charles heard the steam-driven lathes and drills come to rest. Quiet at last. Who cared about the prostration of the furniture business, the decay of prosperity? Not one penny could save one member of his family. A fleeting vision of Samantha holding the hands of their youngest sisters rose before him.

The wagons and unmoved crates stood where the men had abandoned them. Charles took the pitchfork back to the house for scalding. Snow continued to pile up on top of the horse-less wagons.

* * *

Matilda lay in his parents' room, as quiet now as the factory. Snow drifted past the windowsill onto the floor. No hot breath appeared on the mirror Charles held to Matilda's blue lips. "Didn't stop the noise in time." Charles knew he was being irrational.

Freed from fanning the emaciated figure, Cotton pulled the sheet over her dear face. "Xing can fetch da doctor, again. Only work he does." Cotton pushed Charles out of the room.

He stood in the hall, trying to make sense of death. "Never should have let Mother bring him into the house."

"Rue dis and next day rue dat." Cotton shook her head.

Stacked in the hall were books Charles had planned to read to Matilda to drown out death's footsteps. Lord Byron, Disraeli, Browning, Shakespeare, Emerson. "More than sufficient unto the day are the troubles thereof, troubles that thicken like green soup in this house."

"Daily shocks, dat's for sure." Cotton looked up at him and patted his shaking shoulder. "Best go look in on Little Ben."

Charles unearthed 'Uncle Tom's Cabin' from his closet and straightened his shoulders to fight the next fight, soften the approach of death word upon word.

"Caint get dat boy to drink his liquids." Cotton worried, as she passed him in the upstairs hall. "Skin's a fallin off him. Wants me to take an apple to Flicka."

* * *

Cotton was in no mood for the likes of Xing, when she headed for the carriage house. She didn't particularly like horses either, flighty as butterflies they were, but at least their smell was decent.

She handed Flicka the apple. "It's be's from Little Ben." Why was she talking to a horse? He didn't understand more than the broadside of the barn. Flicka looked her right in the eye. Cotton patted his furry neck. His winter coat was thick and deep. Flicka pushed the front of her shawl with his warm nose, gentle like. "Good Boy," she couldn't help adding. "Maybe dey not all dat bad."

After climbing the ladder, Cotton knocked on the loft room's door. When Xing opened his door, smells of sweet pipe tobacco or weeds mingled with old fish-cake odors made her wish for horses. "We needs da doctor again."

Xing waved his arm. "Hsiang tsang ying tau yen."

Cotton didn't understand the words, but she knew by the way he studied her dark skin, spitting his words at the floor, that she hadn't heard a compliment. Anger rose as she clenched her fists. "Go."

Xing mumbled, "Wo hen chei ko ti fang," as he headed down the ladder.

Cotton resisted an urge to kick him all the way back to China. Poor Miss Abigail. Her courtship was ruined by this mangy, nasty fellow. And Taffy. What if she, herself, came down with this fever? Who would mind her darling? And Charles was getting more scary all the time. She saw him take a pitchfork out back. At least the creepy dragging noises had stopped.

* * *

Abigail continued law school as the Van Aker household across town fought their battle against typhoid. Matilda had perished. Abigail heard about the lonely grave-side ceremony from Reverend Tatlock. Charles refused to let him publish news of the funeral. Cotton said Little Ben was just melting away. John Eric was trying to hang on for the little ones, but even Lily was gravely ill.

Grandpa and Isaac periodically visited Madison Street but would only say Charles was distraught. "Give him time," Grandpa said.

Cotton had more to say about Abigail's future bridegroom, his black moods and lack of redemptive future. "Ought to trash dat boy. More fish in da sea."

Abigail would have none of it. "Charles is brave and dashing. A splendid creature."

"Well you' right," Cotton said. "I've seen dat dashing creature's temper tantrums. Tearing up da house. Terrifying it is."

Whenever black moods threatened her day, Abigail ducked into the finished gazebo to pursue the intricacies of jurist prudence. Thankfully, Isaac knew her habits well enough to keep the fireplace roaring. She prayed daily for Charles, hoping the Lord might intervene and bring solace to his raging soul. Other than prayer she was unable to solve Charles's problems. Left to open the Justin estate, leather-bound law volumes and attack the reading requirements for the various courses, she knew she had to row her own life boat or let the dream of being a lawyer fade forever.

Grandpa arranged with Isaac to take her to the train station each weekday morning to await Jacob Hangsterfer's horse-drawn tram to State Street. The light-hearted students on campus bridged the gap between painful realities and the elevated, academic life. Each evening engulfing emotions of loneliness and sorrow waited for her return in the home-bound carriage as another day without Charles passed.

Even after the exertion of finishing the office for Abigail, Grandpa continued having noticeable trouble breathing. One cold November morning, Grandpa read a story in the Courier to Abigail at breakfast. "On Monday forenoon a span of horses attached to one of our city busses and left standing in front of the St. James Hotel became tired of standing and facing the storm, and started for the stables. In passing along Main Street they ran the bus into a wagon, upsetting the former and breaking a wheel of the latter. The pieces were gathered together and the vehicles were sent away for repairs."

Isaac entered the room roaring with laughter, encouraging Abigail to lighten up and laugh too, but Grandpa started gasping for air. They both stopped talking. Each rushed to the old man and took an arm raising them above Grandpa's head as if to pump the air back into his lungs. Their twin reactions so surprised Grandpa air rushed in, and the attack passed.

Nevertheless, Abigail asked Isaac to help Grandpa back to his bed and then called the doctor.

Doctor Wells reassured Abigail. "The man is seventy-eight. He needs to slow down a bit. Don't worry him about anything. He'll be around for a lot of years, if he takes it easy."

Abigail had never doubted a doctor before, but Grandpa's health worried her. She failed at limiting his marathon rambles around Ann Arbor's scenic valleys. Instead, she sent Isaac after him with the carriage, with fictitious errands and small emergencies requiring Grandpa's immediate return from his frigid tramps along the Huron River.

A dutiful granddaughter, Abigail contracted for Billy Edwards, the newspaper boy, to shovel the walks and to curry Old Prescott, their carriage horse. Both chores had been Grandpa's. Abigail hadn't wanted to burden Mrs. McConnell by taking away Cornelius now that they had added four more mouths for her to feed every day. Isaac had enough to look after, chasing Grandpa all over town and dale.

In order to assure Billy she knew her business, Abigail asked the boy, "Do you curry with the hair or against it?"

"Against it, ma'am," Billy stated. "How else will you get the dirt out of him?"

"Yes, but be gentle with him. He is getting along in years."

Billy was a thoughtful boy. She could tell he was thinking, as she was, of her grandfather's age. "I use straps with football cleats for my boots on ice. Would you be needing any for Mr. Breckenridge?"

Abigail patted the boy's shoulder. "Yes, please bring them around. I'm not sure we can convince Grandpa to use them; but if you show up in your pair, he might be persuaded."

One evening Abigail even canceled her plans to attend the Opera House with Samuel Dredford and Dolly. She did want to study, but she also wanted to be near Grandpa if he needed her.

"Don't hover so," Grandpa said, during the long evening. "I thought you were going out?"

Abigail looked up from her law volume. "I wanted to stay in, in case you needed me."

"Your friends need you as much as I do. Don't give people reason to start a scandal about Dolly. Make sure you chaperone them."

"They enjoy each other's company, alone."

Grandpa began a new cigar. "Charles confided in me."

Abigail turned a page to cover her interest. "About what?"

"As soon as he can figure out to beat back old man typhoid, and find someone to help take care of his family, even before the house is finished on Plymouth, he intends to marry you."

Abigail jumped to her feet. "Grandpa!"

"Calm down. You'll get my ticker running away with itself, again. Too much mourning in the Van Aker family to plan a wedding. Keep busy with your studies. You could encourage Dolly to set her date. And Abigail, the boy loves the ground you walk on. I never chastised you about George. We were both deceived, but you need to love a man for more than physical excitement."

"I know, Grandpa." Abigail began to weep. "I thought it was all right, getting all riled up, because marriage would make it holy."

"Some marriages are never holy, but it's good to think in those terms…to seek the higher ground. And Charles is that kind of man. Maybe a bit too young to keep you in line," Grandpa smiled impishly at her. "He means well."

"Yes, Grandpa. I even look forward to hearing his footsteps. He warms my heart, not that earth-shaking thing with George, but a comforting feeling."

"That's it, my girl." Grandpa seemed mightily pleased. "Just wait for him now, until he can put all this horror behind him. You promise me?"

"Of course, Grandpa." Abigail couldn't feel happier. "When will he set the date?"

"Now. I told you to wait." Grandpa rocked merrily in his chair. "It'll be like Christmas coming. Could you wait for a basket of Christmases?"

"I could," Abigail lied, thinking one Christmas far enough away to wait.

Chapter Thirteen

Mid November, 1879

The doorbell rang and Isaac announced to the sitting room crowd the arrival of Mr. Dredford, whose teeth chattered from the chilling walk from the train station. Dolly nearly floated down the staircase, wearing her London concert gown. Abigail couldn't stop smiling at the happy pair.

Dolly pinched her. "What is the secret, cherub? Did Grandpa tell you what he's getting you for Christmas?"

"Almost," Abigail said. "Mr. Dredford, please join us for Thanksgiving."

Samuel bowed first to Grandpa and then to Abigail. "Your table is the best in town."

Later that evening, Abigail's mood hadn't changed when Dolly and Samuel returned in the Breckenridge carriage. Nearly dancing across the room, Abigail pulled the servant bell cord for Isaac. "Brandy and peach tarts, if it's not too much trouble."

Samuel sat across from Grandpa in the matching sofa with the best lighting from the gas lamp. Charles's chair. Abigail took Dolly's hand. Everything might turn out right after all. Abigail remembered the contents of the blue volume Samuel held. When Charles read from a book, Abigail didn't need to ask if the poem was his. She quoted the volume's author, Blake, "*...to see the world in a grain of sand and heaven in a wild flower, hold infinity in the palm of your hand and eternity in an hour.*"

Abigail wished the poem had been more cheerful for Grandpa's sake. To lighten the mood Abigail gushed, "I am happy for you both."

"He's a good person," Dolly said, much to Grandpa's nodding approval.

* * *

Not many days after Charles returned from Matilda's grave, Cotton had to report, "Little Ben has joined his family in heaven, Mister Van Aker." Charles uncovered his brother's dehydrated body, which Cotton had laid out on the dining room table. "I've been washing dis baby for da funeral."

Charles couldn't bring himself to worry John Eric and Lily with the news of their eight-year-old brother's death. "Did you tell the children?"

"No, sir." Cotton wiped her eyes with her apron. "I just brought his body down. Light as a feather, it is."

"We could bring John Eric's bed down to the parlor."

"Better than moldering away in a hospital."

"And put Lily in Mother's room?"

Cotton agreed. "Clean as a whistle in dar. And da air is better."

"We'll tell them Little Ben wanted to stay upstairs." Charles sat down next to the body, holding the cold, small hand.

"Ain't no lie, Mister Van Aker. Dat baby is in heaven, now."

After they settled twelve-year-old John Eric in the parlor, Charles heard Cotton tell him, "Young man, hold on now. Christmas is coming and Charles needs you. Samantha and Beatrice and Cassandra, dey alls needs John Eric up and about."

"And Little Ben and Lily," John Eric whispered. His blistered lips cracked and bled with the effort to speak. "They'd get frightened without me." Rallying his torpid spirit, he vowed, "I've got a couple more skirmishes in me. The fever's not yet in full possession."

Cotton held the boy upright. "Now force dis tea down."

Charles planned to read Thackery's "Vanity Fair" to him. It was a long story, a thick book. John Eric lasted, sleeping from the pain killers for twenty hours out of each day, for two more nights.

Charles sat in the kitchen. His knees were too weak to proceed in any direction. "The very days and months a symbol and nothing signified."

"Dat Saint Job ain't seen nothing like your troubles," Cotton told Charles in a commiserating tone.

"Boils." Charles remembered. He hadn't acquired that peculiarity, but he was one of the unluckiest or most unloved of God. "And a dog to lick them."

"Dat's right," Cotton's bronze mask scowled. "Tempt da Lord. See what else He brings your ornery hide."

"When did you decide to hate me, too?"

"Day you stopped seeing Miss Abigail."

"Reason enough to be churlish." Charles wanted to explain, 'I have no heart left to love her. It's been ruthlessly torn-out.' Dolorous indeed to lose all these unsuspecting angels. What did Job complain to God about? Not giving him safety from suffering? God got angry, flaunted His creation as proof no one had the right to question His motives. Nonetheless, what evil had Matilda, John Eric, and Little Ben called upon themselves? What good did their suffering accomplish? Why were their lives created to die in so much anguish? Answers were buried under the mountains of faith other people held dear. Charles could find nothing in his heart worthy to love in a God.

"Smite me, Lord." Charles dropped his head on the table. "Not my family."

* * *

During Charles's absence, Grandpa provided Abigail's main links to the outside world. School was a world unto itself, once removed from reality. Grandpa could find the strangest things in the local newspapers. The 'Courier' was part of their breakfast table routine. He usually found something to share with her.

Today it was, "The Argus says that the Courier and other republican papers are endeavoring to foment a feeling of dissatisfaction among the friends of Mr. Liesemer by making him appear as a sorehead, etc.," Grandpa stopped reading to roll his eyes at her. She had to laugh or smile each day for him to continue. "…because he did not receive the congressional nomination. The Courier never said or even intimated that Liesemer was *sore*, but what we aim to do is to prove to the German-Americans of this congressional district that the democratic party has no use for a German but his vote."

If Abigail could stop her mind from thinking evil things, it would help her demeanor. Like right then, she was thinking, boring, oh dear Lord, he is boring me to death. Perhaps it was a good thing George hadn't married her, she'd make a grumpy wife…to add to his bevy of wives as a matter of fact. Would she ever stop thinking of the brute? "Will Charles accept an invitation for Thanksgiving?"

"Haven't you taken care of that yet?" Grandpa frowned.

"I'll do it straight away," Abigail said, not wanting Grandpa to have any reason to frown.

"You're a good girl, Abigail."

"Woman, Grandpa."

"A mere slip of a girl, Abigail." Grandpa smiled. "Eighteen is such a little number."

"And seventy-eight is a grand number to be."

"It is." He folded the paper and smiled as Isaac removed his coffee cup, replacing it with a fresh, hot cup.

"Dolly keeps delaying her marriage." Abigail knew Grandpa wanted to see them married as soon as possible. He had told her small-town gossips enjoyed sharpening their claws on the happiness they see in others. Abigail stirred her oatmeal, stewing in her own sour juices.

"Could your feelings against George Lott color your relationship with Dolly?"

"I can't believe you would take their part." Abigail studied her grandfather. First of all he never brought up George Lott's painful name or the past situation. And he was the one who specifically told her to encourage Dolly and Samuel to marry quickly. Grandpa was never inconsistent. Were his headaches affecting his thinking?

"Now, Abigail, you know that's not the case." Grandpa turned quite red in the face. "You are disturbing my digestion."

"Sorry," Abigail said, truly sorry to have upset him. "Read me another story from the Courier."

He smiled, his face dimming in color. "Here's a good and short one, right in between a death and a bar association appointment: "Detective John Manly of Toledo, in one of his visits to this place, detected one of Ann Arbor's fair daughters as being the finest in the world to him, and as a result he and Miss Nellie Hoban were married yesterday at St. Thomas church. Doesn't that sound like Samuel Dredford?"

Abigail looked at her plate. Nellie Hoban was not as pretty as she was, and already married. "Maybe I should get accustomed to my role as an old maid."

"Abigail!" Grandpa yelled, rubbing his shoulder. "I read that for you to laugh at, and you turned it around!" He pounded the table with his fist. One loud crash, then another rattling the glassware.

Isaac came running into the dining room. "Yes, Sir?"

Grandpa stared at them, opened his mouth slightly and then pressed his head against the back of his chair.

Abigail ran to his side. "Oh, Grandpa, not now. Not like this." She unbuttoned his tight collar. His gaze didn't shift. In a panic, she looked up at Isaac. "Run go fetch the doctor!"

Instead, Isaac patted her shoulder. "No reason for that, Miss Abigail. Your grandpa is gone."

* * *

Planning to attend to the sweet-tempered, ten-year-old Lily's burial arrangements, Charles hoped his visit would be the last to the posh funeral emporium. With no one left to nurse on Madison Street, Cotton had packed up the few things she had brought to go back to her Breckenridge home. On her last day, Cotton said. "Mrs. McConnell will expect yous for suppers, now. Show up for Thanksgiving, too, or I'll be blamed for not askin."

Charles intended to go. He had no one else to care for.

"Finally sold that ebony casket," the mortician cheerfully told him.

"Who passed, then?" Charles asked out of politeness, not really wanting to know.

"Israel Orlando Breckenridge," the man said, as if he was proud of his famous customer. A plank in the fragile function of Charles's grief-stricken mind snapped with this extra weight. An unspoken foreboding swamped his reason. Abigail would be next, then himself. Religion, morality, affection all died. Charles thought he could count his final days.

At eighteen he needed to say good-bye to a life he'd never experienced just as his sisters, Matilda and Lily, and his brothers, John Eric and Little Ben, had been pulled out of the world. Abigail and he would not live through the coming new year. Their world was doomed.

* * *

The empty rooms on Madison Street had no heart. Walls stood where people had milled about. At every turn, Charles expected a face, a skirt, a rolling ball, something. In place of laughter, he thought he heard sighs. Maybe his own. No aromas graced the barren kitchen. The sick rooms still smelled of medicines and disinfectant vinegar.

Every time he touched a wall or staircase banister, Charles nearly ran to the kitchen to pour more hot water and soap on his arms and face. Fear loomed in dark corners which familiarity used to call home. Panicked at his own anger of the unknown, he grabbed his father's warmest coat to tramp outside.

He spotted Xing leaving the barn. They'd kept away from each other since Charles's mother died. Flicka cheered up seeing him, but Charles was ashamed he hadn't brought an apple for a treat. He saddled the mare in silence, afraid if he started talking he wouldn't be able to stop, even to a horse.

Astride Flicka, Charles noticed the sunset at the top of Liberty Street. The Breckenridge home on the corner of Wright and Moore

Street meant further litanies of suffering, painful exhibitions, similar to the horror that would eventually snuff out Abigail and himself, distilling their essences into green bile. Charles cringed and returned south on Main Street. There was nothing and no one hieing him home.

At Main and Williams, the house of pleasure for dreary-hearted men rose before him. Pretty lamps flickered in the front windows, beckoning to him. He tethered Flicka across the street at the plank walk railing. A happy rag-time tune spilled out of the door when a dark maid took in the evening paper. Throbbing life called to him, he leaned toward the place.

Charles mounted the steps, pushed by the desire to escape reality. Dalliance he could call it, a slight detour of duty. Betrayal stayed his hand as it reached for the whore-house knocker. Charles dejectedly headed back to the accounting books at the closed factory, angry at his entrenched innocence.

* * *

As old Mrs. Hanson stepped onto the horse-drawn bus to the depot, she turned to check the sky as the last rays of the sun painted a fleet of snow clouds into a brilliant orange. In lieu of beauty, she caught Abigail's fiancé descending the house of ill repute on Williams. Her sympathy could not blot out her disgust and sadness for Abigail's fallen angel. 'Grief can make madmen out of the best of men,' she thought.

* * *

Under Abigail's watchful eyes, Isaac and Cornelius rolled Cotton's largest wash tub into the Breckenridge back yard. They built a stone foundation to hold the tub over the logs and started the vat boiling. Then Mrs. McConnell poured in the black dye as Cotton and Jessie hauled Abigail's fashionable silks and muslins down from her room.

The crowds at Grandpa's funeral panoply confused Abigail. She searched each face, forgetting why she bothered. Stalwart Isaac, Mrs. McConnell, Cotton and Taffy, Cornelius, Jessie, and even Billy Edwards, lined the plank walk in front of Wright and Moore Street. Their love for Israel Breckenridge was unquestioned. Isaac had fitted poor Prescott, their carriage horse, as a military rendition of a riderless Morgan. Grandpa's polished Civil War boots rode backward and empty in the stirrups.

Dolly informed Abigail they needed to excuse Samantha and the Van Aker little ones from attending and to leave them in Samuel Dredford's care. Dolly sat next to Abigail all through the day. The Breckenridge black-draped carriage pulled by the Van Aker's white horse, Flicka, followed behind the Walker Livery's matched Arabian team, hauling its sad cargo.

Lower Town neighbors and businessmen lined Broadway to the Depot. Abigail thought she recognized Gardner and Gates in brushed Sunday clothes. She remembered Grandpa telling her Gardner had predicted their horse's demise and Gates hadn't had much hope for their old carriage. Neither of them had thought Grandpa might not outlast the horse or the carriage.

A string of young workers from the Kellogg Nursery stood together in a somber group. Even Mr. Shyler tipped his hat in Abigail and Dolly's direction.

In the throngs of mourners along Division and Huron to the Forest Hill Cemetery, Abigail recognized one out of every three faces: Mary Foster, the three Hansons, Mrs. Stone and Miss Miley, her dressmakers; the Ladies Library women and their husbands and families, and St. Andrew's and the Fuller Street Church parishioners. Abigail wasn't sure but she thought she recognized old Mrs. Husted. Professor White stood next to older Miss Millen. Then Abigail realized it was Charles Van Aker she searched for and missed seeing at the service.

"He didn't come?" Abigail asked Dolly.

"No, I didn't see him." Dolly hugged the small shoulders of her grieving friend.

Reverend Tatlock's words were as empty as the hole in which they lowered Grandpa's casket. The preacher must have known his words lack of comfort as he took her cold gloved hand to assist her into the carriage.

"Young Mr. Van Aker sent word this morning. Lily is gone."

Abigail broke down. How could she have faulted the man, who had lost six members of his family in less than a year?

* * *

Abandoning the empty house with its dread stillness for a second day without sleeping, Charles mounted the broad backed Flicka again. He missed the very texture of his brothers' and sisters' spirits in the house. He didn't count as courage his avoidance of a further world of illness in ministering to his redheaded, remaining sisters at the Breckenridges'. With Grandpa felled by the dread disease, they would all perish, too. In a stupor, he evaded the Broadway bridge to the Breckenridge home by going up Hill Street and crossing at the Huron Street dam.

At the Plymouth address of his dream home, Charles stared as if transfixed by the upright house joists. His unrealized life with Abigail lay before him with its two story walk-around porch, double balustrades, turned porch posts and lattice spindle work. The sketches of the house rose a momentary edifice, complete with acres of gardens and orchards.

Safe from the snow, he retrieved the sledge hammer among the tools he'd tucked under canvas before typhoid's progress stopped everything. So he knocked down the weather-beaten frame of the house he'd planned for Abigail. Because they would both perish from typhoid he chose not to leave anything of the perfect mansion they'd envisioned. With increased venom Charles destroyed everything standing. No gingerbread gilding or weathered beams for them.

In the midst of his rampage, Charles did notice the black carriage that slowed down and then passed by.

* * *

Bewildered Reverend Tatlock tried to come up with plausible reasons why a future bridegroom might want to destroy his new home. Passengers in his carriage, Mrs. Hanson and the widow, Mrs. Earl wanted answers.

"Life begins in vanity and ends in vanity," was all the wisdom Tatlock could manage.

None of them had the courage to approach the sorrow-stricken figure wielding the sledge hammer and turned feral by the deaths in his family. So none of them learned Charles harbored the fear that Abigail, his remaining little sisters, and he were dying.

* * *

Samuel Dredford waited on Abigail's porch for Dolly. "My muse," he greeted her but refused to let go of her hands. "What happened?"

Dolly met his eyes. She could not break his trust by lying. "Walk with me before dinner," she managed. Tears escaped. Trudging through the snow up Moore Street to the crest of the overlook, they watched Ann Arbor's evening lamps being lit. "Old Mrs. Hanson came by," Dolly said. "She saw Charles at Williams and Main."

Dredford remained silent until Dolly faced him, expecting some comment. "A furniture delivery?" His monotone held no conviction. "I can find out the particulars."

"If he's a regular," Dolly gulped. "I'll have to break it to…."

Dredford lost no time in his quest for the truth, after a moribund dinner with Abigail and Dolly, he knocked on the friendly Williams Street door.

Louise Warner cheerily greeted him. "Another unhappy wife?"

"Fiancée."

Louise's red ruffled blouse exactly matched the flocked flowers of the wall paper and the patternless rug of the entrance way. She motioned for him to adjourn to the less ostentatious office. "Keep a lid on it." She must have bathed in buckets of her perfume. "I'll check for you."

Dredford noted the unladylike tone of the office. Ledgers lined the book shelves. Wooden file cabinets flanked the shuttered windows. An enormous calendar served as an ink blotter on the mammoth desk. Not a painting or flower graced the staid room. Business as usual.

Louise returned with a young maid in tow. "She saw him outside. It's all I got."

"Yes, Sir," the nervous child curtsied. "He stood 'cross the street like he was growing out of the sidewalk. Finally moseyed up the front stairs, but never even knocked. Somes of 'um get scared." She shook her head in disgust. "Big man like that."

Dredford welcomed the good news with two, twenty dollar bills.

"Lord," the child said.

"Good enough," the Madam smiled.

Chapter Fourteen

After lunch was cleared away, Abigail prepared to hear Grandpa's will read at the dining room table. Grandpa's lawyer, Mary Foster was at her side. Abigail said, "Dolly and Samuel have taken the Van Aker children ice-skating. We told Samantha after each death in the Van Aker family, but the younger girls, Beatrice and Cassandra, were spared the sad news. We expect to hear from Charles, but no one had seen him since he visited the funeral parlor for Lily's burial arrangements."

"I'll call the servants," Mrs. Foster said.

"No." Abigail stopped her.

"They need to be told their inheritance."

"We don't call them servants," Abigail sucked in a breath of air to combat the momentary panic of being an orphan. "They are family."

"Your grandfather has provided well for them, but I'm afraid you'll be at their mercy."

"Surely, Grandpa explained when he drew up the will that I was about to marry."

"I should have demanded Mr. Breckenridge change his will as soon as I heard about Lott's perfidy. My apologies, however, will not change the legality of the will."

"I can adjust." Abigail hoped her words didn't betray her own worries. Where would she find enough funds to dress appropriately? Belief in her own resources and the Lord's care prevailed. "Do you need a clerk in your office? Please don't offer the position if you don't need me. Charity would do me in."

"Now, Abigail, you know I offered the position in my office before you became engaged." Mrs. Foster righted the lace ruffles at the throat of her widow's garb. "I need a decent law clerk and I cannot find competent people. Nevertheless, I don't want your studies to suffer."

Abigail forced a smile. "We don't have to worry. Books don't feel emotions. They'll keep offering me all the information I need."

"I expect to see you four hours a day, if you have no conflicts, starting Monday morning."

Abigail rang for the staff. She insisted Isaac sit in Grandpa's chair. After Mrs. McConnell, Cotton and Taffy, and Cornelius were seated, Abigail explained first to Mary Foster, "Jessie, the laundress, and Billy Edwards are absent because they don't live in the house." Then she said, "Grandpa loved you all and didn't want you to leave me or the house. He's provided for your wages to continue until you depart this world."

"Bless his heart, and you'll have enough, child?" Mrs. McConnell asked immediately.

"My tuition is taken care of, and with Dolly's and the Van Akers' room-and-board, I can make it. I'll be helping out at Mary Foster's office, too. I'd like us to include Dolly and the Van Akers in our evening meals as we are seated now. I have so little family. Will that be all right?"

Everyone agreed, except Cornelius. "No, Miss Abigail, I have to make my fortune for to marry Cotton and I intends to be off to one of dem Union schools down South. My family's willing to board me."

"Cotton?" Abigail tried not to cry, but the tears slid down her face.

"I ain't leavin' you." Cotton embraced her mistress. "How could I leave you now with that no-count Van Aker misbehavin'?"

"But Cornelius--."

"Is on his own." Cotton straightened her spine. "Boy makin' plans without consultin' me!"

"Now, Cotton, dat's not so."

"I never agreed."

"True." Cornelius hung his head. "But it's for the best."

"Best for you." Cotton slammed out of the room. Taffy climbed onto Isaac's lap. They could still hear Cotton ranting as she went down the back stairs to the kitchen. "Just like a man, run rough-shod over feelins."

Isaac coughed loudly. Cotton didn't take the hint and busied herself throwing pans onto the stove. Mrs. McConnell got up to stop the racket. Cornelius followed.

"Wait one moment," Abigail said, nodding at Mrs. Foster. "Could we keep the state of my finances between us, in the family? I'd rather not worry Dolly or the Van Akers."

Cotton may have been listening, because another loud banging of pans was heard from below.

* * *

In the echoing house on Madison, Charles lit the cold fireplace logs, then the wood stove kindling in the kitchen. When the tea kettle sang, he prepared a morning pot of coffee, which triggered a new thought. There was no one he could share the hair-minded idea with. Grandpa did say to burn the bedding. Why not the beds, and the house too?

First, he spilled kerosene from the lamps in the parlor, then from the bedroom lamps around the second floor. The kitchen's store of lamp oil was more than he needed. Picking his way warily among the spilled lamps, Charles went outside and poured kerosene around both outhouses.

He considered torching the carriage house, but Flicka needed a place out of the winter wind. Xing would be made homeless, but thoughts of the horse came first to his thoughts. He reflected on the fact that smelly people, like Xing, repelled others, but horses possessed healthy odors even when sweating from hard work. Agitated by Xing's presence on the property, Charles could think of no remedy.

'My books,' Charles remembered. 'Can't burn the house until my books are stored, besides I don't want to stay with Xing and Flicka.' Benumbed, he lit the old outhouse and watched the ubiquitous flames consume the evil disease and the new privy which was closer to the house. When it fell forward toward the stream of kerosene Charles had spilled from the back door to the old outhouse, it sent a stream of fire into the kitchen.

The boards in the kitchen saturated with fuel oil quickly ignited the entire house. By the time the fire wagons reached the place, the flames where higher than the roof. Without meaning to, Charles realized he had successfully destroyed his pestilence-filled house, but his beloved books were lost.

"Keep the factory wet, boys," the fire captain cried.

A second fire company took over as the first refilled its pumps from the cistern.

"Let it burn, too," Charles called out. Money was worthless without his family, without Abigail. What did he need a factory for? No need for trumpery things when life gives out. He wanted the anxious wretches, those fire fighters, to go home.

Hearing, Charles's rant, Constable Martin escorted him down to the county jail. "Arson and endangerment of life," the policeman explained to the small man in the next cell.

Charles understood Cotton was right. His challenge to God had been well met. "Could Reverend Tatlock--?"

"Fat lot he'll do," George Lott sniggered from the next cell.

* * *

With Christmas looming less than a month away, the Van Aker children would have a tree with presents galore if Abigail had anything to do with it. "We must paint the parlor for Christmas, Isaac. Store the plants and pictures in the library."

Isaac shook his head. "The library is full now of Mr. Breckenridge's belongings from upstairs."

"I'll go through them for you to give away, Isaac. I'd like you to move into my grandmother's room, now that Grandpa is gone. I miss having a grown man upstairs. Noises will be less threatening if you are there."

"Nothing wrong with Cornelius and me bunking together."

"Cornelius is moving out, and I'm giving his room to Cotton. She needs her privacy." Abigail wished she could talk to Charles, find out what his plans were for Thanksgiving or Christmas. But in the meantime, life needed to be lived. She had an entire household to care for, now. Grandpa would expect her to do her best. "Should I hire painters? The will covers painting and repairs. Might as well paint the inside of the entire house."

"Yes, Miss Abigail." Abigail thought Isaac had planned a way to escape her dictates, when they heard a knock at the front door. "Reverend Tatlock," Isaac announced.

Abigail hurried into the hall. "Is Charles ill?"

"Worse." Without shedding his coat, the pastor sat down on the parlor sofa. "I'm exhausted."

Dolly joined them.

Reverend Tatlock struggled to his feet trying to regain his Boston manners.

"No, sit." Abigail said.

"I'll get some coffee," Dolly offered, leaving for the kitchen.

"Any brandy in the house? Tatlock asked Isaac.

"That bad." Isaac commented, before heading for the library's cabinet.

Tatlock whispered to Abigail. "He's in jail."

Abigail registered the fact, but no response emerged from her addled mind.

Tatlock continued in a normal tone of voice. "He set fire to his house and wanted to burn down the factory, too. They said."

"Never happened." Isaac had returned with brandy which he served first to the pastor, then to Abigail and then to himself.

"With my own eyes, I did see him tear down the joists on your house on Plymouth." Tatlock emptied his glass and held it out for a refill.

Dolly returned with a coffee tray. She placed it carefully on the marble table, before saying, "Mrs. Hanson says he's been acting like a wild animal."

Abigail could tell from Dolly's blush there was a lot more news from Mrs. Hanson than Dolly was going to share. It was well enough for Isaac to remain loyal, but burning down his own home, destroying their plans for a house, and whatever else the poor boy was up to only showed Charles's grief had taken his mind and actions out of his control.

A siege of anger nearly overtook Abigail's good sense, but Grandpa had trained her well: first things first. She'd find out the truth about what had happened directly from Charles, before she decided anything else. "My wrap, Isaac." Abigail pulled Tatlock to his feet. "Take me to him."

"Not now," Tte three said in unison.

"Now," Abigail insisted. "I want Samantha to come with us, too."

* * *

The jail in the basement of the Courthouse at least was well heated. Abigail handed her winter cape to Isaac. "Wait for us. I doubt we'll be long."

"He's not the same, Abigail." Reverend Tatlock blocked the hallway to the cells. Abigail tried to push past. The clergyman was surprisingly stubborn. He held his ground. "And George Lott is in the next cell."

The jailer waited for her to make up her mind.

"We're going to see Charles," Abigail said. She hoped Lott would rot where he was, but Charles Van Aker was going home with her. "Charles," Abigail called to the hunched hulk of a man in the far corner of his cell. "Samantha is here."

Charles turned his face to them. His eyes were placidly vacant.

"I expected an engagement ring," Abigail said.

Charles moved slightly. "Are you there?"

"Of course." An electric charge passed between them. He came toward them in a rush. Abigail backed away from the bars.

"You…you should be lying down." His voice cracked with emotion. "Have the stomach pains started?"

"I don't have typhoid."

"Grandpa?" Charles's hands went to his dirty blond curls.

"Died of a stroke," Abigail said. "Did you think--?"

"Yes and all of us." His clouded eyes cleared as if a shade had been pulled up.

Reverend Tatlock asked, "Are you ill with it?"

"Don't think so." Charles's transpiercing gaze surveyed first Abigail and then Samantha. "Only mad."

"You're not crazy." Samantha touched his hand on the cell bar.

Abigail added, "It's the grief."

Charles turned away. "Hated God."

Reverend Tatlock took in a shocked breath.

"Guard, open this door," Abigail commanded, somewhat surprised when the jailer did exactly that. "Sit down, Charles."

Abigail and Samantha talked for two hours about Thanksgiving, the girls, Dolly's non-engagement to Samuel Dredford, skating, Christmas coming, even law school.

Their voices appeared to call Charles back from the fearful world of damnation, dark deeds, death and disease. His slumped posture straightened with each word as if they had pumped blood back into his veins.

"Arson." Charles straightened. "It was an accident. Need a bath."

Samuel Dredford appeared at the open cell door. "Judge Pond would like to see you in the morning. For the time being, you are remanded to my custody."

"Thank you," Abigail whispered.

"Go home, you two," Samuel said. "I'll bring Charles over in the morning, after Judge Pond is finished with him. Reverend Tatlock, I'll need you as a character witness."

"The little ones will be excited to see you," Samantha said.

Abigail kissed Charles's smoke-blackened face, his familiar lips.

George Lott had said not a word throughout the proceedings, until then. In a mawkish whine he cried, "Abigail."

Reverend Tatlock informed George, "You're unfit for a lady's notice."

Chapter Fifteen

In the basement cell of the courthouse, Charles's angst produced a humble thankfulness, as well as an explosion of vitality with the good news that typhoid had not invaded the Breckenridge household. When one after another of his family had been wiped out by typhoid, he had the audacity to question God. "Does the Lord hate me?" Charles asked Abigail, during their long discussion.

She reached out to touch Samantha's face. "Charles, the same grief struck your sister's heart. Do you think the Lord hates this beautiful young girl?"

"The Lord loves Samantha," Charles said. He tried to follow the logic of Abigail's reasoning, but anger overtook his emotions. "Please, Lord," he prayed, "help me to understand and to forgive what I cannot understand."

Reverend Tatlock overheard the last statement. He clucked his tongue. "We are not asked to forgive the Lord!"

"Let his soul find his own way back," Abigail defended her hero. "How else will he be able to love our Lord?"

Charles experienced another surge of energy, less restricted, less retarded, less defensive, emerging from his personal holocaust as a refined human. He understood that previously he had operated as a giant propelled by a shy boy's heart. "Thank the Lord," Charles said, ashamed he had ever questioned his beliefs.

Abigail stroked his hair then giggled.

He turned his face up to hers and she showed him the palm of her hand, which was black from the soot in his hair. Charles then remembered catching George's hair dye with his finger. How long ago was that? Fifteen years? This year? "Threatened George here with jail," he had told her during their long talk. "And now guess who is in the next cell, nearly his cell-mate."

When the guard had unlocked his cell, after Samantha and Abigail talked to him for such a long time, Charles stood unsteadily. He embraced Abigail and carried her up the steps out of the basement prison. Abigail's arms stayed locked around his dirty neck.

At the top of the stairs, Isaac took in the situation and merely draped Abigail's cloak over her.

Charles lifted Abigail into Reverend Tatlock's carriage, but he couldn't bear to let her go.

Isaac tapped him on the back. "Time enough for that now."

Soot or no, with his arms still wrapped around Abigail, Charles kissed her again. The fresh fragrance of her hair filled his lungs, cleared out the smells of smoke and typhoid's vinegary odors. "I need you," he said, listening to the ease with which 'I' slipped out of his mouth, but then Abigail had always comforted him. "Heard Grandpa died when we buried Lily." He stopped speaking as the full force of his losses hit him. His beloved father, who had been more like an older brother or dear friend, was gone, as well as the larger part of his family. All gone.

He heard first Mr. Dredford's voice, then Reverend Tatlock's, then Isaac's and finally, Samantha calling him as his neck stayed nestled in Abigail's arms.

"I love you, Charles." Abigail voice was the only one he could interpret. "You have to let me go. I'll see you in the morning."

"Until dawn." Charles's mind cleared and a feeling of space, time, and appropriateness re-established themselves. Charles watched Abigail's carriage until it was out of sight. Then his knees gave out. "Oh Lord, forgive my ignorance and my anger. Help me to trust You more."

Samuel Dredford and Constable Martin each took an arm nearly carrying Charles to Dredford's shay. "When did you eat last?" Samuel asked him.

Charles's head was spinning. "Can't remember. Maybe a couple of days before the outhouse burned down."

The constable produced a hip flask. "Brandy."

The hot vital liquid flowed down Charles's throat, warmed his gut as it hit bottom. The warmth spread and his eyes closed.

He could barely hear Samuel complain, "How am I going to get this lug into the house?"

Charles couldn't remember why he didn't care, but he remembered why he was smiling. Typhoid had not won. "Abigail loves me. We're not going to die."

* * *

Charles woke up on the wood floor of Samuel's house with a pillow under his head and a heavy blanket on top of him. A great hound lay next to him. As Charles sat up, the dog barked once, but didn't show his teeth. "Nice dog." Charles gingerly offered his hand below the mastiff's jaw.

"Brutus," Samuel called from the next room. Brutus sniffed at Charles's own dirty paw but declined a lick. Samuel appeared in white long johns. Brutus bumped into his master. "Good dog. He's half Great Dane, half horse, I think." Samuel rubbed the dog's ears. "He came with the place." Charles looked around the cottage. Samuel interpreted his assessment. "Small. I know. You need to get cleaned up."

Charles stood up, out of balance with the floor. "I'm awfully hungry."

"Sit down before you fall down. Oatmeal? Coffee?" Samuel pushed Charles into a chair in the kitchen end of the room. "Need to get you to Judge Pond's by nine o'clock. It's already seven."

Charles shivered as reality set it. "Don't want to go back to jail."

Samuel handed him a cup of coffee. "Drink this. You might be able to stay here, under house arrest."

"Need to be with Abigail." Charles tried to stand with the aid of the table, but gave it up. "Would she be able to visit here?"

They worked for an hour trying to make Charles presentable. His pants were brushed and his shoes shined, but Samuel didn't have a shirt big enough for Charles. "Wait a minute," Samuel said. He took the laddered steps to the loft two at a time. "Dolly knitted me a sweater.

When he put it on, Charles noticed one sleeve was longer than the other on the red sweater. "Itch from the wool."

Samuel produced a stretchy top part of a set of long johns. "This will help."

* * *

Judge Pond's paneled chambers on the second floor of the courthouse imposed a somber tone to the arraignment proceedings. Samuel showed Charles a stack of daily newspapers with alarming headlines: *"Van Aker's Son Torches Typhoid Home," "Van Aker Forces Workers out of Furniture Factory," "Typhoid Still Spreading," and "Arsonist Freed."*

The constable and Samuel shielded Charles from the crowd of angry spectators. Martin kicked the gate open to the tabled area in front of the raised bench of justice. Catcalls and obscenities hurled at the back of bowed Charles's head. "Abigail isn't here?"

The bailiff entered. "All rise."

Well into the proceedings, Charles lifted his head to hear Judge Pond say, "It is all very well for you to claim you were grief-stricken, but civilized people maintain their decorum through their troubles." The judge's spectacles perched crookedly on his nose. "Benjamin Van Aker did not raise his children to become callow youths."

Charles agreed. "Didn't mean for the house to burn, too."

"Then why did you soak it with kerosene?" Judge Pond asked.

"Wanted to get rid of the pestilence, but then remembered my books."

Judge Pond shouted, "Did you save the books?"

Charles shook his head. "No, Sir. When the second outhouse fell, it ignited the house. Grandpa, Israel Breckenridge, told me to put the new outhouse downhill from the well. He told me to burn the bedding. That's why I thought I should burn the beds. Remembered my books though." Charles couldn't suppress a cough, which helped cover a sob. "They're all gone."

"The books?"

"My family."

Judge Pond adjusted his glasses. "Your three remaining sisters are boarding with Abigail Breckenridge. Now explain to me why you wanted the factory to burn."

A low grumble ensued from the crowd. Judge Pond banged his gavel.

Charles hung his head. "Money couldn't buy any remedy. My mother, Matilda, John Eric, Little Ben, Lily."

"Have you come to your senses, now?" Judge Pond asked.

"Yes. I'm sorry if Xing was frightened." Charles turned toward the courtroom's audience. "Didn't spill any kerosene in the carriage house. The horse you know."

"Xing will need to be deported," Judge Pond said. "Can't allow typhoid carriers to become citizens."

The Chinese cook raised his fist and shouted. "Yaug kui tzu, wo hen chei ko ti fang."

Judge Pond stood and pointed his gavel at Xing. "If that's profanity, Sirrah, I can put you in jail for contempt of court. Jail! Do you understand?"

Xing nodded his head.

Mr. Shyler rose. "Judge Pond I can translate, if you wish." The Judge waved his hand toward Shyler to proceed. "I believe Mr. Xing understands English, even if he doesn't speak it very well. His response to your deportation order was quite distinct. He said, 'Foreign devil, I hate this place.'"

"Thank you, Mr. Shyler," Judge Pond banged his gavel. "We therefore need feel no guilt about our judgment. Constable Martin, escort Mr. Xing to Detroit for deportation after we finish this case."

Oliver Martin motioned to his assistant, who walked over to where Xing stood.

Charles continued his defense to the Judge. "The foundations for my future home are on Plymouth. The factory can expand now to the entire Madison Street lot. My lack of responsibility to the community might be forgiven by the additional jobs created."

"What about our lost wages while you were in your crazed state?" Earl Henry called from the hostile audience.

Charles turned toward the spectators, again. "They will be compensated, gladly." Then addressing the Judge, he said, "It's the least that can be done for endangering the lives of the fire fighters."

"Well at last your mind is functioning," Judge Pond said. "I can't let you off scot free."

Samuel offered, "I'll be glad to maintain custody under house arrest."

"Done. Charles, I hold you to your promise of rehiring your men. Six months." The judge stood as if to leave and then remembered to pound his gavel. "Court dismissed."

* * *

That afternoon, Abigail and Isaac arrived at Samuel's. Isaac hauled in a trunk of new clothes for Charles. Happiness radiated throughout Abigail's senses by seeing Charles's smile. His welcoming embrace and affectionate kiss were all she'd hoped for. "I missed you Charles Van Aker."

"After Mother's funeral, when the children were so ill--." Charles couldn't continue.

"I tried to understand." Abigail placed her hand under Charles's strong chin. "We can forget your courtship lapse for now. Your sisters are outside."

Charles asked her quietly, "Do they know what happened?"

Abigail explained, "I told them there was a serious accident and that you need to stay with Mr. Dredford until spring to make sure nothing else goes wrong."

Charles reached for her hand, withdrew her glove and kissed her palm. Then he looked into her eyes with his great dark pools of contrition. "I love you," he said. Then he repeated it as if relishing the freedom symbolized by being able to pronounce the dreaded pronoun, 'I' without stuttering. "I am so lucky to know you. The Lord has blessed me. I'll love you for the rest of my life." He broke down, his great shoulders shook. "You don't need to marry me," he sobbed, "if this added scandal--."

"Charles, you were ill, crazy with grief. I understand. If anyone else has a problem with my marrying you, it will be their problem, not ours."

Abigail said a quick prayer of thanksgiving to the Lord. Her Charles was truly returned to her. She wiped his tears away and kissed his mouth. "Now, no more nonsense. Your sisters are waiting."

Charles opened the front door to the cottage. His sisters flew at him. Samantha broke down, but Beatrice and Cassandra laughed and hugged his knees. "We have all the time in the world to be together." Charles said. "Our mother…."

"Is in Heaven," Beatrice said. "Samantha said so."

"She sees us," Cassandra said in an awed tone.

While Charles was reunited with his sisters, Abigail took Samuel into the kitchen. "Could you appeal to Judge Pond? We would like Charles to join us for Thanksgiving."

Samuel didn't speak immediately, as if considering the wisdom of her request. "Judge Pond doesn't have any family. Could I invite him, too?"

"Absolutely," Abigail said. "He'll love Mrs. McConnell's feast."

* * *

Abigail thanked the Lord and blessed Mrs. McConnell's Irish heart, knowing the state of things…money was scarce, Isaac, and the cook decided against a buffet for the Thanksgiving meal. Reverend Tatlock, Judge Pond, the widow, Mrs. Earl, and her friends, Miriam Pettibone and Robert Koelz, besides Charles, Samuel and the Breckenridge crew and household added up to sixteen thankful bellies to fill. The table only seated twelve, so Isaac and Mrs. McConnell insisted they and Cotton and Taffy should eat early downstairs, in order to serve at the table.

"Taffy might feel left out," Abigail said.

Cotton smiled at her. "We could play cards after."

Mrs. McConnell agreed, "After we get rid of...sorry. After the guests leave, we can play '*Questions and Answers.*' Isaac, I know that was the biggest turkey you could find, but Miss Abigail, there'll not be many leftovers."

"Dey'll stop eatin when the foods gone," Cotton laughed.

"Judge Pond could take Charles back to Ypsilanti," Abigail said.

"Then Mr. Dredford will be able to spend more time with Miss Colt."

* * *

On Thanksgiving, Charles mostly feasted on seeing Abigail for the few hours he spent at the meal. Still in mourning, her dress revealed a bit of cleavage under thin black netting. As he reviewed her attire, he realized she had dyed the dress she'd worn when they visited the Amish, a lifetime ago. The rick-rack was black as well as the pleated petticoat showing below the hem of her dress. Happy times cloaked with sorrow, now. Dolly and his sisters wore similar outfits, black skirts and white blouses with green ribbons for sashes with all that red hair gracing their shoulders.

Judge Pond elbowed him. "Eat up, young man. You won't be tasting Mrs. McConnell's cooking in Ypsilanti."

"Remembering happy times," Charles said, turning his gaze again on Abigail.

"Earl Henry tells me you've hired back all the workers," Reverend Tatlock popped the last piece of turkey on his plate into his mouth.

"And then some," Samuel added. "I think the Van Aker's have hired half of the town's carpenters."

"Our Plymouth home will be rebuilt in no time." Charles watched Abigail's reaction. He asked the Lord for forgiveness, but he really wanted everyone to vanish, except for Abigail. Of course, he'd missed his sisters. But he admitted to his Maker that his need to touch Abigail, to confirm the reality of her good health, overwhelmed his best intentions to comfort his orphaned sisters.

Abigail ignored him with her attention focused on her chores as hostess: asking Isaac to bring more wine, directing Cotton to notice the emptying serving dishes of sweet potatoes, green beans, corn relish, and Mrs. McConnell's light as feather dinner rolls.

"Abigail," Mrs. Earl said. "Your grandfather would be proud of your skills in running his home."

"Thank you," Abigail said. "Mrs. McConnell and Isaac are my right and left hands and Cotton here is my rod and staff."

"Best leave those to the Lord's 23rd Psalm," Isaac said, as he set three more bottles of wine on the table.

* * *

After Judge Pond interrupted Abigail and Charles's good-bye embrace to take Charles back to Ypsilanti, Abigail started rounding up her Breckenridge-house family. She pulled Isaac out of the basement wine closet. "Inventory our supplies later. We promised to start a card game this afternoon, remember."

Isaac's brow wrinkled. "Miss Abigail, I let Jessie go Friday, what with Cotton back and all."

"That's fine Isaac." Abigail wondered for the hundredth time if she should have made that particular decision. Abigail avoided, lost track of, or let go of such household matters, while her nose stayed close to the law books' grindstone. "I'm thankful when you take care of these matters for the house."

When Abigail entered the basement kitchen, Mrs. McConnell had already untied her apron and straightened her lace cap. "I'll need to be shopping tomorrow, Miss Abigail. That crew nearly ate the wood off the table." She laughed.

"Your such a good cook, the table would probably taste good, too. We don't need those cookies until tomorrow, do we?" Abigail asked. "I know the girls would love to pretend they're baking, if you'll let them."

"Och, and I love having them down, throwing flour at each other." Mrs. McConnell laughed. "Messing up my clean floor and me with no helper to go down on their knees to sweep it up."

Confusing it was, Abigail thought. Did Mrs. McConnell argue with Grandpa like this? Abigail turned to go back up the servants' stairs.

"Go on with you now." Mrs. McConnell gave Abigail's backside a swipe with her folded apron. "Grandpa knew when I was playing with him."

"I know!" Inspiration dawned on Abigail. "Give the girls brooms and tell them it's part of the baking game."

"I'll be doing just that." Mrs. McConnell laughed. "And I'll be right up to beat all of you at that beastly game of Dredford's."

In their third floor bedroom, Abigail watched Cotton add yellow ribbons to Taffy's braids. "Cotton, that child is perfect." Abigail petted Taffy's chocolate cheek. "Stop pestering her. Spend some time with us this afternoon. I know you're tired, but we promised to play cards."

* * *

At the cleared dining room table, Abigail noted Dolly was watching Samuel reshuffle the "Question and Answer" stacks of cards as they waited patiently for the Breckenridge family to re-assemble. Across the hall in the parlor, Cassandra, her striped cat, and Beatrice attended Samantha's practice of scales.

"Hurry, hurry." Abigail swept up four-year-old Cassandra in her arms. "The game is starting."

"We need three more men on the 'Questions' side of the table." Samuel directed the seating arrangements. "Beatrice, you pretend you're Charles and sit across from Abigail."

"I'll be Jesus," Cassandra said, sitting opposite Mrs. McConnell.

"The darling child, couldn't be more innocent." Mrs. McConnell smiled at Abigail's slight frown.

Taffy pulled herself up to the chair next to Cassandra's. Beatrice, the family's problem solver, settled the matter with the least resistance. "Samantha, Taffy can be your pretend beau."

"Cotton, you sit across from Isaac." Dolly pulled her into the seat beside her.

Samuel took the first card on the question stack and said, "Let's start with the smallest. Taffy, ask Samantha, 'Like Cinderella, will you disappear at the stroke of midnight?'"

Taffy looked at Samuel, then Cotton, then Samantha. "You gonna dis a peer?"

"Shh, shh," Abgail stilled the giggles.

Samantha picked a card from the answer pack and smiled at Taffy. "On the 25th hour of the day."

Abigail studied the young girl who had become a young lady in less than a year's time. Men would find her quietness enchanting, thinking they had time to claim this woman with charming, reddish blonde hair. Little would they know of the stubborn, capable woman hidden behind those sad and mysterious green eyes.

"My turn, my turn." Cassandra jumped down from her chair and pulled on Samuel's arm.

"Get back in your chair, Sweetie. Now remember everyone, she's Jesus." Samuel shifted through the cards. Abigail wondered if it was fair to read the questions before picking one. Samuel asked, "Do you value money?"

Cassandra leaned over the table to Mrs. McConnell. "Money?" she asked.

"Render to Caesar the things that are Caesar's and to God the things that are God's." Mrs. McConnell smiled.

"Read da answer card," Cotton said.

Mrs. McConnell picked up her card and read, "'Light the candles, that I may see more clearly.' My now, ain't that just as I was saying. We all know the Lord's will, only we hide it away in the dark."

Beatrice reached for the cards. "I want to pick my own for Aunt Abigail."

Samuel gave Beatrice the unused portion of the deck. "Remember, you're Charles."

"Yes, Charles." Abigail wished Charles was sitting across from her instead of his six-year-old sister. The three Van Aker redheads in the Breckenridge household matched Dolly's hair more than Abigail's dark curls. Charles's curls were blond. Samuel's straight hair was black with a few brown strands. Instead, Samuel said Earl Henry was taking up the bulk of Charles's time. Charles told her Mr. Henry visited the cottage in Ypsilanti daily taking down instructions for the factory's expanse and directions for rebuilding their home on Plymouth Road. Charles's sentence of house arrest stretched for five more months into the future. The month of May would see him free to marry her.

Without shuffling the cards at all, Beatrice turned over the top card. "Would you steal a kiss?"

The family laughed at Abigail's blush. Thus justified to blatantly cheat, Abigail looked through the cards for the right answer. "In the dark," she read, showing it to Dolly.

Beatrice shook her head.

"Come up with a good one, Mr. Dredford," Mrs. McConnell giggled.

Samuel turned over the next top card and handed it to Dolly. "Shall I express my affection?"

When Dolly turned over her answer card, she laughed heartily, "Only in a fit of apoplexy."

"What dat?" Taffy asked Cassandra.

"Temper tantrum," Cassandra whispered.

Isaac hadn't laughed during the game, so far. He went through 20 cards before he asked Cotton, "Would you permit me to speak more freely?"

"Can't read dem things." Cotton crossed her arms, pouting. Taffy started to sniffle, but Cassandra comforted her. Dolly picked a card and whispered its message to Cotton, who lifted her chin and said, "Okay, big fella here goes." Cotton took the card and held it out for Isaac to read. "I will relieve you of dat decision, Sir."

"That," Isaac corrected.

Cotton stormed out of the dining room. Isaac excused himself and followed Cotton into the adjoining serving room. Abigail knew they were well aware everything they said could be heard, but the fact didn't put a damper on their tempers.

"Don't talk down to me, front of my baby." The fervor in Cotton's tone let the table know there wasn't room for debate.

Samantha herded the little chickens into the parlor. Mrs. McConnell followed them across the hall and closed that door. Returning, she slowly picked up the stray cards. Then, they all listened unashamedly to the hidden couple.

"Cotton, you know I care as much for that child."

"Don't," Cotton sobbed in a muffled way, as if pressed against Isaac's chest.

"Yes, I do," Isaac said. "I care about you, too. I've been reading up on this speech thing."

Silence. Finally they heard Cotton say, "What do dey say?"

Abigail, Mrs. McConnell, Dolly and Samuel all held their breaths.

Without correcting Cotton's mispronunciation, Isaac said. "That children only learn from their parents. Listening to others does no good."

The table collectively sighed in relief.

Mrs. McConnell opened the parlor door again. "Who wants to bake cookies?" All four of the children rushed in. Mrs. McConnell marched them through the room where Cotton and Isaac stood.

"Come in here, Isaac." Abigail boldly called the couple in. "Samuel wants to see my office and you two need to talk."

"I prefer the library." Isaac was holding Cotton's hand.

"Sure," Cotton winked at Abigail. "Pull me 'round like a rag doll."

Chapter Sixteen

In Abigail's gazebo law office, Dolly sat next to Samuel on what Grandpa called the client side of Abigail's desk. "Will Cotton listen to Isaac?"

"Isaac knows the right things to say," Dolly said. "Cotton loves that child."

"Cotton's over thirty," Samuel worried his left eye brow. "Speaking one way for all those years is a lot to correct." Samuel reached for Dolly's hand, keeping it in his lap. "We don't know who to speak to first, you or Charles." He rushed his words, staring down at Dolly's ring less fingers. "After we marry…."

Dolly reclaimed her hand. "We both love the Van Aker children and don't want to be separated from them."

Abigail stared at them. Neither readily expounded on their plans. What had she missed? Samuel cocked his head, as if waiting for her answer. She held her hand over her mouth, she didn't want to voice an obvious question, but couldn't discover what they were asking for. Dolly was smiling, hopefully. Abigail smiled back, inspired to ask a question. "What do you think Charles would say?"

"We thought you might know," Samuel said.

'About what?' she wanted to shout, but kept calm. "I'm sure Charles would welcome your influence with the children."

"Abigail," Dolly looked for approval from Samuel before stating clearly, "We haven't mentioned this to the children. You're the first to know our plans. We're hoping to adopt Samantha, Beatrice and Cassandra."

Abigail smiled approval. But she withheld any direct response, while she considered the ramifications. Where would they live? Dredford's place in Ypsilanti was unsuitable. It might be all right for a newly married couple for a few years, certainly not for a couple with three young girls. Dolly was only twenty-six. Surely they would want children of their own. Abigail admitted she was jealous of the closeness Samantha and the girls shared with Dolly, instead of her. Dolly's mothering skills were already in evidence, for instance, she could conjure up ideal accents for reading A. B. Frost's "Uncle Remus" with all the right inflections for dumb Brer Wolf and clever Brer Rabbit.

"Have you contacted Mary Foster," Abigail asked, wondering how all her questions would be answered.

"Should we wait until you and Charles marry?" Dolly asked.

Abigail tried to think about the right and wholesome thing to say, encouraging but non-committal. She looked out the window of the gazebo to stall for time. Her mind was not functioning quickly enough.

Outside the window an amazing caravan was headed straight for them. "Look," she said, pointing out the window.

Samuel acted as if he'd seen the old trick before. His chin jutted out. "Answer me."

"Let me think about it," Abigail said as she continued to point at the window. "Who are those men?"

Dolly was on her feet and out the door with Abigail. Fifteen to twenty men with their hitched teams surrounded the gazebo.

"Going to be a big job." Abigail recognized Earl Henry's voice.

She marched up to him. "What are you doing here? Get those men and horses off my property. Now!"

"Take those animals into the street," Earl Henry barked at his men. "Mr. Van Aker wants this building moved to the Plymouth address."

"He does, does he?" Abigail's hands were on her hips. "This is my property. I'm not married to Mr. Charles Van Aker, and if I were, this property is still my property. Get your interlopers out of here!"

"Now, now," Earl Henry said. "Just a misunderstanding, I'm sure. We'll be back after this is cleared up between you and Mr. Van Aker."

Abigail's anger was increasing, instead of subsiding. She noticed her voice was well above a polite volume. "A misunderstanding! Theft is not a misunderstanding. I'll put that cracker, that recalcitrant charger back in jail!"

She didn't need Samuel's hand on her shoulder to know she'd gone too far. "Grandpa's gazebo." Abigail dissolved in angry tears on Dolly's shoulder. "Why didn't he say something at dinner, today?"

"The pernicious fool," Dolly said, "Men can be so heedless."

Samuel backed away.

Abigail turned on him, "Go tell him," Abigail yelled after him. "This gazebo is never moving and I'm having second thoughts about his value as a future husband."

*   *   *

The day after Thanksgiving, Mrs. McConnell advised Abigail. "Let's call that Sister Grace over here for you. Didn't she tell Mrs. Husted where to find Confederate gold, those English sovereigns, under her jars of carrots, remember? Seems like your being a member of St. Andrew's pope-less congregation and all, she would be doing you no harm."

Abigail couldn't find a reasonable objection, so Mrs. McConnell did invite Sister Grace over on a day when the girls were out gallivanting around with Dolly and Samuel to buy Christmas gifts.

"Come right in, Sister Grace." Isaac ushered her into the parlor and shut the doors in case the shopping crew returned early.

Abigail even dropped her tea cup on the new Persian blue carpet. Wasn't pursuing an oracle against the Lord's lesser instructions? Sister Grace wasn't dressed as a soothsayer, one of those fortune tellers the Lord cautioned against listening to. Instead she wore a somber dress of brushed silk, sensible shoes and a sweet cameo at her throat. But would Grandpa have disapproved? Could she trust Sister Grace's advice, if she told her to marry Charles?

"Hold your hands up in front of your face," the psychic said. "Now turn them palm out." Abigail did as she was told. Sister Grace asked, "Are you right-handed or left-handed?"

After Abigail acknowledged she was right-handed, Sister Grace asked to see the left one first. Abigail laid her hand palm up in Sister's hand. "This is the hand you haven't changed from the time you were born. Gravity implants a pattern of the stars on your hands at birth, but then you change them by your actions."

Abigail looked at the fathomless lines on her own hand. 'Lord,' she prayed, 'forgive this foolishness.'

"See these worry lines? If you don't stop your worry habit and trust in the Lord more," Sister Grace said, "those lines will cut right into this life line. Odd, you have three short life lines. Do you know what that means?"

Abigail shook her head. Was she tempting the fates, mocking her own belief in a caring Creator by entertaining a soothsayer? But this woman mentioned the Lord. Where was the evil in trying to delve into all of the Lord's ways to make his will known? She tried listening to the still small voice from her soul's contact with the Lord; but lately, actually since her grandfather had died so suddenly, perhaps her busy mind had blocked out any incoming messages. Abigail earnestly prayed, 'Lord, help me trust you more.'

Sister Grace was still speaking, "You're an old soul. You've been around before on earth. You know things other people are just now learning. Haven't you wondered why you are able to be so ladylike without a mother hounding you?"

Abigail began to pay closer attention to the prattle. "Is there a way to improve my money situation?"

"Let's see the one you're working on." Sister Grace took her right hand. "Your love line is very strong. We've all heard about Charles Van Aker's troubles and the healthy legacy his mother left him. But you...," Sister Grace put her nose closer to Abigail's hand. "You have a hole in your hand."

"What?"

"See how my palm is flat. Yours has an indentation, which means money runs right through your hands, before you can even know it's there."

Abigail closed her hand. "My life line is strong?"

"Except for the worry business. Do you want to know how many children you'll have?"

Abigail said. "I think I'll wait for my future husband, Charles Van Aker, to decide."

Sister Grace laughed heartily. "You'll be all right, child," she said as Isaac escorted her to the front door.

Abigail knew her money management skills were sadly underdeveloped. Her grandfather Breckenridge covered the house repairs, repainting costs, even the fireplace replacement in his will. Dolly picked out the lincrusta for the hall. The costly, cream colored linoleum, which simulated embossed leather, brightened the windowless entry way. Christmas presents were another matter, not included in the will's provisions. The proceeds from the auction of the old furniture might cover the cost of the bountiful gifts. Abigail admitted she didn't know how to scrimp, never had to before.

When Dolly and Samuel took the girls shopping for new dresses for Thanksgiving with the money Charles meant for their boarding costs, Abigail was truly amazed at how far they had stretched the funds. Abigail envied their skill. Samantha and Mrs. McConnell had set to sewing and completing an entire new wardrobe for each of the growing girls, including Taffy.

Cotton had taken offense. "My baby don't need charity. Grandpa Breckenridge took good care a me and I don't need stuff from nobody."

Isaac intervened. "Cotton, you love that child, but how is she going to feel if she doesn't have dresses just like the Van Aker girls. She's only a child. Gifts are not always charity."

Cotton sniffed, but gave her consent.

Abigail could not restrain her curiosity. "Dolly, how can you afford this?"

"Oh, I saved all of Samantha's piano lesson fees. Remember, Grandpa insisted Charles pay me for them."

Abigail had forgotten, which proved her inability to run the finances for the home. She didn't even know how much the kerosene for the oil lamps cost.

Dolly was a comfort all through the disappointment of Charles failing to continue their courtship. Dolly had filled her time, making plans with Samuel to include Abigail and arranging entertainments with the Van Aker children. Especially after Grandpa died, Dolly kept constant watch. When she married Samuel, of course, Dolly wouldn't be able to spend as much time with her.

If only Charles would rescue her from these bookkeeping duties, Mrs. McConnell's cooking and Isaac's skills might help run a profitable boarding house business. Abigail had intended to leave Grandpa's house to become Charles's bride. As it stood now, Abigail knew she might need to sell something else to keep up her standard of living: new spring outfits for church, new shoes. At least Dolly hadn't noticed Abigail was counting her pennies. Abigail had explained she'd always hated the front-room furniture and Charles disliked Grandmother's bedroom suite. Who could she blame for hating the china and crystal, which would be headed for the auction block next?

Abigail's household staff treated her as a dear member of the extended family, but Abigail missed Charles and the promise of her own home. Even though Grandpa had made the will in order to keep George Lott from profiting by his marriage to her, and then made her nearly destitute by *not* rewriting the document before he died, Abigail missed Grandpa. His good opinions of her and Charles's love had helped to buoy her spirits.

As it stood without Charles as a husband, the straight 'A's' in law school would be the only tangible sign of her worth. Even among books, Abigail couldn't find enjoyment in regular fiction. The clarity of the law made the rest of literature silly, unimportant. Besides, fiction sounded out her feelings, her longings. She couldn't read fiction for twenty minutes without ending up in helpless sobbing. Melodramas touched her vulnerable feelings too deeply.

Matriculation proceeded without similar responses. Grandpa's gazebo-study was a god-send. The gothic lancet windows provided enough winter light to study during the day. Gaslight strained her eyes badly enough to demand reading glasses. They made her look the part of the old maid she was becoming at 18 going on 19.

Reckless Charles had wanted to move the gazebo away from any connection to the courthouse. How would she see clients? No one would be willing to drive out to Plymouth Road to talk to her. It was ridiculous. Had he forgotten she was studying to become a trial lawyer? Was he so dense only *his* plans mattered?

Abigail had invited Mrs. Hanson and Miss Pettibone to visit. She needed their help to appraise the furniture in the parlor, except for the piano, and Abigail's grandmother's bedroom in preparation for auction.

Punctilious Miriam Pettibone arrived at the Breckenridges, jumping down from the front seat of a large dray wagon. She pointed to two lumber-jack sized men. "They'll help me move everything to the depot in Ypsilanti. You should have the bank draft in your hands by next Saturday."

Abigail did remember to ask, at Mary Foster's earlier promptings, "What happens to the items not sold?"

"Oh, they'll all be sold. Some won't receive the asking price, but everything will leave the floor by the end of the auction. Now don't worry. I expect you'll receive $10,000, at least."

Abigail hoped she could provide for herself for at least three years with that amount, maybe even longer. Long enough for Charles to get his house and his act in order.

Miriam Pettibone marched through the house. Her eyebrows rose at the emptied parlor.

Abigail opened the doors to the stuffed library. "Jake," Miss Pettibone directed, "take all the upholstered chairs in both rooms."

"Leave two of the arm chairs and the piano," Abigail said.

"Which pictures do you want to keep?" Miss Pettibone asked, "Any of the lamps?"

"You can auction off all the lamps except the green glass one on the library table."

Miss Pettibone pouted. "I wanted that one. It would have fetched a pretty price."

"I plan to move it to my office." The day was going to be more difficult than Abigail had planned.

"Karl," Miss Pettibone motioned to the other unoccupied man. "Strip the dining room of chairs. We'll have to make a second trip for the table."

"No," Abigail fought to control her tone. "We eat there."

"Yourself and…Dolly?"

"The staff, the Van Aker girls, Dolly and I enjoy taking our meals together."

Miss Pettibone's humph was muffled by the door knocker.

Isaac pushed past the lounging men in the hall. "Mrs. Hanson," he announced.

"With less staff, Abigail, the money will stretch farther," Miss Pettibone offered.

"Israel Breckenridge would roll over in his grave," Mrs. Hanson said. "Looks like I arrived in the nick of time."

Abigail agreed but asked Isaac to show Miss Pettibone to her grandmother's bedroom where every piece of furniture could be moved out. Jake and Karl followed Miss Pettibone's fulminations up the front staircase.

"Come into the dining room," Abigail directed, "Mrs. Hanson. Mrs. McConnell will have fresh coffee and tarts sent up."

Old Mrs. Hanson was not one to mince words. "Can you handle the vulture?" Abigail shrugged her shoulders and smiled politely. "Also, I suggest you entertain a new beau." Mrs. Hanson appraised Abigail as if she were a piece of furniture or a new horse she might want to bid on. "My daughter-in-law's younger brother, Joseph Kerner, would be perfect."

Abigail was grateful Mrs. McConnell arrived with the coffee and tarts.

But Mrs. Hanson was unrelenting. "You cannot possibly accept Charles Van Aker. He has been brought before Judge Pond."

Joseph Kerner was a few years older than Abigail; but Abigail knew the gossip around town was true. After Joe returned from a stint as a lumberjack in California, his drunken exploits were enough to fill three columns in the Courier's gossip column. No amount of money would induce Abigail to undertake the restoration of the handsome, wine-bibber's soul. Grandpa had told her hair-raising tales of how her own father, Orlando, had nearly made Grandpa destitute with his gambling and unpaid bar tabs. Of course, the Lord spent time among the drinkers in His own day, but Abigail knew she was no saint and would not be able to endure the suffering marriage to a drunk would entail.

Abigail stood, hoping she could control her temper, without impugning Joe Kerner's character. "If I can't have Charles, I won't marry anyone. If you had been allowed into the hearing before Judge Pond, you would have discovered Charles did not burn down his home. He meant to burn the privy which spread the pestilence, not his parents' home or his books!"

Mrs. McConnell walked to the hallway as if to escort Mrs. Hanson out the door. "Isaac is employed upstairs," she said. "May I be of help in opening the door for you, Mrs. Hanson."

"Well!" Mrs. Hanson said as she laid down her un-tasted peach tart. "You are a determined lass. I'll say that for you. Got a little Van Aker stubbornness in you without yet being married to one. And, Mrs. McConnell, I'm not finished here. If you don't mind, I'll take myself up to Dolly Colt's room. I understand she has some sway with you, Abigail. Ask her about the details of the gossip I've seen for myself. Heard you were not happy with the way Charles has been rampaging around your gazebo."

Abigail watched the tall matriarch march up the stairs, squeezing past Jake and Karl as they each hauled down drawers from Grandmother's dressers. Doubt seeped like smoke through Abigail's sense. She was losing control of the situation. "Isaac," she called.

At her side in seconds, Isaac waited for orders. "What are Miss Pettibone and Mrs. Hanson up to?" Abigail asked.

"I can tell you what they are *not* doing. They are *not* knocking on Dolly Colt's door, who is *not* receiving visitors, *nor* on the Van Aker children's door, and they are certainly *not* heading to the third floor or the kitchen."

Abigail's tears welled up. "Isaac."

"It's my job, Miss Abigail. Think of me as big guard dog."

"You may be the only male I trust today," Abigail admitted.

"Charles is a gentleman. Grandpa told you to give him time. It is not Christmas yet."

Abigail took heart. "We'll need an extra big tree for the children."

"Their first Christmas without their parents." Isaac agreed.

"My first without Grandpa." Abigail leaned toward Isaac, who put his giant arms around her, offering his handkerchief for any service it might render. '…giving comfort to the destitute,' Abigail thought in a freshet of new tears.

* * *

A month later, the Christmas presents were stacked in Grandpa's library. The dining room doors across the hall from the parlor were closed. Mrs. McConnell and Dolly started a card game after supper with the girls, while Isaac and Abigail slipped out to transfer the gifts from the library, placing them under the tree in the parlor.

Isaac stopped to gaze at the tree. His arms were filled to his chin with presents. "Great tree."

The giant spruce towered to the ceiling in the freshly painted blue room. The satin, striped blue sofa faced a new ceramic fireplace mantle, which cheered the room much better than the old slate monstrosity. Arm chairs on each side of the tree were already filled with presents for the adults.

What would the parlor look like without the tree, after Christmas? The room echoed even now, emptied of its heirlooms, shed of its sound softening plants and abundance of over-stuffed chairs. No wonder Grandpa had kept the room filled to capacity. Loneliness rallied to echoes. Abigail missed Grandpa's gruff twang, Charles's literary eloquence.

Abigail had the cherry breakfront cabinet painted white. The painter insisted it was a sin to paint over the beautiful wood, but she'd persisted. Photographs of the Van Akers and Grandpa in his civil war uniform, his face untroubled by the events to come, were displayed on the white cabinet. Two wedding photographs, one of Salome and Grandpa and one of Bernice and Orlando, vied for space with tintypes of Salome and Bernice. One other off-centered photo of Abigail in her engagement dress completed the display. George's side of the picture had been thrown away.

Large black-and-white photographs of great sailing ships and a few steamships decorated the walls. A model ship in full sail sat on the piano, the result of a late hobby of Grandpa's. She found a blue paisley scarf of her mother's as its indoor sea. But Abigail missed the robin's-egg blue sofa still sitting in Charles's factory. Abigail missed her Charles, too. "Maybe he's still on his way. Judge Pond said he could come."

Isaac only shook his head. "We need to pray that boy will wake up soon and realize the only good food in town is Mrs. McConnell's.

Cotton started running around the parlor jingling the sleigh bells. The voices in the dining room quieted down. Dolly slid the dining room door open slowly, and the faces of Taffy, Cassandra, Beatrice and Samantha lit up with the spectacle of the candle-lit Christmas tree and the stacks of presents.

"See," Cassandra pinched her bigger sister. "Santa Claus knew where we lived."

After the exhausted, satiated children retired, Dolly stayed with Abigail in the darkened parlor. "Maybe Charles will still come?" Abigail hoped beyond reason.

Dolly scooted closer to her on the sofa. "It's late."

"I thought tonight he might want to tell me when to announce the banns."

Dolly played with the ribbons on her skirt. "Charles might want to re-start building your house, even completing it in the spring, before you announce your engagement."

"I want him with me now," Abigail said.

"I know," Dolly showed her sympathetic green eyes.

Abigail's temper flared. "You don't! Sorry. It is just that you and Samuel don't seem in any rush."

"We haven't agreed on a time, that's all." Dolly twisted on the sofa. "I would like to see you and the girls settled before I make a decision."

"I'm settled." If Charles wasn't going to marry her, Abigail knew she'd never settle for anyone else. "Charles has to come." Where would she go if Charles didn't bring her a ring? She couldn't bear the dirge her heart prepared. Life without Charles, without Grandpa was too hard. It was all very well to become a lawyer but she needed someone to love.

* * *

Earlier on Christmas Eve when Charles Van Aker and Samuel Dredford were headed for the door, Samuel stopped Charles. Samuel cleared his throat for the fifteenth time. Charles knew their Christmas visit to Abigail's had been sanctioned by Judge Pond as had the Thanksgiving Day dinner. "What is it?" Charles guessed either an unpleasant or unseemly subject clogged his friend's throat.

"Dolly and I." Samuel stopped, unable to go on.

Charles thought he could help the poor man. "Are to be married soon."

Samuel smiled, but shook his head no. "Dolly wants children."

Now Charles was at a loss. "What is the problem?"

"Not her own children," Samuel looked in every corner of the room trying to avoid Charles's face, "Yours."

"Mine?" Charles put his hands on his hips, then crossed his hands, then let his arms hang loose. "Why?"

Samuel realized his error. "Not yours, exactly, your sisters. To take care of as our own."

Charles knew his silence might be a problem for Samuel, but the news took the wind out of him. Nevertheless, a problem could be solved. This way Abigail and he could start a fresh, a new family of their own. Not that he didn't love his sisters, but if they were taken care of. "How do you feel about the idea?" he asked Samuel.

"I love those girls. Samantha is such a brave trouper. You should have seen her with the little ones after your mother passed. Beatrice is sharp as a whip, wiser than the rest of us at times. And Cassandra, no one could ask for a sweeter child."

"Have you both talked to Abigail?" Charles wondered why she hadn't said anything at Thanksgiving.

"We talked to her after the Thanksgiving dinner, but your men interrupted when they showed up to move the gazebo, and she didn't give us an answer. We worried we were presumptuous. I mean to take the only thing she had of yours, your sisters, when you stopped courting her, because of typhoid, but now…."

"I'd have to pay for their upkeep; that's the only way I would agree to your taking care of them. Abigail will have to be consulted, too."

"We want to adopt them." Now Samuel looked Charles straight in the eyes.

Charles smiled. His sisters were loved. "I'd still need to provide for them. The Van Aker trusts will help, too."

"There's something more." Samuel pulled out a kitchen chair and sat down. "Mrs. Hanson saw you at the Williams Street house."

"Does Abigail know?" Charles leaned against the outer door, unbuttoned his great coat.

"I found out you didn't go inside," Samuel said wiping his brow. "Dolly knows but she hasn't told Abigail." Silence reigned. "And, Charles." Samuel looked at the empty table, as if to help him spill out the rest. "Mr. Breckenridge failed to take care of Abigail in his will."

"Impossible."

"He made the will when she was…engaged to Lott."

"How is she managing?" Poor Abigail, Charles thought. I've given her so much trouble while she was coping with her own problems.

"She has a trust for running the house and school tuition, but that's it. She's been selling the furniture."

Charles laughed in relief. "We both hated Grandpa's old fashioned furniture."

Samuel seemed scandalized by Charles's laughter. "The china and crystal are next."

Charles stopped his guffaws. "I'll take care of her." But, Charles couldn't imagine how to approach Abigail about Dolly and Samuel's suggestion to adopt the girls.

***

Near midnight Isaac opened the door for Charles and Samuel. "The ladies need to retire. Come back in the morning."

Abigail came rushing into the hall. She had heard Isaac's suggestion. "Oh, stay," she said. "Neither of us will sleep until you tell us why you are so late."

Charles said, "I love you, Abigail. I'm so sorry about the gazebo. I didn't think the men would work on Thanksgiving Day. I thought they had enough other work to do and planned to ask you about the gazebo. They knew I wanted the gazebo out on Plymouth road and took the initiative to move it on their own schedule. Please announce the banns the first Sunday in May. By then, the house-arrest will be over and you'll have an engagement ring from me."

Abigail fell against Charles, clung to his waist as he bent down to kiss her. But out of the corner of her eye Dolly and Samuel's' behavior stopped her pleasure. "What?"

"Charles needs to talk to you about Dolly and my plans," Samuel said.

"Why can't you tell me?" Abigail asked. Samuel actually blushed. "You can't be shy about marrying Dolly?"

"Entirely different matter," Samuel said.

Dolly agreed. "We'll wait in the library, until you decide."

Abigail turned to Charles, who had seated himself on the striped sofa. He patted the place next to him. "You're sitting on the wrong sofa."

Charles's brows lowered, then he laughed. "The robin's-egg sofa is safe. I'll send Earl Henry over to the factory with the delivery information."

As Abigail spread her skirts out next to him, a small foreboding clung to her thoughts. "Is everything all right?"

"It certainly is," Charles said. "Did I tell you how beautiful you are this evening?"

Abigail bounded off the couch. "Do you want your present, now?"

"Let's talk, first," he said. "I know you love my sisters, but Samuel told me the particulars of Grandpa's will."

Abigail remained silent. Something untoward was afoot. She laid her hand on his shoulder, scooted closer to his side.

"Dolly and Samuel want to adopt my sisters as their family," Charles said, then added, "as soon as they marry."

"His house is too small," Abigail said.

"When you're living with me." Charles grasped both her hands in his. "We could let the children and the Dredford's rent out this big house."

"Did Samuel ask for the house?"

"My idea, entirely," Charles said.

Abigail rose and reseated herself on the piano bench. "Oh, the Dredford's can stay here with the children. I think adoption is a great idea. But I want the gazebo in town, to keep an eye on things. The Plymouth Road site is too far for business for a lawyer. I need to be close to the courthouse. And I need to be close to my family: Isaac, Mrs. McConnell, Cotton and Taffy."

Charles joined her at the piano. "And Dolly and Samuel and my sisters. Of course, moving the gazebo was not a good idea."

"Should we join them in the library?" Abigail asked.

"After you feel you been kissed enough," Charles said, taking her into his arms.

Chapter Seventeen

Through the long winter months while Charles and Abigail were separated by his house arrest, Abigail prayed for patience. But one Saturday morning on Valentine's Day, Abigail could no longer restrain her frustration. Her law studies could wait for now. She needed a love potion or cloying religious ritual to seal her bargain with Charles. Maybe she could bring up the subject of magic with Cotton. After breakfast, Abigail followed Cotton down the back stairs.

Cotton was rehearsing her diction lessons, "This thing, and dat..that thing. Believing and loving and everything that lasts."

"That's almost a poem," Abigail said, to lighten her embarrassment of eavesdropping.

"Hard work," Cotton said, emptying a basket of sheets onto a rough table.

"Is magic hard work, too?" Abigail reached for the empty basket and turned away to hide her blush.

Cotton laughed. "Not like remembering '*th's*' and '*ing's*.'" Abigail stood around, shifting from one foot to the other, not knowing what to ask for. Cotton caught on. "You need yourself some?"

Abigail tried to correct the question but gave it up. "Charles," she said.

"Not sure I should help you with *TH*-at one."

"Please, Cotton."

Cotton nodded her head as she stoked the low stove under the wash tub. "Guess we should concentrate on some spells. When does you plan ta see him?"

"This morning, after I talk to Mrs. Foster."

"I could make da candle dance." Cotton leaned back on her haunches, stirring the fire.

Abigail bent down to hear her advice, just as Cotton stood up. They knocked heads and laughed.

"Rub dat rose petal cream on da inside of your legs, way up."

"That's not magic."

"It'll work. And under your arms to make the sweat smell sweet." Abigail chewed her lips. "Dat…that's good," Cotton said. "Do that right before you goes in ta see him, makes your lips puff and da blood comes up to make 'em redder. But, if you mama was here, I'd let her tell ya. It ain't never easy da first time. Virgins bleed a little bit. Don't let it scare him. I knows he ain't never done it. Dat'll help."

Abigail wondered what she should wear.

"Dat velvety Christmas skirt, with the lacy silk top." Cotton seemed to read her mind.

"Don't wear no underclothes but stuff some in your reticule."

"Charles will say I'm as shameless---

"Well, marries him 'fore you do anything. Dat will solve dat." Cotton turned around to hug her briefly. "Ain't no shame in lovin, and it's time you both stop talkin. I taught you how to shave your legs with a straight razor, so's you could give dat man a clean shave. Can't have you comin home wid your face all tore up."

"Oh," Abigail said.

"Dat boy loves to jaw, so if he starts, put your finger in your mouth, get it nice and wet and place it on his lips to quiet him."

"Wow," Abigail said.

"You wants children?" Cotton asked frankly. "I could fix a nice vinegar douche after, to stop dat."

"No, that's all right. I'd like to have children, quickly."

"And lock da door, bolt if it you can. Men feel safer dat way."

"Thank you, Cotton." Abigail was humbled by all the new, applicable knowledge. She hugged the older woman. "I don't have anyone else to ask."

"Magic lasts, so make sure you knows whats you want."

"I do," Abigail said. It sounded like a wedding rehearsal.

After attending to all of Cotton's directions, Abigail took an apple to the carriage house for Flicka where Isaac was harnessing Prescott to the carriage for her.

"Miss Abigail, take Miss Dolly with you." Isaac cautioned.

"I don't need help with Charles." Abigail surprised herself with the depth of her determination.

However, Dolly climbed into the buggy. Cotton must have been watching their shenanigans. She hurried out with two lap robes. "Too cold to let the wind whip around you like dat...that."

Isaac smiled from ear to ear.

'Goodness,' Abigail thought. 'Everyone can manage their men except me.' Prickles of dissatisfaction ran up her spine. "Isaac, please stop first at Mary Foster's."

After all, the lady had been widowed three times, Hopefully, she had gleaned some morsels of wisdom about obstinate men. Abigail's mind emitted stormy displeasure in Charles's direction. Her agitated nerves needed Mrs. Foster's calming viewpoint. Dolly's position as boarder and friend didn't always provide an unbiased view.

Mud everywhere, the February thaw set the morning tableau. Bouncing along in the carriage, Abigail wished they could drive out to Plymouth Road to see how far work on the house had progressed.

Dolly ventured a quiet comment. "You're in a momentary state of frustration. It will pass."

"Where's loyalty when I need it?"

"Based in truth, that's where." Dolly didn't blink.

"I'm getting sick of everyone giving Charles excuses. I've had my own troubles." Abigail smoothed down her black skirt. "Do you find me burning down the house?"

Dolly winked at her.

Abigail laughed. "Dolly, you're a brick. I should throw you through Dredford's window."

At the lawyer's, Abigail told Isaac, "We'll be a minute. Will you be warm enough out here?"

"If required," Isaac answered.

From her open front door Mary Foster heard the response. "Plenty of warmth to go around in here." She motioned for Isaac to come inside. "Kitchen," she pointed down the hall.

Safely ensconced in the front parlor with Dolly, Abigail marveled at the duplicate layout of the house. "Did you notice our homes are identical? Our kitchen is in the basement, too."

Mary shook her head, ignoring the remark. "Hired help can be as much work as they are useful."

Abigail wasn't feeling disloyal. "It is Charles Van Aker I'm having trouble with."

"Men." Mary Foster poured them tea out of pot with a perched chickadee painted on its lid.

Dolly turned the teapot around to appreciate the garden of flowers on its sides.

Aware of her friend's thoughts, Abigail said, "Winter must be getting on my nerves."

"Last year, you did *not* have it easy," Mary said. "How's school?"

The subject eased Abigail's immediate distress. "Every time I think of the progress I'm making, a solid contentment comes over me. Why doesn't thinking of Charles produce the same effect?"

"Facts are facts. Emotions carry us in all directions." Mary refilled their cups.

"Charles tried to have the gazebo moved to Plymouth Road."

"Without his family, Charles has no one to gainsay his projects." Mary handed around plates of cream-puffs. "My mother only told me one thing about marriage, 'After you raise your children, you have to raise your husband.' I didn't have any children, but I raised three men to be good husbands."

"Charles thinks he needs to be master of his household, no doubt." Abigail frowned at Dolly, who was already sampling her pastry.

"Not necessarily." Dolly used her napkin to catch a hint of lost pudding from the corner of her mouth.

"If he had discussed moving the gazebo with you, you could have explained the benefits of keeping your legal office closer to the court house," Mary, the lawyer, reasoned.

"And my family."

"The servants?" Mary asked. "I've let all of mine go, years ago. I manage."

"I rarely think of people as servants," Abigail said. "I've loved them for years."

"Yes," Mary shook her finger at Abigail, "but they don't love you above their own interests."

"Cornelius left," Dolly said to prove that the staff had considered Abigail's need to stretch her dollars.

Mary gathered their empty plates and transferred them to the bottom shelf of the tea service cart. "What happens to the house on Wright and Moore when you marry?"

"They, Isaac, Mrs. McConnell, Cotton and Taffy, are allowed to live there, but it is still mine."

Dolly grasped the picture more quickly than Abigail. "They can't change the house without her approval, can they?"

"Will they pay you rent?" Mary excused herself to take a pastry down to the kitchen for Isaac. Abigail still didn't have an answer when she returned. "Do you pay the property tax?" Mary prompted.

"Yes." A certain defensiveness led Abigail to add, "I may not marry."

"Nevertheless," Mary said, "let's not confuse disparate issues."

Dolly sipped another cup of tea and got into the swing of drilling Abigail. "Will you move the books in the library, when you marry?"

"The Van Aker children, Taffy, and Isaac need them." Relieved, Abigail was to finally answer a question. "And Cotton is determined to learn to read."

"Have you discussed the books?" Mary poured Abigail another cup of tea. "The household items?"

"Abigail sold furniture to buy Christmas presents," Dolly said.

"Charles never liked the furniture I sold. I didn't spend all the money." Abigail was surprised to hear Dolly speak of Charles's place of priority in her life. Evidently, Dolly knew how much she'd spent on Christmas for everyone.

"Selling your belongings can't go on forever," Mary said.

"I'll have my law practice." Abigail's chin lifted.

"If you marry?" Mary asked. "Might not children overwhelm you?"

"Men aren't overcome by children." Somewhere in her heart, Abigail knew these two were friendly challengers, but she was starting to think they considered her stupid, or at least ill-prepared for marriage. "Men keep working." Then Abigail remembered having a similar conversation with Charles's mother on the train to New York. "Cotton would care for mine."

"That's better." Mary poured herself another cup of tea and brought out a decanter of cream sherry. She handed Dolly and Abigail each a stemmed glass, half full. "I'm selfish," she said. "I'm not going to waste my time advising you about your fiancé, if you're not willing to control your own life."

Abigail stretched taller, which reminded her of a book she'd read as a child, where the characters had magic dust they could sprinkle on themselves to get very small or very tall. "I need to take control of my family's situation on Wright and Moore, too."

"You could ask Samuel and me to rent the house from you," Dolly said.

"Grandpa's provision for the staff to live there would need to be included in the lease," Abigail said. "At least I can write up the contract."

Then Dolly turned to Mary. "After Charles and Abigail marry, Samuel and I want to adopt the Van Aker girls."

"So, Abigail," Mary said. "If the contingency, your marriage, is planned, they will realize their own security faster."

"They must wonder about their future," Dolly said.

"I'm sure they do." Mary poured them each another glass of sherry. "Excuse me. I'll foist a glass of this warming liquid off on Isaac, to keep him happy with his environs. I see he has a book with him. We might be a while."

"He could take me home," Dolly offered. "Your discussions might be a bit delicate."

Oh, stay," Abigail finished another glass of sherry. "...for the interrogation."

Mary laughed. "How do you intend to handle Charles?"

"He's not going to move my office." Abigail handed Mary her empty glass. "As soon as he's out of the county's custody, I'm going to marry him…if not sooner. This sherry is better than tea.

"I could call Judge Pond," Mary looked into her glass of sherry as if the answer might be found in the dark liquid. "Maybe house arrest doesn't preclude marriage ceremonies."

Abigail sat her glass down and clapped her hands. "Dolly, we could have a double-wedding ceremony."

Mary asked, "Will the university let you continue to teach?"

"No." Dolly said. "That's another reason I keep putting Samuel off."

"We could fight that outdated restriction." Mary poured Dolly the last glass of sherry from the crystal decanter. "Abigail, is your name going to be on the house on Plymouth?"

"Or, I won't marry him."

"Good girl. And here's another thing to work out with Charles. You'll need an allowance until you're making a profit from the law. Some of the Van Aker legacy can be put in your name. Any other questions?"

Abigail's spirits had lifted considerably. "Will you come to the wedding? Maybe Judge Pond could meet us at Samuel Dredford's, for to marry us today."

Mary laughed. "Why not? I'll pick up Judge Pond and you two go by St. Andrew's to see if Reverend Tatlock won't join us for the ceremony."

* * *

In the Ypsilanti cottage, Charles had spent a sleepless night on the couch. When all the sounds of commerce had ceased and only a startled bird's cry lighted on his hungry ears, the stillness filled Charles with a restlessness.

Was Abigail growing angry with him? That wouldn't do, and he couldn't go to her to explain. All the days he'd wasted not seeing her when had the freedom to, galled him. Wrapped in his arms, Abigail would have prevented everything bad from happening. His shoulders ached. Abigail was the center of his world. He touched his chest where his heart thudded out of control.

In the dark room, he could see the dim white blotch on the wall that was his calendar. He knew the line of X's on the days already gone in February were not nearly enough. March, April, May, could he get their house done by the time he was released in May?

As dawn approached Brutus whined at the door, but Charles wasn't allowed to walk him. House arrest was not that cheerful an alternative to jail. He surveyed the mess he'd made. Plans for the Plymouth Road house and the new factory lay about on the table and floor. Some sketches were tacked to the wall. Another roll of drawings, for the factory's expansion, had been propped into a corner.

After clearing the table by switching the drawings to the couch, Charles moved to the kitchen end of the room. He tried to quietly make a pot of coffee, but Samuel must have heard him moving around.

Brutus almost knocked Samuel down, herding him from the loft's ladder to the door. "Be right back," he said. "Brutus needs a run."

"So does Charles," Charles said.

When Samuel returned, they rehashed the gazebo disaster. "What would I gain by making Abigail unhappy?"

"Exactly," Samuel said. "Women live for emotional dramas. Female logic. They raise the stakes whenever they can. They want to see if you'll fold your cards and slink away."

"Dolly does it, too?"

Samuel stopped scrambling the eggs. "Do you want to be harangued about losing a university job for two hours?"

"I'll do whatever Abigail wants," Charles said, then prayed, 'if it be your will, Lord."

"They know that," Samuel said with a tone of resentment.

Charles's mind was spinning. "I've got to get out of here. My sisters, Abigail. I can't be in jail." Samuel handed him a cup of coffee. Feeling like a silent zombie, Charles retrieved the factory plans from the corner and spread them out on the floor. If he could be released, see Abigail again, maybe he could make a life with her.

"I'm making a list of wells in the city to find out where the cleanest water is." Charles was surprised that Samuel's presence was *un*threatening enough for him to use the pronoun, 'I'. "I was trying to find uncontaminated water to pipe into the factory, and to the house on Plymouth Road, besides for Ypsilanti's citizens." His words tumbled out as if propelled by his fear of restraining any communication. "The factory might be able to use the water from Brown's spring on south Main. They're using hollow tamarack logs as pipes. I'll have a well and septic tank dug at the Plymouth property for Abigail." The tongue-tied, eleven years of youth terrorized Charles into verbal rapidity.

"You've researched all the wells in Ann Arbor?" Samuel didn't notice Charles's struggle for composure in order to keep speaking.

"The University has a few," Charles said. "There's one between two professors' homes, but I don't know exactly where. Another one is supposed to be on the other side of campus." Charles was on the road to seeking his freedom. Maybe Judge Pond would find his work commendable enough to release him. "The Regents gave Silas Douglas $5,000 to lay six inch iron and wood pipes from the spring on Emmanuel Mann's farm." Charles relaxed. "You know, near the State Street hill."

"Sounds like a community-minded project to me," Samuel said. "I think Judge Pond would agree."

"I wanted to locate those closest to my new building projects. And the construction boom needs water-access information. Most families dig their own wells, and stores put tanks on their roofs for rainwater. I think there are about eight more springs than I mentioned."

Samuel brought over a red Crayola. "Let's mark them on a map."

Charles produced the 'Everts & Stewart's plot map of Ann Arbor. "Do you think I could be released early?"

Samuel marked down the six water sources Charles had mentioned. "We can only ask. Read off the other addresses."

"The Breckenridges use Dr. Kellogg's water from the Mineral Spring House in Lower Town. Last year the well was dug down to a depth of 800 feet. Grandpa still boiled all their water."

"In jail, you said you thought Abigail had typhoid."

"When I buried Lily, the funeral director told me Grandpa was dead. I wasn't thinking clearly. I thought we were all going to die."

Samuel shook his head. "I'll make sure Judge Pond hears about that outside of the court room."

"Thanks." Charles roused himself. "Let's get this finished. The Court House Square has two wells: the one on the south side was closed in '49 then reopened in '72. I was twelve when they put the pump in. That seems more than a hundred years ago."

"If you add up all the ages of the family members you lost," Samuel said, "it was."

"Enough of reminiscing about the dead." Charles pointed to the map. "Put down the well on the west side of the Court House Square. They posted a sign when they were drilling, '775 feet deep.' I'm sure it was Grandpa who put up the other one."

"You mean the sign that read, '$3,500 high?'"

"He never admitted to it." A small smile of remembrance cracked Charles's face, then tore a gash in his heart. "The veterans did collect water after the war. Sold it door to door."

Samuel asked, "When did the city council give out the contract for pipes to be laid in the streets?"

"August 1874. And not a pipe laid. Let's keep at this: two on Huron: one at First Street and one at Fifth Avenue. Two on Main: corner of Liberty and the intersection of Washington."

"Doesn't Dr. Cleland run a mineral spring house?"

Charles corrected him. "Dr. Hale built that in '66. Are you marking these down?"

Samuel nodded busy with his Crayola.

"There's a well at the corner of Jefferson and State, another on the southeast corner of Maynard and Liberty. I thought I might get a subscription to use their water, but 50 families already have the rights. It's stone walled and 90 feet deep. That's all there is." Charles laid his head on the table.

Brutus put a huge paw on Charles's lap.

Samuel placed a cup of soup in front of him. "Sometimes, Charles, I think women throw us a golden ball, just out of reach, to keep us interested."

"She was my anchor in a safe harbor," Charles said. "But I think she might set me adrift. I'm always saying unwise things to her. And who would want a jailbird for the father of their children?"

* * *

Mary Foster and Judge Pond had arrived at the Ypsilanti cottage before Abigail. Reverend Tatlock had been reluctant to join Dolly and Abigail for a visit to see Charles. "Does Judge Pond allow visits when people are under house arrest?" Reverend Tatlock had asked.

"Oh, Judge Pond will be there, so you can ask permission." Dolly winked at Abigail.

"Ladies, have you been drinking to excess?" the reverend asked. "It's not yet noon."

Isaac's dignity convinced Reverend Tatlock that he might *not* be on some fool's errand. The minister took nearly half-an-hour collecting his missal, communion trappings and vestment. "Have you obtained a license?"

"Judge Pond has both of them with him." Abigail hoped she wasn't lying to a man of God.

* * *

Abigail heard Charles laughing as she knocked on Samuel's cottage. Mary opened the door. "Come in, come in," Mary said. "Charles and Samuel have already signed the licenses. You're later than we expected."

Reverend Tatlock conferred with Judge Pond for a moment in the corner farthest from the door. Dolly and Samuel spoke quietly in the kitchen end of the room, where Mary was making coffee while the dog, Brutus leaned against her.

Charles held Abigail's hand. "Did Reverend Tatlock agree to marry us?"

"That's why he came," Abigail said. She couldn't tell if the cream sherry was still heightening her senses or if her happiness was radiating straight from the middle of Charles's chest. "I've prayed and prayed and then finally gave up and look what happened."

"It's not the church wedding in St. Andrew's that Grandpa might have wanted to see," Charles said.

"He knows I'm happy," Abigail said. "Did Judge Pond agree to let me spend my honeymoon here with you?"

"Mary convinced him it was the best way to rehabilitate a person like me." Charles readied a cough, a sure sign tears were being kept at bay. "You know, I love you?"

"Everything is going to get better now," Abigail straightened the lace on her white blouse, thanking the Lord for Cotton, who had given her all the magic she needed to undertake this happy step.

Isaac stood next to the door. "Abigail," he called, "Who is going to take care of the dog?"

"I am," Mary Foster said. "My house needs a guard dog. And, Abigail, Did you hear that next year the school term will be nine months instead of six?"

* * *

After the wedding vows of Samuel and Dolly and Charles and Abigail were exchanged, Charles and Abigail were left alone. Isaac had promised to bring supper along with Charles's sisters, Cotton and Taffy, and Mrs. McConnell. "She'll be needing time to bake a proper cake for you," Isaac said. "Grandpa would agree that today is a happy day."

Abigail started folding the architectural drawings on the couch.

"Could you roll those, they're for the factory?" Charles pointed to the stack of plans littering the table. "Come look at the plans for the house. Should I explain anything to you?"

Abigail began to study the Plymouth plans. Was he as shy as she about uniting as husband and wife? Maybe there was a bed in the loft. The couch even without the drawings didn't look comfortable enough for two. She wondered how long Mrs. McConnell would take to bake a cake. She wasn't hungry for food. Looking up at Charles, she noticed his face was red with embarrassment. Her own cheeks grew hot. Nighttime would be a more romantic time to start tearing each other's clothing off, wouldn't it? She took in a long breath of air, trying to appear calm and collected. "Too bad we couldn't have discussed the gazebo."

"I'm sorry, Abigail," Charles said. Both of his hands stayed on the table but he leaned in her direction. "That was thoughtless."

His voice sounded lower than she remembered. "As I explained, my office needs to be near the courthouse for clients." Abigail pointed to the front hall on the drawing. "I want windows in all the halls, upstairs and down."

"I don't see how---"

"Put a window in the back wall, here on the first floor. The door needs a full length window in it, and side panels. Put another window in this slanted roof to give light to the upstairs hall." Charles began making notes directly on the drawings. "Put a water closet and a bathing tub in this room. I want a door here, too; so I can go in from the nursery."

Charles pulled out a chair and directed her to sit down; then he placed one next to her on the same side of the table and sat down, too. "Remember when I scolded you for talking about a nursery."

"When you hurt my arm?" Abigail thought they might as well clear up all the misunderstandings.

"I never intended to injure you." Charles laid his large hand over her smaller one.

He was difficult to resist, but she wanted no hurdles in their way, once they decided to consummate the marriage, later that evening. "When you wouldn't go to England with Dolly and me? When you stopped courting me? When you didn't come to Grandpa's funeral?"

"I wanted to."

"Oh sure, now you have a great excuse. I'm in jail." Abigail whined plaintively and then burst out laughing.

"It's no joke," he grumbled.

She batted his chest with the back of her hand. "I'm here, aren't I?"

"You are," Charles stood, pulling her to her feet. "We are alone." He kissed her mouth then, but she stepped quickly away from him.

"Your whiskers hurt."

"Give me a minute, I'll shave." Charles rushed toward the stove for hot water.

Abigail calmly found his shaving mug and brought it to him. "Is your edge honed?"

"Yes." He gulped.

Abigail planned no further diatribes. "Let me do it."

* * *

"Did Grandpa let you shave him" Charles sat down at the table, watching her expertly lather the brush.

"Isaac did that." Abigail put her face close to his, teasing him. "Won't you let me try?"

Charles rubbed his stubby chin. "Sure, why not?"

"It's not the gallows." Abigail soaped his face and then his eyebrows.

"No," he said, remaining very still.

"Just kidding." She toweled his forehead dry, hiked up her skirt and straddled his lap.

"Abigail," he said.

She rested one hand on his collarbone, while she deftly scraped his whiskers off with her other hand. Charles placed his huge hands on her waist to steady her. His fingertips touched the back of her lace blouse. "Sit still," she said. "You don't want to get hurt do you?"

Silence reigned. Abigail laid the razor down in the basin on the table and unbuttoned her blouse to the waist. She wore no chemise. Then she cupped his giant hand in hers and brought it to her inner thigh. "Life mates deserve pleasure," she said.

Charles let out a harsh sigh and pressed her to him. They held onto each other as if they were slipping into a deep sea, going down together for the third and final time.

Abigail drew back her head. "I graduate two years from now." She reached up and pulled on his curls, before getting off his lap. "I expect to have had two children by then."

"Abigail," Charles said, then began picking up the remaining drawings from the couch.

"No," Abigail said from the loft ladder. "Up here."

All the sorrow drained from Charles's heart as a surge of joy coursed through his body.

"My Charles," Abigail said, again and again.

They remained entwined with each other for hours. Abigail nestled in the safe 'L' cure of Charles's body. She pulled the quilt from the side of the bed to cover them. "Thank you, Lord," he prayed aloud. She seemed unwilling to move. He smiled at the shaving ploy she had used. His breath rustled her hair. He hoped she was as satiated as he was.

His father's saying came back to him. "All they needed was good loving and cool spring water." The Lord had been forgiving of Charles's anger, answering his prayers for his remaining sisters' health, and rewarding him with Abigail's affection.

Now all he needed to do was get out from under house arrest.

Chapter Eighteen

Three days after her Valentine Day marriage, Abigail returned to her Breckenridge home. Charles remained confined to Samuel's house in Ypsilanti. Isaac encouraged her to come home after he delivered another day's supply of Mrs. McConnell's cooking for the newlyweds. "The children miss you, Miss Abigail, excuse me, Mrs. Van Aker."

Abigail reached for Isaac's sleeve. "I'll always be Abigail to you, Isaac."

Abigail missed her family, too. She wanted to talk to Cotton, to thank her for her great ideas, even if they were not strictly speaking any magical elements included. And she missed Mrs. McConnell, and Dolly, and her studies. The small cottage was all very well and good for a honeymoon, but life had to go on and poor Charles couldn't leave, yet. She planned to visit Mary Foster again to bring up the subject of Charles's release from house arrest…as soon as she was up-to-date with her law classes. Exams loomed in four law courses.

When Isaac stopped old Prescott in front of the Breckenridge house, Abigail couldn't move. She heard the piano as Samantha practiced scales. She was suddenly shy about facing her family as a married woman. "Isaac, please drive around back to the carriage house." She searched her mind for a logical reason not to be let off at the front door. "I want to see if Flicka is adjusting to her new surroundings."

If Isaac doubted her intention, he was gentleman enough not to mention it. "Beatrice is out fawning over that animal every day."

"I'm glad," Abigail said, distracted; but remembering to go into the carriage house to pet Flicka. Creeping up the servants' steps, Abigail wondered how life would proceed. Did she look different now that she was married?

She was relieved to meet Cotton first. Cotton's arms were filled with a heaping laundry basket, which she promptly dropped, stepped over and nearly knocked Abigail back down the steps, hugging her tightly. "Yous back!" She righted Abigail on the steps and asked. "He treaten you way he should?"

"Yes, but I might as well be married to a man in the zoo." Abigail laughed. "All your ideas worked, but Charles is still caged up in the cottage in Ypsilanti."

"Never you mind." Cotton picked up her basket. "Go down and see Mrs. McConnell 'for you sees the girls. She'll be wantin to add another portion to da meal. I'll pack you another suitcase to take back to Ypsilanti."

In the basement kitchen, Mrs. McConnell's tears flowed freely. "Oh and it's good to see you. That boy of any good to you?"

Abigail laughed, hugging her friend and cook. "That he was, Mrs. McConnell, that he was."

"We're having a pork roast this evening," Mrs. McConnell said. "Best, give all those girls a hug before you go out to the gazebo to study. That'll give Isaac time to get your fireplace up and warming."

"Already, done, Miss Abigail," Isaac said, "Shall I bring up tea for you in the parlor."

"That would be heavenly." Abigail was suddenly homesick. She sniffed to hide her tears. She was home, what was the big deal? Nonetheless, her heart was in her throat as she climbed the stairs from the basement kitchen to the first floor.

Samantha immediately stopped playing, when she spied Abigail. "Oh you're home." She got up from the piano bench and hugged Abigail. "I suppose I'll have to wait to see Charles?"

Abigail wasn't sure she could speak without crying her silly eyes out.

Dolly moved in and hugged her. "Mrs. Van Aker," she whispered.

Abigail smiled. "And, Mrs. Dredford, tea is being brought up."

Beatrice, Cassandra and Taffy made a circle around her skirts, holding hands and skipping. Beatrice stopped first. "Samantha told us you would come home; but I thought once a woman is married she had to stay with her husband."

"Not me," Abigail said. "I have things to do, books to read, family to hug."

"I'm glad," Cassandra said. "I don't ever get enough hugs."

Abigail sat down on the piano bench and let Cassandra and Taffy both climb onto her lap. "Me either."

Isaac brought in tea and motioned for Abigail to speak with him in the hall. "Will you be staying the night, Miss Abigail?"

"I better not, Isaac." She wanted to go up to her old room and forget all about being a married woman. "I love Charles so much." Abigail eyes filled with tears. "I've missed you all."

Isaac shook a bit with emotion as he patted her shoulder. "Don't, don't let's make the children think anything is amiss, when of course all's well. I believe it's natural to feel a little nostalgic coming home after you're married. Miss Dolly has requested I not call her Mrs. Dredford. It's a shock to me to realize you're all grown up. Maybe we need a church wedding for it to be official and easier to adjust."

"You're a very wise person, Isaac. Maybe after Charles is released we will have a proper double wedding ceremony with Dolly and Samuel."

Samantha had followed Abigail out to the hall and heard the last statement. "Oh that would be so much fun for the girls." Samantha pulled Abigail back into the parlor. "Could we, Abigail? Listen, girls. We might see Charles and Abigail married in St. Andrew's church!"

"Reverend Tatlock would need to approve," Abigail said. "What do you think, Dolly? Would Samuel want to be remarried in church?"

"I'm sure he would, Abigail." Dolly smiled. "We could make arrangements. When is Charles going to be released?"

* * *

After her heart-warming homecoming tea, Abigail put on her coat and retired to the gazebo. The gazebo's fireplace glowed from Isaac's ministrations and the lamps were lit overhead to keep out the February gloom. But the books stacked on each side of her notes failed to protect her from waves of frustration. Being at the top of the Law Department's 90 students did allow some reason for pride, but Haven Hall couldn't compete with her passion for Charles.

She adjusted her glasses to read the titles of the books next to her right hand: 'Tort Law' and "Michigan Property Precedents.' Professors Felch and Walker's notes lay before her. To the left, the stack of books read: 'Constitutional Case Studies' and 'Common Law and Verbal Contracts.'

If she could concentrate for five minutes. She began to turn over the pages of her notes. Words swam before her eyes. Charles! His sweet hide, his burly shoulders, even the scent of his shaving cream invaded her thoughts. "Please, Lord," she prayed, "I need to study."

The words readjusted on the page. She could do this. Blaming Charles for not concentrating would only exacerbate the problem. The cooling ideas of justice and the methods of courtroom presentation slowly filtered through the agitated storm of her emotions into the safe haven of her mind. The more she read, the more she forgot Charles.

She intensified her activity. Read the words, sort the ideas, memorize the terms.

As her glasses slipped down her nose and she brushed a lock of hair off her forehead, Charles appeared before her.

"Abigail." His head was cocked to the side, arms akimbo. "You look like an old maid."

Abigail threw one of the heavy law volumes straight at his head. "Get out of here!" Two hit his chest. "Out!"

Charles ducked the fourth tome and rushed out.

Abigail laid her head on her worthless notes and cried for half an hour. That fool could hurt her worse than any disease. She wiped her wet face and dabbed at the splotched and soggy sheets in front of her. He probably escaped his house arrest, and now they wouldn't even be able to marry in June at St. Andrews.

"Abigail?" It was Charles again, ducking his head in the front door of her office. "Please forgive me. I'm not under house arrest anymore, in the daytime." He didn't sound penitent.

"Why did they let you out?" She deliberately re-shuffled the limp stack of papers.

Charles picked up the books she had thrown and placed them out of arm's reach on the desk. "Seems your bungling husband is needed to head up a drain commission, but we still need to spend our evenings dingily lodged at Dredford's." He smiled in the most charming way. "Please forgive me. I need you to stand up for me."

"To whom? You have everyone's approval." Abigail ran her fingers through her hair. She must look a fright. Before her stood the only man she ever noticed, who had the biggest shoulders, muscled neck, giant hands. A new suit coat didn't hide a fresh shirt that her hands itched to unbutton.

"To the lawyer I see before me. My wife that I carelessly insulted, who I love dearly, whose passions show through the short fuse of her temper, who I'll be lucky to take into our new home, if she can continue to forge the idiot who loves her to distraction."

Abigail didn't feel like giving in quite so easily. A picture of Cassandra's cat, Fluffy, cuffing at a fly came to her mind. It was cruel not to let him know how her feelings. No amount of pride could hold back the longing. Abigail took off her glasses. "The day Grandpa died, he wanted me to laugh at an article he read, and all I did was call myself an old maid." Abigail shuddered. "And then he had a stroke and died."

Charles came around to her side of the desk. He knelt next to her. "Please, Abigail. Let's kiss and make up. This will be the end of our first misunderstanding. That's how my father and mother did it. And they never brought up hurts from the past."

A bolt of happiness struck her heart. "You should read your mother's letters. She loved you all, most tenderly."

"Will you keep loving me that way?" Charles moved closer. "Being released from my room, my heart ran pell mell to yours."

Abigail could see perspiration on his upper lip. The lip she couldn't bear not to kiss. She flung herself into his brawny arms. "Charles, I'd die without you."

He kissed her. Then he helped her stand under the bright gas fixture. Her hands entwined themselves in the hair at the back of his head. "Turn the gas lamps off," she said, pulling him into the file closet. Their passion for each other reached uncivilized heights. "We're like animals," Abigail said, "or magnetized metal."

Charles shook his head. "We need each other entirely."

"Grandpa told me some marriages aren't holy," Abigail said. "Will the need for each other ever subside?"

"Never," Charles said. He wrapped her in his arms. "Our love and trust of each other will only grow."

Abigail asked, "Will Judge Pond allow you to marry in St. Andrew's, if we return to the Ypsilanti house?"

"I'll ask," Charles said. "Would Samuel be willing to have a church wedding, too?"

* * *

The very next day, the used-book dealer, Robert Koelz, busily re-arranged books in Grandpa's library. Isaac had called Abigail in from her studies in the gazebo.

"Abigail." Koelz embraced her.

Isaac rolled his eyes at the older man's familiarity with his mistress.

"Charles sent me over with a list of books you might want sent to the Plymouth address. Have you seen your library there? Very impressive. Wall-to-wall cherry bookcases with glass pull-down lids."

Abigail pushed him into the parlor. "Isaac, if we don't have any more sherry, could you make a special trip to the corner?"

"There is the Madeira."

"Oh splendid." Koelz nearly clapped his hands.

As Isaac poured out the amber liquid, the mailman rang the bell. Abigail skipped to the door and found a note from Charles. "I need a shave," it read, signed, "Your loving husband."

Abigail stuffed the note into her pocket. "Now about Charles's orders," she said advancing on a pliant Koelz.

The End

Other Books by Rohn Federbush

Salome's Conversion, 2011
North Parish, 2014
Floating Home, 2014
Sally Bianco Mystery Series, 2014

About Rohn Federbush

Rohn Federbush retired as an administrator from the University of Michigan in 1999. She received a Masters of Arts in Creative Writing in 1995 from Eastern Michigan University, where she studied under Janet Kauffman and Larry Smith. In 1998, Vermont College awarded her a summer conference scholarship to work on her novel under Ellen Lesser and Brett Lott. Frederick Busch of Colgate granted a 1997 summer stipend for her ghost-story collection. Michael Joyce of Vassar encouraged earlier writing at Jackson Community College, Jackson, Michigan in 1981. Rohn has completed fourteen novels, with an additional mystery nearly finished, 120 short stories and 150 poems to date.

You can find Rohn on:
Facebook / Twitter / Goodreads /LinkedIn

And on her website:
www.RohnFederbush.com

Made in the USA
Charleston, SC
12 April 2014